THE MAYOR'S TONGUE

a member of
Penguin Group (USA) Inc.
New York · 2008

The Mayor's Tongue

NATHANIEL RICH

RIVERHEAD BOOKS

Published by the Penguin Group

Penguin Group (USA) Inc., 375 Hudson Street, New York, New York 10014, USA

Penguin Group (Canada), 90 Eglinton Avenue East, Suite 700, Toronto, Ontario M4P 2Y3, Canada (a division of Pearson Canada Inc.)

Penguin Books Ltd, 80 Strand, London WC2R 0RL, England

Penguin Ireland, 25 St Stephen's Green, Dublin 2, Ireland (a division of Penguin Books Ltd)

Penguin Group (Australia), 250 Camberwell Road, Camberwell, Victoria 3124, Australia (a division of Pearson Australia Group Pty Ltd)

Penguin Books India Pvt Ltd, 11 Community Centre, Panchsheel Park, New Delhi–110 017, India

Penguin Group (NZ), 67 Apollo Drive, Roseland, North Shore 0632, New Zealand (a division of Pearson New Zealand Ltd)

Penguin Books (South Africa) (Pty) Ltd, 24 Sturdee Avenue, Rosebank, Johannesburg 2196, South Africa

Penguin Books Ltd, Registered Offices: 80 Strand, London WC2R 0RL, England

Published simultaneously in Canada

Passages have been quoted from Jan Morris's *Trieste and the Meaning of Nowhere* (Simon & Schuster, 2001) and Johanna Spyri's *Heidi* (trans. Helen B. Dole).

ISBN 978-1-59448-990-7

Printed in the United States of America
10 9 8 7 6 5 4 3 2 1

BOOK DESIGN BY STEPHANIE HUNTWORK

THIS IS FOR MY MOTHER AND MY FATHER

T‖E
MAYOR'S
TONGUE

THE CIBAEÑO TONGUE

It was June when Eugene Brentani took the job at Aaronsen and Son Moving Company and subleased an apartment in Inwood from a man on his crew named Alvaro. Like many of the men who worked at Aaronsen and Son, Alvaro had recently emigrated from the Dominican Republic. Unlike the others, however, Alvaro was from the Cibao Valley, a small rural region in the northern part of the country. Separated from the rest of the island by the Cordillera Septentrional mountain range, the isolated farming communities of the Cibao Valley had developed their own dialect. This dialect, Cibaeño, was virtually incomprehensible to natives of the other Spanish-speaking countries in the Caribbean. Cubans thought that it sounded excessively affricative, like Catalan; Puerto Ricans found it soft and melodious, like Portuguese. Even the other Dominicans on the moving crew were baffled by Alvaro's speech. To Eugene, it sounded like Alvaro was speaking with a mouth full of porridge. Alvaro's attempts to learn English were, despite his most strenuous efforts, pitiful, but he was able to make himself understood in other ways. Since words failed him, he communicated through vivid intonation; forceful hand gestures; and dynamic facial expressions, made with contortions of his rubbery face, the muscles of which were flexible to an uncanny degree. An arched lip or a wiggled ear was a disquisition in itself, conveying meaning far more articulate than, say, one of Eugene's father's monosyllabic lectures. After several weeks, it no longer mattered that Alvaro couldn't speak a word of English. Eugene believed that he could understand him just fine.

Alvaro's flexibility was not limited to his facial muscles. Like Eugene, he looked too small to be a mover—he was lithe, almost bony—but his suppleness compensated for the lack of bulk in his back and upper arms. During a furniture-moving job, his body would arch, twist, and buckle out double-jointed, engaging each muscle to its greatest capacity. He could support a loveseat on the straining tendons of his neck, an ottoman on his bulging rib cage, and even an armchair on his flexing toes, if he walked on his heels. He was blessed with a jigsaw anatomy.

Although Eugene often feared that his friend's spine might rupture, or his fingers snap back in compound fractures, Alvaro never suffered any serious injuries. After an especially arduous job, however, his whole body, and not just his arms or his back, throbbed madly. Each vertebra, rib, and abdominal muscle, his pelvis, his quadriceps, his collarbone, and even his jaw rallied together, a ragged band of crippled assassins, raising hammers, gouges, and pliers to his frayed nerve endings. Using a wild array of gestures, Alvaro explained to Eugene how he spent entire nights limping between a bath filled with ice cubes and a bed insulated by a carefully choreographed patchwork of electric heating pads. He also mimed tears, for the sadness he felt about this sorry state of affairs. But he was good at the work, and he needed the salary. He had to feed his family.

When Alvaro showed his apartment to Eugene, he apologized for its meager furnishings. He had scavenged everything he owned from moving jobs. The front door opened into a long living room, occupied only by a broad player piano, an orange floor lamp, and stuffed into the space on the parquet floor behind the piano, a king-sized mattress. A rough kitchen nook had been built into one corner, delineated by a wooden counter and two stools. Pipes jutted out from the crumbling white brick behind the stove. A doorway, minus door, led to the sole bedroom, which ran parallel to the living room and was almost as long. This, Eugene realized, would be his room. It contained a second mattress, a single; a crumpled sheet was balled up on the floor next to it. Blushing, Alvaro shook it open and laid it over the mattress.

"I can make my own bed," said Eugene. "It's really no problem."

The sheet was spotted with discolorations like diseased flowers; Alvaro smoothed it apologetically. Eugene was about to repeat himself, to make certain his friend understood, when Alvaro let out a loud, embarrassed chortle. Eugene took that to mean that they had reached an accord.

As it turned out, Alvaro was rarely in the apartment. That was because he had another home down in Washington Heights, which he shared with his wife and their two young sons. He was there for most of the connubial hours—breakfast, supper, and bedtime—but would visit the Inwood apartment on off-shifts during the day and on the weekend. He usually brought with him a nurse, a secretary, or sometimes a physician's aide—women from St. Valentino, the hospital that regularly employed Aaronsen and Son to move machinery. On Sunday nights, he brought home prostitutes. Eugene had never seen one before, at least not up close, not within his own living space. They were less exotic at close range, in the apartment's murky orange light. They dressed cheaply, but not as ornately as he might have guessed (though perhaps that was a reflection of Alvaro's tastes). They looked a lot like the secretaries.

Eugene usually knew when to expect Alvaro, so he was able to avoid any real unpleasantness. Even though there was no door to his room, and the walls were dangerously thin, the king-sized mattress was on the opposite side of the living room, so the sounds never rose beyond muffled grunts and creaks. If Eugene put on his headphones, it was only to block out any of the noises the girl might, accidentally, let escape. Eugene didn't actually mind listening—in particularly lonely moments he sometimes removed his headphones—but for the most part his modesty, and his respect for Alvaro, kept him from spying on his friend.

At least until one bright, full-mooned night, several months into Eugene's stay. Alvaro had brought home Betty, a Filipina nurse whom Eugene knew from St. Valentino. During a night shift in October, while Eugene and Alvaro's crew had been hauling in three new CT-scan machines, she had brought Eugene a paper cup full of instant hot chocolate. When the other movers protested, Betty told them to shut up. Then she cupped Eugene's face in her soft, latexed hands, and winked at him. Though the men had catcalled and cackled, Eugene was elated. Part of the goal of this period of self-imposed exile was to meet a girl, and this was the closest he had come yet. But he had barely seen Betty since then. His habitual timidity prevented him from going out of his way to seek her out, and soon she seemed less desirable to him. In recent weeks, the other guys on his moving team told him that she'd been hanging out in the hospital stairwells with Alvaro off-shift.

They arrived late that night, whispering and giggling. Eugene stepped quietly to his doorway just as the couple fell to the mattress. He could see only the edge of an indeterminate body part—a back, or a shoulder, or maybe knees—protruding just slightly over the top of the piano, but the slanting moonlight projected a vivid silhouette onto the wall. It was horrible. It looked like a shadow-puppet show of a chrysalis tearing through its cocoon, its wings trembling and straining to separate from its body. Eugene soon realized that he was watching Alvaro, bound up in some kind of inhuman contortion. Betty's round, fleshy body was on the bottom, this was clear; she lay on her back, her hips raised slightly off the mattress. Alvaro, taut and spindly, was on top, face-to-face with Betty; but he had arched his spine so dramatically that, with his knees fully bent, the tips of his toes rested on the back of his head. He had curved himself backward into a loop. His forearms, planted on the mattress on either side of Betty's head, bore his entire weight. Betty's hips rose to accommodate him. The chrysalis quivered, almost lost balance, and tightened once again. It looked painful. It looked like meditation. Betty started screaming—in ecstasy or terror, it wasn't clear. Eugene tiptoed quickly back to his room. Sliding into his bed, he found the sheets still warm with his own body heat. He shivered, and laughed with relief. Living in this apartment, working in this job, he really believed he was free.

Inwood was a foreign city, as far away from Manhattan as Eugene could travel—without actually leaving Manhattan. The neighborhood's geography was exotic, his friends were Dominican, and the meals Alvaro taught him to prepare induced dyspepsia in ways his childhood maid's traditional Italian cooking had never prepared him for. He saw no one he had known before moving there. His oldest friends knew where he was and what he was doing, but none of them lived in New York anymore, and he did not respond to e-mails from those few college acquaintances that had settled in lower Manhattan or in the subway-proximate neighborhoods of Brooklyn. In his more expansive moments, he fashioned himself a refugee, or at least some sort of psychic immigrant.

Eugene telephoned his father several times over the course of the summer, collect, from phone booths in Inwood. He could tell that his father was happy to hear a familiar voice, but neither one of them knew what to say. When he came home after college graduation, Eugene had told his father that he was moving to Florida, so in their conversations he made sure to mention his job as a lifeguard, his house near the beach, and the afternoon thunderstorms that would come and go without warning. He added that he had made some nice friends, though he said they were Cuban, not Dominican. His father would chuckle or make curt remarks, but reveal nothing about himself. He was alone in

Eugene's childhood apartment on Sutton Place, enduring the first years of his early retirement in solitary, nostalgic reveries for the old world.

Unmoored and exuberant, Eugene made an effort to lose himself to the cadences of his new life. He purposefully worked erratic shifts at Aaronsen and Son, so that his life lacked any semblance of routine. In his spare time, he sat and read by the pond in Inwood Hill Park, or visited his friends on the moving crew, meeting their families and playing with their children. He bought Spanish instruction tapes and tried to practice speaking the language around the neighborhood—at the grocery store, in the library, and at bars with skeptical Dominican women—but found he was best understood when he spoke Italian.

One night, after Alvaro and Eugene had lived together for more than six months, Alvaro invited Eugene to visit his other apartment. Alvaro's two sons called him Tío Eugenio and showed him how they could carry chairs and tables over their heads. Alvaro's wife, Milagros, was strong and squat, with gentle facial features and shapely, carefully painted lips. She cooked pork neck in salsa verde and never made eye contact, though she often smiled in Eugene's general direction. For the occasion Milagros had laid out a white cotton tablecloth, and the boys' hair had been washed and combed. When Pepecito used his fingers to push corn niblets onto his fork, Milagros reprimanded him in a hushed voice. Otherwise, she was silent. Eugene figured she didn't speak English. She was from Santo Domingo, and did not know Cibaeño either, so Alvaro had to talk to her, like all the women in his life, in a deformed, pidgin Spanish.

After dinner, while Alvaro put the kids to bed, Milagros

served Eugene a cup of sweet, highly concentrated coffee. When she sat down to join him at the table, her smile vanished. She surprised him by speaking, for the first time, in English.

"Uncle Eugene," she said, "I know about Alvaro's nurses. I have been to the hospital. They took my children out of my body and I let them. They have given my children private consultations. I let them."

"I'm sorry," said Eugene, trying to sip his coffee. "I'm sorry."

"I know that when he goes to sleep at your place, there are women present. I know that you allow this."

"I'm so sorry," said Eugene, his coffee cup gibbering on its saucer.

"I know you are not from here, but you are trying to live in this community. I know what Alvaro is capable of. I know what he can do with the shape of his body."

"No, please, God no, I'm sorry, it won't happen—"

"I want you just to know this: I forgive you. I forgive you." She smiled again. A red glow seemed to rush into all her features, coloring her cheeks, her ears, her nostrils, radiating out of her eyes.

"Thank you. Thank you," said Eugene, coffee splattering on his chin and neck. "Thank you—"

"Leave my house now," she said. "Don't return. My children will never look on you again."

Eugene stumbled out, but later that night, he was not surprised to hear Alvaro creep into their Inwood apartment. When Eugene peeked out of his room, he saw a shadow on the wall that resembled a cow giving birth—the trembling skull of a newborn calf, distending an elastic caul. Eugene was too tired to perform the necessary extrapolations. As he tried to fall asleep, he heard the shifting weight of the player piano, and the inadvertent tin-kling of the keys.

By March, Inwood—once a vibrant pastiche of florid bodegas, clapboard religious centers, and exotic family-style cafés—had all the muted familiarity of a childhood closet, brimming with items discarded and worn from use. Eugene turned corners without looking for street names; he crossed avenues without checking both ways for traffic, relying only on his hearing and peripheral vision. The public library, housed in a blocky mansion built in the Dutch colonial era, now seemed the only logical architectural bridge between its neighbors on Broadway, the Doppiando pizza parlor and the El Encantar del Principe Hair Salon for Men. Even the shadowy forms of Alvaro and his women projected on the orange-lit wall of the living room seemed as innocent as the most rudimentary of shadow puppets. Instead of a bloody chrysalis or a birthing cow, he saw doves and panda bears.

Alvaro started spending a lot of time at the library, and one night Eugene decided to accompany him there. He followed Alvaro to the third floor, and then into the men's bathroom; through what appeared to be the middle stall was a hidden passageway that led into a private study. A long conference table filled most of the room's floor space, though an ancient bookcase and small stained-glass windows were reminders of a time when the mansion served as a summer retreat for a family of wealthy Dutch merchants on the Hudson River. Soon the two friends were sneaking in several nights a week, shortly before the library's closing time, and would stay there undetected, late into the night. When Eugene asked how he knew about this room, Alvaro

pointed to the conference table and then to his sore back, and
Eugene understood.

They sat at opposite sides of the false-wood table. Eugene
spent his time there trying to get through the eccentric late-
career short stories of Constance Eakins, whom he'd studied in
college—his thesis had been titled "Eakins: The Man, the Myth,
the Monster." (He got a B—the professor complained that Eugene had gone out of his depth in trying to take on the entire
career of a writer so prolific.) Alvaro didn't read at all, but wrote
obsessively on a yellow legal pad with a long blue pen, scrawling
a chaotic, looping Cibaeño across the page.

One night, Alvaro started to read his writing aloud. Eugene
couldn't understand a single word, but he loved the sound of
Alvaro's voice, and lost all interest in the book he was reading—
Eakins's *Keftir the Blind and Other Stories.* He played back the
music of Alvaro's prose in his head, and started to suspect that
his friend was a beautiful writer.

Alvaro looked up at Eugene, and spoke in his Cibaeño dialect.

"So? Did you like it?"

Eugene still couldn't understand a word his friend was saying,
but he figured he could usually grasp the general idea. "That was
nice, what you read," he said.

Alvaro nodded and brought over his writing pad. Eugene had
not realized how much work he had done. Dozens of pages were
filled with Alvaro's loopy, hieroglyphic scribbles. It was difficult
to determine where words ended and began, since they were all
cramped together, with little or no punctuation except for stray
accent marks.

"Do you think you might be willing to translate it?"

Eugene squinted, trying to divine the meaning of his friend's words.

"It looks like you've worked very hard on that. You should be proud."

Alvaro frowned.

"But do you think you might be willing to translate it?"

"I do like the way it sounds. Like some enchanting Mexican song."

The two men stared at each other baffled. Eugene had never seen his friend this stubborn. Alvaro sullenly walked back to his side of the room and let his manuscript fall to the table. Although they were laughing again by the time they left the library, Eugene felt responsible for their mutual incomprehension. Alvaro wanted to ask him something urgent, but Eugene couldn't figure out what.

The next night at the library, Alvaro couldn't concentrate on his manuscript. He strolled past the bookshelves, pretending to read the titles, and then ripped from his legal pad a fresh piece of paper. He wrote deliberately in a large, stiff hand, referring often to his old draft. Eugene watched as wrinkles formed on Alvaro's face in places he had never seen them. A culvert indented the patch of skin under his nostrils, faint gullies coursed along his jaws, and a network of trenches disfigured his forehead. Still frustrated by their miscommunication a day earlier, Eugene pretended not to notice.

Alvaro walked the length of the table and slid the yellow lined paper over the book that Eugene was pretending to read. When Eugene looked up, Alvaro was smiling, eager. The script was neatly written, but no more comprehensible for it. Alvaro pointed

to the manuscript, and then to Eugene. He continued to repeat
this gesture while he spoke.

"I would like you to translate it. Do you understand me?"

"Is this a story?"

"Please understand what I am saying to you, Eugene."

"Do you want me to . . . translate it?"

"Translate it," said Alvaro, nodding. His eyes flashed black.

"But Alvaro, I can't speak Spanish, let alone Cibaeño."

Alvaro took the Eakins book out of Eugene's hands. He
slammed it shut and, with a dramatic flourish, threw it against
the wall.

*"Translate it. Please, Eugene, please translate it into English. Oth-
erwise, it will be lost forever. Almost no one here understands my
dialect, but I think you can."*

Eugene began to read the dense scrawl, wondering what kind
of story Alvaro would write. He pulled out his own notebook and
laid it side-by-side with Alvaro's. Then Eugene began to write
himself, stopping every sentence or so to consult Alvaro's text.
Alvaro watched all this closely, encouraging his friend whenever
he looked up. The further Eugene went along, the less convinced
he became that he was getting it right. But Alvaro looked on with
such a hopeful expression that Eugene started to believe.

The story that began to take form on those pages seemed to
be at least partially autobiographical in nature. The narrator was
an immigrant from Jamao, a village in the Cibao Valley of the
Dominican Republic. Like Alvaro, the man, who Eugene determined was named Jacinto, spoke in the Cibaeño dialect. Jacinto
had moved to an apartment in northern Manhattan with another
man, who was a depressed, fatherless loner. Jacinto was very poor,
so he took a job as a moving man. This was unfortunate, because

he had been one of the more prominent young men in Jamao, a member of the priest caste and the village's only surgeon. He delivered babies and issued last rites, performed exorcisms and blood transfusions. He taught children the Bible and cleaned their scraped knees with an astringent he distilled from a black mountain berry that he himself had discovered.

But Jacinto had been unhappy in Jamao, and craved a larger existence. He dreamt of a vast metallic metropolis, with spires rising from cathedral-like structures made of steel. He imagined hundreds of people tripping over one another, and tunnels that formed a secret network under the city like the caves dug out by moles, except these tunnels extended not only deep below the earth but also straight up, to the top of the highest buildings. Jacinto boarded a boat to Santo Domingo and then a flight for New York City. Once he arrived at the apartment, several rote secondary characters were granted introductions: a wicked old landlady, a boisterous, incoherent drunk, and an infant who might or might not be the Son of Man. They all lived together in a large high-rise in Inwood.

The real action begins when Jacinto meets Alsa. She's the teenage daughter of a downstairs neighbor, who is also from Cibao. Alsa is beautiful and plump, with straight black hair that hangs below her waist. When she smiles, which is often, she has a habit of covering her mouth, until she gives way to laughter and breaks out in loud, irrepressible bursts. Eugene hoped very much that Alsa would fall in love with Jacinto.

Eugene completed translating this opening section of the story several weeks later, on an unseasonably mild night in April, relying heavily on guesswork, intuition, and the fragments of knowledge he was able to gather about his friend. When he was done, he read it aloud to Alvaro, who, despite his incomprehension of the English words, listened with an ecstatic expression on his face. Alvaro kept interrupting in order to shake his hand. Eugene began to suspect that his translation might have been accurate after all.

He was amazed. It was a rare and mysterious thing when two people could understand each other with such perfect clarity.

PART I

NEW YORK CITY

1   Rutherford
                    and Mr. Schmitz sit smoking
              on a public bench at the northern edge
           of Central Park, trying not to exhale into each
       other's face.

"Rutherford," says Mr. Schmitz, "I've started writing down the story of my life."

"The story of your—"

"The ENTIRE story of my life."

"I don't remember you ever writing down so much as a grocery list. Even your checks are signed by Mrs. Schmitz."

"I'm already in the middle of writing the first chapter, the story of my birth. After this, I will chronicle my childhood, my young adulthood, my advanced adulthood, and finally, my maturing years. I'm telling you this in absolute confidence. Lock and key."

Rutherford accidentally coughs a cloud of smoke into his friend's face.

"You're writing about your own birth? What could you possibly have to say about it?"

"I have a vivid memory of my own birth." Mr. Schmitz exhales slowly and rests his chin against his great boulder of a chest. "I even remember what happened before I came out."

Rutherford flicks his cigarette against the back of the green wooden bench, and waits.

"There were milky red-and-black clouds swirled up all around me, and I was suspended in a substance that had the consistency of fruit preserves."

Rutherford frowns, watching as Mr. Schmitz's eyes converge slightly.

"Under the strongest lock and key. Listen to my story."

"I'm listening."

"When I came out, I entered a state of mild shock. I couldn't even cry. I felt only that I was being pushed on from all sides, like I was caving in. When the doctor slapped me, the pressure burst. I was never the same afterward. I was a new person." He scratches his cheek. "This is all included in the first chapter."

Rutherford regards his friend's profile. Mr. Schmitz wears an undersized yellow checked jacket over a collared T-shirt and a bright speckled tie. An oily stain in the shape of Michigan peeks out from beneath his belly whenever he sits up straight, which is often. He has flat, happy eyes and is fond of rubbing his chin. He has combed his sandy hair loosely to one side, with an air of studied tidiness that is disrupted only by a single recalcitrant tuft that ribbons up behind one ear. His rigid sedentary pose was acquired over a half-century earlier at the Menno Simons School-house of Lancaster County, Pennsylvania, where he took a course every morning called Rectitude; the robust nuns lashed the students' curved backs with aluminum metric rulers.

Sitting in this fashion Mr. Schmitz towers over his friend,

despite being several inches shorter in height. Perhaps it is because of the disjunction of sight lines that Mr. Schmitz does not notice his friend's scrutiny. Rutherford has the attitude of a man who stares hard at his own reflection in a sparkling lake in order to make out what lurks in the water beneath. Mr. Schmitz sits oblivious and still, except for his wayward tuft of hair, which jogs in the steady uptown breeze.

"I once kept a diary," says Rutherford. "But I never read it over. I didn't want to remind myself of all those days when nothing happened—the long passages of time between memorable events. Days like that make up most of our lives. We miss those days only if we keep track of them."

"I think I know exactly what you mean," says Mr. Schmitz. He lets his smoldering butt fall gently to the ground. After coughing several times into his armpit, he spits out a hunk of matter that resembles loose egg whites.

"Recently I've been having this dream, every night," continues Mr. Schmitz. "Though I forget it as soon as I wake. I haven't remembered a dream for over three months. I'm certain that I'm dreaming—I always was an active dreamer. But now, whatever dream I'm having, it vanishes the very second the sports radio comes on. That's at five-fifteen a.m."

"I sometimes have that dream," says Rutherford. He is transfixed by the loose egg white matter and does not quite follow his friend's words.

"I wake up to nothing—no memories of dreams. It's like I stopped existing for the night," says Mr. Schmitz. "I'm calm at first, but seconds later, I start to panic. I pull on my hair sometimes and once in a while"—he leans over to Rutherford, whispering hoarsely—"I turn the radio up so loud that my ears start vibrating. This usually wakes up Agnes, even when her hearing aids aren't in. And when she wakes up, she starts screaming."

"Mrs. Schmitz can, at times, be easily disturbed," says Rutherford, frowning again, and straightening his cuffs. He wears cufflinks, even on a Saturday morning like this one, at the beginning of spring.

"I have a theory about what happens in these lost dreams," says Mr. Schmitz. "I think they take place in a foreign land. A land that appears different to everyone who visits it."

"I think I know this place," says Rutherford, suddenly alert. His arm flies up; his forefinger jabs at a gray cloud above. "The strangest things happen there." Rutherford removes his hat, a black bowler, for a moment, before resting it back down on his matted hair.

Mr. Schmitz watches him closely, his eyes asquint. He speaks in a whisper: "You know what land I'm thinking of, then?"

"Of course I do," replies Rutherford, his voice lilting like a musical saw. "We spent the best days of our lives there, oh, fifty years ago."

"Yes. Tell me about it. Maybe it will help me remember my dreams."

The two men pause for a moment, taking in a deep, cold breath of air. They light new cigarettes, adjust various articles of clothing (a dirty collared shirt; a black bowler), and make brief surveys of the park in front of them. Finally, after exhaling the first mouthfuls of smoke over their outside shoulders, the two old friends turn again to face each other.

2

One morning in May, nearly a year after Eugene had begun working at Aaronsen and Son, he was assigned, with Alvaro, a job on a shady block between Park and Madison on the Upper East Side. Their moving van rumbled to a stop in front of a three-story redbrick Georgian townhouse. Alvaro, who seemed never to have ventured south of Harlem, removed a crumpled red polo shirt from the floor under his seat, and stretched it over his wife-beater. Eugene was wearing a heavy winter hat, his company's sports jacket, and Alvaro's gold-rimmed aviator glasses.

He realized it was irrational, but Eugene hadn't been this close to his childhood apartment all year and he was terrified of running into his father. He had no idea what he would say to him—that he was back from Florida on vacation?

Alvaro seemed to sense his anxiety. He stared at Eugene for a moment and then broke into a wide grin, his dimples popping craters in his cheeks. He wrapped his arm around Eugene's shoulder and led him to the house. The front door stood ajar, so they peeked inside and announced themselves.

"Hello?" boomed a man's voice. "HELLO? God damn it, who's down there?"

Alvaro and Eugene raced up the stairs and into a hall decorated with large oil canvases of British hunting scenes that depicted eager spaniels prancing gamely around fallen elk and wild boars. The old man was in a room at the end of the hall, dark except for a single lightbulb that hung on a wire from the ceiling; it had all the charm of an interrogation chamber. Several moments passed before Eugene's eyes could make anything out in the dim light. Crowded blackwood bookshelves began to take shape before him. They lined every wall of the room from floor to ceiling, and the rows of books were interrupted here and there by gold-framed photographs. An elderly man with a large head and wide, sunken shoulders sat upright in the middle of the room on a stool. His arms lay dead across his knees so he looked like a man waiting for a dog to return with his throwing stick. He wore a crisp, finely tailored suit and had chalky white hair that gleamed under the hanging lightbulb, which swung back and forth ever so slightly in the room's stuffy air.

The man appeared not to have heard Eugene and Alvaro's footsteps, for instead of acknowledging their presence he made an unpleasant retching sound, hung his head back, and opened his mouth, yawning like a lion. Two rows of bright white teeth sprang up to his lips, with such force that it looked as if they would leap out of his mouth altogether. The man convulsed, and the teeth popped back into his jaw. With a deep sense of relief, Eugene realized they were dentures.

"Hello, sir," he said, stepping forward.

"Yes? Ah, there you are," said the man, suddenly amiable, though on another face, his smile would have seemed a grimace.

"Excuse the light. You see, we have this curious situation with our BOOKS." He hit his palms against his knees whenever he stressed a word. "They simply cannot abide the light. And so we're stuck here," he said, beginning to chuckle softly to himself, "in the DARK!"

"Are you Mr. Chisholm?" said Eugene. Alvaro appeared distracted, and was drifting off to one side.

"What's that? Oh yes. I'm Chisholm. ABRAHAM Chisholm," he said, slapping his knee. "Well what brings you here today? How can I HELP you?"

"We're from Aaronsen and Son—we had an order to move some furniture from this house to an office uptown?"

"What is it? I can't see so well. What are you looking at? Ah. Yes, there's Connie." Chisholm had followed Alvaro's gaze to a bronze bust that stood on a pedestal in front of one of the bookshelves. "Good old Connie."

Eugene walked over to the bust. It had been modeled after a young man, robustly proportioned; his caved eyes and pear-shaped cheeks gave him the rugged look of a prizefighter.

"Why don't you take a look around," said Chisholm. He raised his palm high above his knee, ominously, in preparation for an extra large smack. "I don't mind. AT ALL!"

Eugene nodded and, with a glance to Alvaro, he began to survey the thousands of books that had been packed into the cramped space. The first title that he was able to make out was a familiar one: Eakins's *The Darkness and the Devil*. As he went to take it down he noticed that it was one of over a dozen copies of that novel on the same shelf. Each of them was laminated and marked by a sticker on which was printed the edition's publishing company, printing, and date.

"The Darkness!" shouted Chisholm from his chair, his voice filled with delight. "What wisdom, what daring! What ecstatic madness."

"You like Eakins, Mr. Chisholm?"

"Like? Like? Why, LOOK," said Chisholm, with a triumphant slap. He swept his arm around wildly to indicate the entire room. Eugene, his eyes finally adjusted to the light, realized that every shelf was filled with books by Constance Eakins. Chisholm hadn't only collected the novels, essay collections, poetry collections, plays, and memoirs, but he also had anthologies, books of photographs taken by Eakins and books of photographs taken of Eakins, artworks inspired by his writing, scholarly studies, histories in which he was mentioned, and old literary magazines containing his short stories. A whole shelf was devoted to the Jaymes Silk detective novels he wrote under a pseudonym; another shelf included several editions of a Cajun cookbook written by his aunt, Jinnie Eakins, and even a slim volume of topographical surveys of the swamps of southern Louisiana, collected by Duane R. S. Eakins, Constance's cartographer nephew. Framed photographs among the shelves showed Eakins in various poses, at different stages of his life. In one, he was thrusting a spear through a cheetah's forehead; in another, he was wearing only a towel across his hips, lying in a yacht beside a topless woman who, if Eugene wasn't mistaken, was Rita Hayworth.

"Let me explain," said Chisholm. "I am a biographer. Eakins is my closest friend in the WORLD and I am writing his biography. I have been put off by endless delays and problems. My health—that's one. Public skepticism about Eakins's survival— that's two."

"You seem like you're in pretty good health."

"That's exactly wrong. I'm ill beyond belief. Just this morning I spent two hundred minutes in the loo, on the growler. I call that ILL. Where am I?

"Ah. Space difficulties, that's three. You see, I need an office. I'm moving, to 190th Street and Riverside. I'll work there until I finish my project. I need someone to move the books and the desk. I have only my daughter. She helps me greatly with my work and she is able-bodied, but not physically robust. And I'm not in book-lifting condition, alas. So I asked you. That is, my daughter called your company, because I'm terrible with the phones and cannot manage. I have a HEARING problem. I can HEAR you only because I am wearing these absolutely miraculous hearing aids."

Chisholm pushed his fingers deep into his ears and removed two beige plastic devices. They had been custom-designed to fit into his ear canal, which must have been unusually narrow and spiraled: the hearing aids looked something like corkscrews.

"I understand now," said Eugene, trying to placate the old man. He feared that Chisholm was working himself up into a hysterical fit.

"WHAT?" Slap.

"I understand now," said Eugene, louder.

"WHAT! WHAT! Ah. Please hold on." He remembered his hearing aids, which he now screwed back into his head. "There. So now you understand."

Alvaro and Eugene spent all morning stacking the books into boxes and moving them, along with the furniture, to a small studio apartment by the river in Washington Heights, not far from Aaronsen and Son. The room, on the top floor of a nondescript prewar elevator building, had a single window that gave onto

views of the George Washington Bridge. A large lacquered mahogany desk filled nearly half the apartment, so they had to stack
the boxes of Eakinsiana on top of it and even in the bathroom,
on the toilet and in the shower. They couldn't wash their dusty
hands or splash water on their faces because they had plugged
the sink and filled it with commemorative coins issued by the
Italian government, bearing Eakins's profile.

There was no way they'd finish the job before the evening, so
Chisholm said they could go home and come back the next day.

"I can stay longer," said Eugene. Alvaro glared at him. "I don't
mind being around all these books—I'm happy to work late and
start shelving them."

"Very good," said Chisholm. "I'll pay overtime."

Alvaro lingered a moment after Chisholm left.

"Are you OK? Why do you want to stay late?"

"What? I'm fine."

Alvaro cocked his head to get a better look at his friend, but
when he seemed satisfied that Eugene was determined to stay, he
bounded out of the apartment. Eugene was alone. There was
once a time when this would have scared him, but now he was
surprised to realize that what he had been craving was not the
time to study Chisholm's Eakins collection, but the isolation it
would bring.

He began by organizing Eakins's books in chronological order,
creating separate sections for the biographies, criticism, and mis-
cellanea. He paused often to read certain passages, and dwelled
particularly on rare material that he had never encountered in all
his thesis research. He did not know, for instance, that Eakins

had dedicated several volumes, erudite though drily academic, to a critical study of Norse mythology: *The Legend of Idavoll.* But Eugene was most excited to find an obscure collection of short stories, published by a small Triestine publisher called Casa Esperanta. The volume included an early story that he had never seen before, called "The Saddest Man." It was very late by this time, so Eugene decided to take a break and read.

The story begins with Lorenzo, the young man of the title, spotting a plain brown-haired girl sitting at a bus stop. She is wearing a misshapen gray dress that her mother, the wife of a farmer in the Dolomites, has sewn for her out of flax. Her braided hair bounces against her nape, and the neck of her dress falls off to reveal a scarlet bra strap. She's not gorgeous, but she has lively, emerald eyes and mischievous dimples that Eakins describes as "indicative of some vast undisclosed intelligence." Lorenzo watches her, waiting for a nod or a smile. In response she squeezes her face disapprovingly and concentrates on the ground in front of her. Lorenzo leans toward her to get her attention, smiles in mock defeat, and then leans in again. Her frown only deepens. The bus does not come. Soon another girl comes by, younger and urban, Aryan and haughty. Lorenzo's "cheeks puff out." He mumbles to himself and shakes his head in disbelief at her cold beauty. When the farm girl sees that Lorenzo has found a new quarry and forgotten about her, she grows anxious and even sneaks looks at Lorenzo and the Aryan.

The bus finally arrives, but it is packed and no one can get on. Finally it "exhales" several people, and the Aryan girl, who is closest to the door, slides aboard just before the door closes. Lorenzo gives chase, but it is too late. The Aryan girl waves at him behind the glass, laughing, and mouthing words that he cannot decipher. "I'll go with you anywhere!" shouts Lorenzo. "Open up!" He pounds the door and jogs beside the bus for a dozen feet before it pulls away. He skulks back to the bus stop, furious at himself for not speaking to the Aryan girl, but also secretly thrilled by the interaction. At that moment the plain farm girl, grinding her teeth, walks up beside him and introduces herself. Would you like to walk to the next stop? Eakins's description of her speech sticks with Eugene—she talks "in a laughing kind of voice."

While they walk, the girl can't help but notice that Lorenzo is still staring at the departed bus ahead of them as it disappears over a hill. She clenches her hand in frustration. Soon, however, Lorenzo touches her fist, and she opens her fingers into his.

Eugene put down the book and lay on the floor among the piles of Eakins memorabilia. His head rested on a history of American literature whose cover featured a small picture of Eakins, squeezed between portraits of Henry Adams and Mark Twain. A *Life* magazine from the autumn of 1971—the cover image showed Eakins during his failed congressional campaign, dressed as George Washington—was spread across Eugene's face, shielding him from the sunlight that had begun to slant through the apartment's single window. As the sounds of traffic rose from the highway, he absently pulled several paperbacks over his chest as if they might together form a blanket.

There was a rapping on the front door, and he shifted abruptly, sending his foot into a stack of Eakins's out-of-print third novel, *Better Days Will Haunt You.* When the spine of an annotated hardcover edition landed on his forehead, he saw black spots wherever there was light.

"Dad? Are you in there?"

Eugene's head throbbed in protest.

"Dad? Open up!"

Eugene stumbled up, and tried to straighten out the piles around him, not noticing the many books he trod underfoot. The knocking on the door was insistent and increasingly frantic.

Eugene found the door and opened it. A young woman stood in front of him. When she saw Eugene, she opened her mouth, and then lurched back.

"Who the hell are you," she said. It was spoken like an accusation.

"Eugene. Um. Brentani."

"Where's my father? Is he all right?"

"He's coming back soon." He could not help noticing, in his muddled state, that she was beautiful, even as her pale lips formed a defiant moue and her arms dangled in a mix of exasperation and perhaps fear. Auburn hair falling to her shoulders, a wiry voice stifled in her long pale throat, and a thin red shirt missing the top and bottom buttons. A small white scar cupped the hollow beneath her left eye. The only trait she seemed to have inherited from Chisholm was the almost rabid intensity of her glare.

"I'm working for him," said Eugene. "Shelving books. Organizing."

Standing on tiptoe, the girl peered over his shoulder. After determining, from what she saw, that he was telling the truth, she seemed to take account of him for the first time.

"You're not doing such a good job of it," she said. "Can I—?"

She pushed past him into the crowded apartment.

"Were you sleeping?"

"I started reading and . . . it was very warm."

"You don't look like the moving-man type."

"Hey—I'm stronger than I look," he said. He was joking but she didn't pick up on it, so he felt like an idiot. "I mean, it's just a job. It lets me see how other people live."

She ignored him and began cleaning up the mess of books scattered across the floor. After a minute she looked at him and laughed.

"Do you happen to know anything about the man who wrote all the books you're moving around?"

"Of course," he said. "Eakins? He's the greatest writer I know."

"Then you'll be sorry to see this." She opened her purse and handed him a folded newspaper. Eugene read the headline: U.S. TO REDUCE CASE AGAINST SCIENTIST TO A SINGLE CHARGE. The article was about the trial of a former Los Alamos scientist accused of stealing nuclear weapons secrets.

"Oh, I see," said Eugene, relieved to make the connection. "This is like Eakins's short story about the nuclear scientist Velibor Topic, who feeds small radioactive pebbles to his neighbors' dogs."

She looked at him blankly.

"*Was* it Velibor Topic? Maybe I'm confused. It's early and I've been up reading stories all night."

"Look farther down."

He uncrinkled the newspaper and saw, at the bottom of the page, the headline CONSTANCE EAKINS, LEGENDARY AUTHOR OF *TOBIN THE LESSER* AND *SACRAMENT*, IS DECLARED DEAD.

The article followed:

> Constance Eakins, a colossus of the last American century, who changed the face of literature with his bold,

imaginative novels, poems, plays, and essays, has been declared dead by authorities in Trieste, Italy, the last city in which he was known to have lived. Mr. Eakins's whereabouts have been unknown for three decades, ever since he disappeared during a hiking trip in the Carso, the high mountain countryside region surrounding the city. In Italy, the statute of limitation on a missing person case is thirty years—if a person is not found by that time, the case is closed and the state issues a death certificate. Mr. Eakins would have been eighty-three this year.

In recent decades, Mr. Eakins was rumored to have been working on a final novel—his twenty-sixth—provisionally titled "The Mayor's Tongue." No manuscript, however, has ever surfaced. "He has left a profound literary legacy, diabolically daunting and likely never to be matched," wrote Barney Dylan, the Director of the Eakins Center at Yale University, in his foreword to the Modern Library's new edition of Eakins's major novel trilogy, *The Slayed, The Slaying,* and *The Slaughter.*

With his Churchillian brio and Falstaffian appetites—for adventure, glamour, violence, sport, and most of all, women—Mr. Eakins may have been equally recognized for aspects of his life that had nothing to do with his writing. Over the years, he had stood accused, by critics and occasionally in a court of law, of excessive prodigality, brutalism, graft, lechery, whoremongering, thievery, murder, and even cannibalism (though these last two claims have been largely discredited). Mr. Eakins has long been described as a figure "larger than

life," and it is likely that his legacy will prove larger
than death as well.

Mr. Eakins was born on the bank of the Mississippi
River in St. Rose, Louisiana, where his father worked
in a sardine cannery. . . .

"You see?" said Chisholm's daughter, tapping the page in Eugene's hands. "I need to find my father. You can keep that copy, I have dozens. If you see Dad first, tell him I'll be back later."

"OK!" said Eugene, much louder than he had intended, to the slammed door.

Eugene sat down on a crate by the desk and gingerly unfolded the newspaper. Next to the obituary, the newspaper ran an old picture of the writer, taken in the late forties. The face of young Eakins had an angularity normally associated with the features of the desiccated elderly. Eugene wondered why they hadn't used a more recent author photo, such as the one that appeared on the dust jacket of *The Man with Holes in His Cheeks,* Eakins's last published memoir. Perhaps it was because the author, as photographed in the years before his disappearance, was not easy to look at. His head had become jowly and grotesquely elongated, his shaggy blond hair and beard darted out all sides of the frame, and his eyes were sunken from exhaustion. Young Eakins's face had just as many sharp angles, but they were distributed more favorably. They were there in his sharp widow's peak, in the diagonals that slanted downward from the corners of his mouth, in his broken-glass stare. Here was a man who had lived. As the obituary pointed out, by the time he was twenty-three—Eugene's age—he had swum the breaststroke in every continent (even Antarctica), mastered nine languages (including three dead ones), received a war medal, and conducted epistolary correspondences with such writers as H. L. Mencken, Yasunari Kawabata, and Simone de Beauvoir. Furthermore, as Eugene knew from the first volume of his memoirs, *Gashes*, Eakins had already amassed dozens of lovers, including six women who could not speak a single word of English (one of them a mute, hirsute Inuit), four men (one of them a heterosexual), and a first cousin.

On reading the obituary, Eugene realized that he knew more about Eakins's life than his own father's. He knew that Signor Brentani had been raised in Milan and had lived there until he met his mother, who was traveling with her Wellesley friends over the summer, and they eloped. But most of the years that his parents spent together were vague in his father's retelling. As long as he could remember, Eugene had been collecting details from that period, based on disclosures made during his father's rare moments of expansiveness—which usually coincided with episodes of inebriation or somnambulance—but ultimately he wasn't left with much information about either parent. He had seen only a couple of photographs from that time, and he wondered whether he would even recognize his father as a young man were he to pass him in the street. Were a young Signor Brentani now living in New York, would he frequent the same libraries, movie theaters, and subway stops that Eugene did? Would they strike up a conversation if they found themselves sitting next to each other in the upper deck at Shea Stadium, way at the top behind home plate, where they could see the stadium under their feet and the Long Island Sound through the orange iron grating in the distance behind them?

Eugene could only recall, in fact, a single picture of his father as a young man. He had found it in an old photo album hidden in the hall closet, where they stored his mother's old belongings—a floral slip, a single pearl earring, a sketchbook from a life-drawing course she took in college, and a book of expired raffle tickets from Eugene's preschool. The photo album was, perhaps, the most telling of all the items there. It was filled with grainy pictures, framed by white upraised borders, of his mother's family. Eugene's father appeared in the background of one of these photos. Signor Brentani was standing with his wife's cousins on a sailboat, his hands on his hips. The Bay of Naples was a gray wash behind him. His face seemed to shudder with some kind of violent energy; his eyes were jumpy and his hair was wet and whorled. The horizontal bands of his shirt stretched outward like staves on a barrel about to burst.

Eugene imagined sitting on a wooden bench in the subway late one night and seeing his twenty-three-year-old father sitting there next to him. Would Eugene dare to talk to him? Perhaps they would notice that they were reading the same book: an Eakins novel, say, such as *The Rude Violence of the Poor* or—more appropriately—*Dolman Hardy*. "How do you like the book so far?" Eugene would ask his young father, nodding at the book. "The character of Dolman is vivid to me," the signore would reply, in perfect English. "I feel as if I know him, or have met him somewhere—yet I am sure I haven't had the pleasure!" He'd laugh nervously.

EUGENE BRENTANI (AGE TWENTY-THREE): What did you think about the scene in the city, when the streets are empty—have you made it that far?

SIGNOR PIERO ODOLFO BRENTANI (AGE TWENTY-THREE): Yes, it's marvelous. All of the people are inside, sitting at their windows and waiting for something to happen, when—let's see . . . yes, here's the passage:

Their pale faces lined the avenue like dim streetlamps. Dolman wandered on, exhausted and febrile, hoping to find a hospitable stranger. But there was no candlelit beer-hall, no inn, not even a bordello to welcome him. With a growing sense of alarm, he realized that he had not yet seen even a single door.

EUGENE: That's it.
PIERO: Eakins was only twenty-three when he wrote that.
EUGENE: He had already fought in a war, and murdered a man.
PIERO: His whiskers grew nigh up to his eyes.

The two men would sit in mute appreciation of Eakins, and wonder privately if they had become friends. It wouldn't be long before they would realize, with a shock, their uncanny resemblance to each other. They would not converse further, but when the train finally arrived, they'd discover happily that they were getting off at the same stop.

But it didn't happen!"

When Eugene woke this time it was full morning and Abraham Chisholm was towering over him. His white hair flopped the wrong way over his head so that it hung over an ear, his lips were bright red with denture marks, he wrung his hands like claws—and he was shouting.

"It did NOT happen!" Chisholm was no longer slapping his leg. He was slapping his own face.

Eugene rushed to his feet, books cascading down his back and arms. The old man was holding two copies of the newspaper, one in each hand. He stared unseeingly across the room, his cheek inflamed scarlet.

"Alison!" he shouted. "Alison! Alison! ALISON!"

"It's just me," said Eugene. He backed away from Chisholm into the recesses of the room, his hands reaching for purchase as he stumbled over falling books and planted his sneakers into cardboard boxes.

"ALISON! ALISON! ALISON—"

"I'm here, Dad," said a voice from the doorway. The overhead lights went on.

"Ah, Alison. I don't understand. Why do they print this?"

"I don't know, Dad." She embraced him gently but he did not seem to notice. "I think you should calm down now," she said, in a voice so relaxed that it seemed robotic. She held his hand firmly to stop it from shaking. It looked as though she had experience in this.

"You'll have to go back to visit Connie."

"Dad, do you remember Eugene? The moving man. He's right there."

Eugene smiled at her.

"I see . . . oh! Eugene, yes. And how has the moving gone?"

"It might take a little bit longer," said Eugene. "I have to admit I've been a bit distracted by all the books."

"The books, yes, of course. You do know what I'm doing here, with this new office?"

The telephone began to ring and Chisholm answered it with a howl. He had an unusual telephone manner. When he spoke, he held the apparatus straight in front of his face, his mouth directly on the receiver. This ensured that the person on the other end of the line would have no trouble hearing him, but had the disadvantage of forcing the earpiece so far from his ear that he couldn't himself hear anything that was said to him.

"Hello? No, no no, no, NO!" He shifted the phone so that the earpiece was even with the bridge of his nose. "He's very much alive. What? I can't hear you," he said, and abruptly hung up.

"They've been calling me all morning at home," said Chisholm. "The bastards."

With a start, he wrested free of Alison's grip and charged at Eugene, adroitly dodging Eakins detritus along the way. He didn't stop until he was only inches away from Eugene's face, and Eugene was backed against the wall. Chisholm's breath, that close, was shocking.

"Eakins is my friend and we keep in close touch. He has long avoided public scrutiny, you see, but we have a close personal relationship: we correspond regularly. Why, I received a note from him not three days ago!"

"You mean—Eakins is alive?"

"Of course. We correspond regularly. Alison visits him often, and she gives me reports. You see, I am too WEARY to travel. How old do you think I am?"

". . . Sixty?"

"WRONG! Seventy-four!"

All of a sudden a strange phantom seemed to overtake Chisholm's features. The corners of his mouth stretched back, his eyes squinted shut, his carbuncled nose wrinkled like a frightened snail, and his ears perked and turned mauve. If the process progressed any further, his skin might have retreated entirely off his skull, but at this moment his features froze. After several seconds, his hands began to grasp at the air, kneading invisible balls of clay. It occurred to Eugene that the old man was having a heart attack. Should he grab his chest, massage it? An enormous burst of noise issued from deep within Chisholm's belly. Then, with a gasp, he began to jiggle and nod uncontrollably. Spittle burst from his mouth and, it seemed, his nose. It dawned on Eugene that this was the old man's idea of laughter. Chisholm's eyes slowly opened, glassy and wet like two bivalves, and appealed mirthfully to Eugene to join in the fun. Eugene laughed hollowly, looking to Alison for help. She was staring out the window, as if lost in some private thought.

The phone rang. Chisholm turned and raced back to pick it up.

"Hello? No! Alive. Not dead! WHAT? Ah, hold on." He transferred the phone to his ear. "Yes. It's under way. 'Constance Eakins: A Life.' In three volumes, maybe four. Thank you." He slammed the phone down.

Chisholm's convulsions came to a rest and his voice grew somber. He turned to Eugene.

"You see, this is my life's final WORK."

Alison appeared relieved to see her father go back to slapping his leg, and not his face. Chisholm narrowed his eyes at Eugene.

"What does the moving company pay you hourly?"

"Nine dollars an hour, Mr. Chisholm."

"Call me Abe, son. Now understand this: Alison must leave

in a week for Italy to meet with Connie. I will need an assistant. You are strong: a moving-type fellow. You need to make money. I have money. I can pay you. You know Eakins's work. You LIKE Eakins's work. You can help me. It will be a purely clerical position, I should say. But you will be able to be around . . . all this." He repeated his flailing gesture, and in the process launched several volumes off the top of the nearest pile.

He suddenly looked very nervous, almost desperate. "What do you think?"

"I'm sorry, but I have a job already. Aaronsen and Son treats me well."

"I'll double your wages. Eighteen dollars. No, make it twenty-five an hour."

"I'd have to think about it," said Eugene. The possibility, perhaps, of working one day with Constance Eakins—if he was truly alive—was tempting, but Eugene didn't want to give up his job with Alvaro only to serve as some kind of a stooge for a deranged, and perhaps violent, old man.

Abe sighed and stooped over, his body seeming to fold into itself like a collapsible cot.

Eugene turned to Alison. She was looking right at him now, her lips parted and her gray eyes wide and imploring. It was as if she wanted to convey some secret knowledge.

"I'll do it," he said, staring at Alison as he spoke. "I'd be happy to take part—"

A spasm shook Abe's face. He began to pound his fist on a stack of books piled high on his desk.

"A-HA!" he yelled, as the stack teetered and listed precipitously. "Here we go! Here we go! HERE—WE—GO!"

3

Mr. Schmitz wakes up from a dream he has already forgotten. His fingers are wet. He removes his hand from the mattress and touches it with his other hand, smearing the fluid.

He flicks on the light with a dry pinky finger, and has to blink several times before he can see anything. His wife slowly comes into view. She is sitting up in bed, staring at him. Her fleshy torso is bent over, so that her nightgown strap falls from a shoulder. Scratchy white hair flies askew in curlers and a dentureless mouth gapes. Her eyes are wild.

"Agnes?" says Mr. Schmitz. The bedsheet between them is stained a pale pink. His hands are smeared with it. Agnes hiccups a sob.

"Let me get some tissues," says Mr. Schmitz, rising from the bed. He comes back a minute later with clean, damp hands and a bath towel.

"My darling," he says. Her face is craven and distorted with confusion. "It's OK, darlingdear."

He hands her the towel, which she promptly puts under her bottom.

"I'm so sorry," she says.

"What happened?"

"I couldn't sleep, and then I felt this strange feeling, like I was spinning." She breaks off in tears.

"Oh dear," says Mr. Schmitz. "We'll ask the doctor tomorrow. He will tell us what we need to do."

"Yes," she says. She is distracted and still shaking. "I think it's over now. I suppose I'll take a shower."

"Best to do just that," says Mr. Schmitz. "I'll change the bedding."

When she returns from the shower twenty minutes later, the soiled sheets are crumpled up on the turquoise rug. Mr. Schmitz is lying in a fetal position across the half-made bed, his feet by her pillow, fast asleep.

Later that night, past three in the morning, Rutherford finishes taping a massive sheet of bubble wrap to his dining room table. He needs only to cover the table's legs and the dining room will be fully wrapped. He has already done the entire library and the guest room, but there is still his bedroom, both bathrooms, and the set of Etruscan pottery. He will save the sink and the wine cabinet for his final night in the apartment. The kitchen phone rings. Padding and popping, he makes his way down the hall. When he picks up the receiver he hears panting and immediately knows who it is.

"I had the strangest dreams," says Mr. Schmitz. "And now I can't go back to sleep. I didn't want to wake Agnes. It's just that she—she hasn't been sleeping so well recently. Are you still up?"

"Of course," says Rutherford. He eases himself onto a William

IV–style flame mahogany chair that he has found to be much gentler on his arthritic back ever since he padded it with three layers of bubble wrap.

"What is that popping noise?"

"I just opened a new box of wine. The packaging. So you were dreaming . . ."

"Yes! I think so. The same dreams. I was wandering lost in a foreign city. But what city," sighs Mr. Schmitz, "was it?"

"Let's see. . . . Was it Perugia? Where the people are excessively polite and have a rigid sense of decorum?"

"It's possible," says Mr. Schmitz. "Yes, I think you're right."

A single bubble expires under Rutherford's weight as he leans back in the chair. He closes his eyes and begins Mr. Schmitz's nightly lullaby.

"In Perugia," says Rutherford, "a man doesn't just hold a door open for a lady, but he bows at the same time. His humility forbids him from so much as glancing at the woman's face. When a man proposes marriage, he doesn't only have to ask the permission of his fiancée's parents, but must go begging to every single one of her living relations in a strictly defined hierarchical order, from grandparents down to cousins and little nieces. But if the father accepts him, the rest of the family usually agrees. For it would be considered improper if any other family member were to oppose the decision made by the patriarch for his own daughter. The suitor must also place white lilies on the fiancée's family plot in the graveyard, in order to appease her forebears, who have been cruelly barred by death from this important consultation.

"Fortunately, Perugian families are highly concentrated in number. Relatives rarely move more than one city block away from one another, fearing they might offend their kin. As a result, the families are very large and very close. Over the centuries, these strong familial bonds have been responsible for the forma- tion of the city's peculiar street design. Whereas Bologna began as a collection of towers, radiating out from the city center, Pe- rugia has grown linearly, to accommodate the expansion of fam- ilies over time. That's why Perugia is called *'la città della vista infinita'*—the city of the infinite view."

Mr. Schmitz is silent, but Rutherford knows that he is smil- ing, his head lolled back against his pillows.

"What lonely families," says Mr. Schmitz. "No, I think I was in a different city—the one with the impossible name."

"Ah, that's Ferrara, the most difficult Italian city name to pronounce. To do it, your tongue must distinguish between the roll of a double *r* and the roll of a single *r*. Only Ferrarans can get it exactly right. Their double *r*'s are works of wonder—they roll off into the distance long after the neighboring syllables have faded away, like a bicycle gliding down a hill long after you stop pedaling.

"It's fitting, then, that Ferrara is known as the city of bicycles. There are no automobiles of any type. The air is clean and still. The streets are quiet except for the purr of spinning spokes. The people ride and ride. And since the town is shaped like a giant wheel, they never feel like they have to compete. The faster you go, the faster you return to where you started. In the middle of the town, in the hub of the wheel, there is a small garden. If you stand there during rush hour, you can hear nothing but the cy- clists, their spokes spinning softly on all sides, making a noise that sounds like 'Fe-rra-ra, Fe-rra-ra.'"

"What beautiful bicycles," says Mr. Schmitz, in what sounds to Rutherford like a British accent.

"Excuse me?"

"The sound of wheels," says Mr. Schmitz. "Spinning."

From the steady breathing at the other end of the line, Rutherford can tell that his friend has fallen fast asleep. There is an abrupt grunt, followed shortly by a brief whistle, and then Rutherford gently replaces the receiver.

He goes to the hall closet, where he tears out a new sheet of bubble wrap. He folds it around his bedside table, careful not to cover his airplane ticket, which is sitting there. He sees he has exactly two weeks before his departure, during which time he must transfer his funds to an Italian bank, clean out the refrigerator, cancel his newspaper and magazine subscriptions, and finish packing. And, of course, he still must break the news to Mr. Schmitz.

4

Eugene told Alvaro about his new job that night over two steaming bowls of menudo, which Alvaro had smuggled from his wife's house in a large Tupperware container. He didn't seem to take the news too badly.

"You weren't cut out for manual labor anyway. It's OK, we're still friends."

"I thought you'd understand. You understand, right?"

"This came in the mail for you."

Alvaro handed him a long brown envelope that was stamped with red ink. It had been forwarded to Eugene from the post office box he had registered in Jupiter, Florida. He tore it open and removed a piece of his father's pale-blue stationery. "Piero Odolfo Brentani" was embossed in elegant, slender gold print across the top of the page.

Dear son,
Eugenio,

It's about time I wrote. I had misplaced the address you gave me but have now found it. I hope Florida is fine. New

York is. Today a plumber arrived to fix the bathroom sink, which has been giving me trouble ever since you left but now it is better, thanks to the plumber who came today. How are you? Have you found a job?

Are you learning? Let me know how you are.

With love,

Sig. Brentani,

Your Babbo

"From your father?" asked Alvaro. Eugene looked up.

"You're not going to believe this. It's from my father."

"Can I read it? One's handwriting can be quite revealing—"

"What's in this anyway?" asked Eugene, spooning a sharp-nailed claw out of his red, steaming broth. He set it on the table next to the bowl.

"Gracias," said Alvaro, as he took both the piece of pig's foot and the letter from Eugene.

"This note is quite revealing, actually," said Alvaro. His clenched mouth emitted a sucking noise and Eugene could see a porcine toenail poking through his cheek. *"It looks as if it was written by a child. It seems that you must have been the adult in this relationship. He must be sick without you."*

"You know, I sometimes wonder what the hell you're talking about. It sounds like your mouth is full of crackers. You might as well be telling me to screw myself."

"I have a feeling you're not talking about your father anymore."

"Ah well. I'll be spending a lot more time at old man Chisholm's house from now on."

"If you are maligning me, then you can go screw yourself."

Eugene smiled at Alvaro, as he pried a piece of fatty tissue from behind his molars with the point of his knife. Alvaro smiled back.

"You like menudo, huh? You'd never guess what's in it."

"Alvaro, I have to tell you about this girl at the new job, Abe's daughter. Gray eyes, long reddish-brown hair, beautiful skin, a wide smile—"

"Intestines. Feet. Gut juice. Dried pork skin."

"You said it—she's stunning."

The job was not particularly demanding, especially coming after the arduous work at Aaronsen and Son. Often, after lunch, Abe would ask Eugene to lower the shades, complaining, "The sun at this hour is staring me right in the eyes!" Then Abe would bend over on his papers and fall asleep with his cheek on his desk. And a deep slumber it was. After some cautious experimentation, Eugene determined that nothing would be able to rouse him, short of a defibrillator. In these moments of calm, Eugene tried to work on his translation of Alvaro's manuscript. It was coming slowly. The more he stared at Alvaro's muddied text, the more confused he became, until his frustration reached such a pitch that he considered abandoning the project altogether. But whenever he got to this point of despair, he recalled Eakins's "Keftir the Blind," the short story he was reading the day Alvaro first showed him his manuscript. In his word blindness and his struggle to understand what Alvaro had written, Eugene could sympathize with the grasping, angry Alain Keftir and his wrecked eyes.

In Eakins's story, Keftir is a blind artist who has become moderately famous for his effulgent, kaleidoscopic paintings and his assiduous technique. In preparation for any painting, he studies his subject with great devotion. Eakins is meticulous about this point. For Keftir's famous landscape series of Kansas cornfields, for instance, the artist collects agricultural histories of the state and annual USDA reports on crop yields dating back fifty years (and has them translated into Braille). He questions farmers about their harvesting techniques, the equipment they use, their family histories, and what they daydream about in the fields. He dresses in the farmers' dungarees while he paints. He sleeps in the fields, listens to the wind soughing through the stalks and weeds. He has an affair with a farmer's daughter. He eats corn: corn pone, corn mash, corn on the cob, corn chips, corn syrup. He licks atrazine off of a stalk.

Although his landscapes sell well, Keftir receives his highest commissions for his portraits. Many of his wealthy subjects simply pay for his company. It is just as gratifying to have a charming, humble man listen attentively to one's every murmur and explore every nook of one's home for inspiration as it is to have a portrait of oneself painted. Besides, Keftir's portraits, as Eakins describes them, are not particularly accurate. They mostly consist of splotches of bright color melded together by fine brushwork. Still, the result is impressive for a blind man. His admirers and his subjects agree that some essential character has been captured in these lively amalgams of light and color that an ordinary, "seeing" painter might not have achieved.

Still lifes are easiest for Keftir. Preparation for a fruit bowl painting, for instance, takes no more than an afternoon of fondling the fruit and the bowl, tasting the fruit, and gently pressing the fuzz of a peach skin against his eyes. His favorite subject, in fact, was a still life: a glass filled with water. To Keftir, this was the most pleasing image, perfect in its simple serenity. And yet there is also something infinite and inaccessible about it, since he has no way of determining the exact contours of the water in the glass. As soon as he touches the water, no matter how delicately, its shape fluctuates, becomes something new. The more his paint-stained fingers try to approximate the shape of the water, the more he disrupts it. This inability to understand his subject obsesses him, and he returns to the water glasses again and again, between larger projects, whenever he seeks inspiration. By the end of his career, in fact, he has lost interest in all other subjects.

Despite his many repetitions, the paintings of water glasses are wildly inconsistent. Sometimes he paints large canvases in which a whole ocean of blue and white swash against the sides of a thin glass, raging like a tsunami. Other times the glass itself takes on gigantic proportions, becoming an immense border that subverts the water, simplifying it into abstract shapes. Occasionally, however, what Eakins calls the "waterglass paintings" seem to depict other scenes altogether: a naturalistic portrait of a line of Union soldiers posing in full regalia before a battle; a vista of the Moab desert, complete with cacti prickling the big country sky; a classical rendition of the Pietà. But in each case Keftir would stubbornly deny that he had drawn anything other than the very glass that was sitting on the table in front of him and which his assistant had filled with tap water just an hour earlier.

The tone of the story shifts dramatically when a man in a white lab coat appears at Keftir's door, introducing himself as one Dr. Anton Sorokin. Keftir tells him he no longer does portraiture and begins to close the door in his face, but the visitor blocks it with his foot.

"That's not what I'm here for," he says. "I'm not just an admirer—I'm an ophthalmologist."

Keftir invites him inside, and after some polite conversation, Sorokin explains the reason for his visit: he's developed a new procedure that may allow Keftir to regain his vision.

Keftir is silent, but his hands fumble over his face and under his glasses. To Sorokin, writes Eakins, "it looks as if Keftir were using his knuckles to knead his eyeballs deep into his brain." Sorokin fears he's caused pain, but when Keftir looks up, it's clear that the artist is crying tears of joy.

A week later Sorokin performs the surgery. Keftir convalesces, with the help of heavy painkillers, at Sorokin's lab, his entire head wrapped in bandages. After a few weeks, a nurse wheels Keftir into a circular, subterranean chamber sealed off from any light source. A second nurse trundles in a wheelbarrow filled with clunky plastic objects that protrude copper plugs. They are shaped like animals: elephants, giraffes, hippopotamuses, and tyrannosaurs. The nurses, holding the nightlights in their hands, stand along the walls of the room, their mouths slack with anticipation. Sorokin positions himself next to Keftir, holding a pair of scissors. A nurse flips a switch, and the lights go out.

Sorokin cuts off the bandage and, one by one, the nurses plug in the nightlights. The first, a blue cow, is so dim that its aura does not even reach across the room to Keftir's wheelchair. The second, a red antelope, causes Keftir to moan in pain.

Sorokin orders the nurses to plug in a third light, and Keftir protests: he says he's in agony.

"It's not pain you're feeling," says Sorokin, with great solemnity. "It's vision."

One by one the nurses plug the animals into the band of outlets. An electric menagerie flickers into being. To the nurses' astonishment, Keftir starts to laugh.

"Is he dying?" asks one of the nurses.

"No," says Sorokin. "He's confused—he can see only pale forms and shadows. Later, when his eyes have developed more fully, everything will become clearer."

"But I can see perfectly now," says Keftir. "What marvelous animals."

The nurses cheer.

After some further rehabilitation, Sorokin decides that Keftir is ready to be exposed to daylight. He wheels Keftir into his private garden, under the hanging boughs of a live oak tree. Sorokin then hands Keftir a pile of matted drawings and sketches—prints of Keftir's most renowned works. He has purchased them at the gift shop of the nearby art museum.

Keftir is confused. "The colors," he says, "they're faded." Sorokin explains that Keftir's sensitivity to color may still be partially impaired, but Keftir isn't placated. He demands that Sorokin give him a glass of water, without ice.

Sorokin runs off, leaving Keftir amid the dappled sunlight under the bright-green leaves of the live oak. Sorokin returns with the glass, and rests it on the armrest of Keftir's wheelchair. Keftir watches, not breathing, as the surface of the water trembles slightly and rocks back and forth in its container; after some seconds it becomes still.

"The water," he gasps, "the water!"

"Just like your pictures."

"No—just now—it was flat. Completely flat."

"Yes," says Sorokin, "but now, the second you talk about it, it is bouncing about right there on your chair, look at that, and even spilling, oh dear—" And the glass falls to the soil.

But Keftir does not notice the glass falling, doesn't even feel the water spill on his bare foot. He sits stock upright and glances around him "like a drunk who has awoken in a place he has never seen before, without remembering how he got there or even who he is." Keftir, defiant, slams his eyes shut. He refuses to open them again until his implants are carved out and the cataracts, mistlike, begin to spread over his eyeballs once more.

Alison came by the office one afternoon to help Abe revise a chapter he'd drafted about Eakins's Hollywood years. Eugene watched them work together from across the room, where he pretended to be copyediting a previous chapter. Alison was sweet with her father. She made each of her editorial suggestions with great delicacy, posing her criticisms in a gentle, self-deprecating manner. "It's probably my own obtuseness," she'd say, "but I don't understand exactly why you've decided to go on at such great length about Eakins's firsthand research for *Humboldt in the Amazon.* Perhaps the section could be shorter?" Or, "Is it really possible that Eakins not only got Elizabeth Taylor pregnant, but delivered their child as well? I'm sure it's just me being foolish, but maybe it would help to have more evidence."

Abe would pat his daughter softly on the back of her hand and say something like "No, my dear, don't doubt yourself, you're right on this point." And Alison would smile secretly to herself as her father marked the change.

Abe left early for bed, but Alison lingered for some time, making further edits on her father's manuscript, rewriting passages, and even, it seemed to Eugene, writing entire new paragraphs. Eugene finally convinced himself to approach the desk, and uttered her name. He realized as soon as it crossed his lips that he was surprised to hear the word spoken aloud, in his own voice.

Alison looked up. She had heard him coming.

"Actually no one calls me Alison except for my father," she said. "You can call me Sonia."

"Right. Sonia, then." Eugene said her new name to himself, and realized he had nothing else to say to her. "So, Sonia. I wanted to ask you, what is Eakins like? I can't believe he's actually alive. Can you tell me where he lives?"

"I don't know."

"What do you mean? Where are you meeting him?"

"Don't you understand?" she asked. A mocking smile played at the corners of her mouth. "I've never met the man."

Eugene watched her closely. Her smile froze.

"You mean he's dead?" said Eugene.

"I couldn't say for certain. That is what everyone else seems to think."

"What about the letters?"

"Look, you may work for my father, but you don't see how he really is. He's older now, and maybe a little less patient than he used to be, I realize that, but he was a legend in his time—one of the most respected critics and historians of literature around. He's a passionate, serious man."

"Serious about Eakins, that's for sure."

"Yes, and if it wasn't for Eakins, I'm not sure he would last another month. Eakins keeps him alive. They knew each other since the sixties, when Eakins was living in a houseboat on the Seine and my father was in a flat on the Left Bank. Which is when he met my mother. I think she might have known Eakins. In fact, she might have been quite close to him, at least briefly."

Sonia looked back down at her father's manuscript, as if she had forgotten to fix something there.

"But the letters?" asked Eugene. "Who writes those?"

"Who do you think? The funny thing is, he doesn't even recognize my handwriting."

"You're joking."

"I've gone to 'visit' Eakins four times. I love Italy, I love Trieste, I have friends there. By the central piazza, there's this beautiful boardwalk where I like to sit and read. I meet strangers, practice my Italian, go on adventures. When I come home my father is grateful, content."

Eugene watched her until he was certain that she was telling the truth.

"I had a similar thing happen in my family," he said at last. "My great-grandfather Ozzie—my mother's grandfather—opened a shoe store after he emigrated from Germany. It was called Zrel's Shoes—Zrel was his name, at least according to the authorities at Ellis Island. The store was the pride of my family, their gift to their descendants, the proof that they'd made it in America. All the Zrels worked there. Even my mother, as a young girl.

"The store was destroyed during the 1968 riots. Ozzie was dead by then, and his wife, Lily, was living in an old-age home.

My family went to visit her the week of the riots, and realized that no one had told her about what had happened to Zrel's. So they decided not to mention it—no need to make the old lady any more upset. But she stayed alive for a long time after that. Anytime someone visited, Lily would ask how business was going. They'd tell her it was going great. My mother would make up all kinds of stories about our customers and Lily would laugh like a baby."

"Did you ever tell her? Or did she die not knowing?"

"The last time I saw her I was fourteen. She was ninety-seven but still alert. The first thing she asked me was if we were still selling Keds. I said yes, of course, they were flying off the shelves. I knew no one had ever told her the truth about the store, but just the same I was taken aback. I wondered whether, on some level, she knew what had happened. She wasn't senile, after all, just old. She didn't die for another few years—she was one hundred and one."

"So it worked? The lie?"

"I suppose so."

"I have a pair of Keds."

"Oh yeah? What kind?"

"Well," she said, looking down, "they're powder blue, with beige rubber soles, rounded at the toes . . ."

Eugene noticed her sneakers beneath the desk.

". . . and spotless white laces."

"Exactly," she said.

A steady wind was blowing off the river now; it whistled through the old building's air vents like a muted scream.

"Check that out," said Sonia, pointing outside. Framed by the window, in the overcast sky, a half-moon glowed a bilious green hue. A thin white frill of cloud skidded across it.

"I've never seen anything like it," said Eugene. His chest was swollen, felt like it was going to explode.

"It's just strange is all," she said, crossing her arms over her chest. "I need to go home. You can walk me to a cab, if you like." She got up abruptly, her hair whipping over her eyes.

They walked to Broadway and Eugene hailed her a taxi. Sonia gave him a weak handshake. Eugene was desperately certain that he had bored her into leaving.

"I'll see you soon?" She said it in a tone that seemed to signify to Eugene the opposite. "Maybe before I leave."

"I hope so," said Eugene. With a curious, sideways glance, Sonia slunk into the taxicab. Eugene could tell that, behind the dark backseat window, she was still looking at him. He wondered if she would ever look at him that way, or any way, again.

5

Although they rarely speak in bed, it's there that Mr. Schmitz has his most profound interactions with his wife. These are not of a sexual nature, although for Mr. Schmitz, they are passionate. During the moments just after Agnes falls asleep, the semidarkness has a strange tendency to transform some physical detail into the shape of an old memory. A lock of hair, brittle and white by day, morphs into a healthy blond curl, bobbing as it did under the klieg lights of the football field at Lancaster County High School, where Agnes had been a cheerleader and he the editor of the school newspaper. Her lips, in a certain sleepy pose, remind Mr. Schmitz of the mischievous look that used to come over her face when she wanted to be kissed—like on their tenth wedding anniversary, on the boardwalk in Atlantic City, when she leaned against his chest to escape the spray of the crashing surf. But the detail that strikes him most devastatingly is her fist. When she has bad dreams, she balls up her hands, and Mr. Schmitz remembers something she wrote him in a letter that summer of 1944—the summer he met Rutherford.

Both men were stationed in Udine in the final year of the war, operating out of the Campoformido Airfield. Mr. Schmitz served as a runner, charged with sprinting up and down the line of command with encoded messages. Rutherford, a pilot, was greatly admired in camp for his garrulous wit, ribald storytelling, and most of all, his cooking—even though the scant provisions provided to the soldiers (cheese bars, ten varieties of canned meat, and something called "soluble cream product") presented few opportunities for him to display the culinary expertise he had acquired working in his uncle's Mulberry Street restaurant. When the men grew dizzy from hunger and malnutrition, and could eat no more variations of canned meat, they pleaded with Rutherford to describe his favorite dishes. So as the men spooned out clumps of Irish stew, he would explain to them the exact method for whisking eggs for a frittata, simmering onions for a Genovese sauce, or stuffing squid with breadcrumbs, parsley, and garlic to make calamari ripieni. The men would swallow their military rations with smiles and closed eyes, dreaming that they were digesting venison instead of waterlogged beef, bistecca alla fiorentina instead of preserved lamb chunks.

Mr. Schmitz, then Private Schmitz, was not nearly as portly in those days, though his hips were still wide enough to prevent him from squeezing into the cockpit of an Avenger or a Mustang. So during the day, while the fighter pilots flew drills overhead and left on surveying missions, he would stay behind in the camp, supervising the flight log and decoding signals sent by telegraph. The pilots—the camp's leaders and larger personalities—tended to ignore him. If he laughed at a joke during dinner, they would stare at him crossly, until he shifted his seat farther from the campfire, receding into the shadows where he couldn't be seen.

Rutherford didn't pay him any attention either. Most of the time Rutherford was surrounded by a cordon of his comrades, regaling them with lascivious stories, recipes, and anecdotes about his freewheeling youth on the Lower East Side; otherwise he retired into his tent with books sent to him by one of his girlfriends from New York. Private Schmitz suspected that Rutherford got all his stories from these books. He once even sneaked inside Rutherford's tent to gather evidence, so that he could expose the phony chef and get his revenge. But he was shocked to discover that the books were not the dimestore novels he and the others occasionally leafed through. Instead, there were scholarly books on the history of art, a philosophical treatise on Epicureanism, a worn edition of *The Canterbury Tales*, and an Italian grammar textbook. Private Schmitz never mentioned his discovery, but he was no longer angered by Rutherford, only puzzled.

One week, when the division was in Trieste on a supply run, a ship carrying fresh produce from Split capsized in the Adriatic Sea, just several hundred yards from shore. The captain and his small crew waved distress flags, as the boat tilted and slowly plunged. The port's starving deckhands and unemployed sailors took off in rafts for the sinking ship. As soon as their ravenous, sallow faces came into view, the ship's captain and his crew threw down their distress flags and jumped overboard, swimming wildly to shore.

When the starving men climbed aboard the sinking ship, the smell overtook them—a stench so acrid it made their eyes water. Below deck they found the source. There, illuminated by two twinkling oil lamps, was a low-ceilinged hold that stretched back the length of the ship. Thousands of heads of garlic filled the room, piled nearly two feet high. The men howled with rage, and in their despair, took out their guns. They fired into the garlic carpet, sending cloves flying like shrapnel, smashing against the walls, spraying their faces with the bitter juice. The rampage was interrupted by a yell behind them—it was Rutherford, running into the hold, begging them to stop. The garlic was valuable: didn't they know anything about Italian cooking? It could transform what food they had into something edible, maybe even tasty. Chastened, the men stopped firing, and backed away. Then, at the other end of the room, the garlic mass started shifting. A single flabby arm shot out, waving frantically. The men jumped at the sight.

"It's OK," shouted Rutherford. "You can come out now. We won't shoot."

But it wasn't one of the ship's crew.

"I thought," said Private Schmitz, "you were going to kuh-kuh-kill me."

As he straightened, garlic tumbled off of him, like boulders off a mountain. Rutherford and his men looked at him in disbelief. Crushed garlic flecked his chin and cheeks. He had been weeping, and his face was scarlet.

"I was starving," he said. "I was just so . . . ha-ha-hungry."

At that moment, everything changed. Rutherford dedicated himself to cooking, mixing heavy portions of crushed garlic with shrimp, mussels, and octopus, to create such dishes as gamberoni all'aglio, cozze all'aglio, and polipi veraci all'aglio. And he always saved the first bite for Private Schmitz.

"Not enough garlic," Private Schmitz said, after trying an early concoction: porca selvaggia all'aglio. Rutherford realized that Private Schmitz was not joking at all.

"My ideal eater," said Rutherford, his voice brimming with

awe. And Private Schmitz, though he was confused, laughed and laughed, humoring his new friend. From then on, Private Schmitz was Rutherford's sous chef and favorite companion. When they were sent up to the mountains north of Trieste for rest and relaxation, to a small secluded country village called Ternova, they bunked together. At night, Rutherford organized dances in the local monastery, to which he would invite the local farmers' daughters, and introduced his friend Private Schmitz as a war hero. The fighter pilots grumbled at this favoritism, but not too loudly, since they did not want to lose their food.

After the armistice, the friends parted with faint promises to stay in touch, though neither had any idea what would happen to them beyond the next few months. Rutherford shipped off to visit cousins in Rome; Private Schmitz returned to Lancaster County and to Agnes. Soon afterward, under Agnes's influence, Mr. Schmitz took a job in Manhattan at Providential Insurance. About a year passed. Maybe three.

One day Mr. Schmitz received an overseas call from Rutherford. He had not heard from his friend since the war, and was beginning to suspect that he would never see him again. As it turned out, Rutherford had been living in high style, conducting his own postarmistice eating tour of vanquished Europe— Germany, Italy, France, and back up to England. Prices were dogcheap, and he had found out, through a friend in military intelligence, which great chefs had survived the war. He searched for them systematically, and learned that many of them would, in the postwar depression, prepare him a feast for a dime. In the same manner he sought out the best of the wine collections stored in bombproof cellars, and bought what had not yet been destroyed or chugged in desperation. Rutherford explained that he was now living in a rented room in Bari with his new girl-friend, a wild, black-haired Siciliana named Carlita Passamonte. Hearing him talk about her, Mr. Schmitz thought Carlita sounded like something out of Rutherford's dreams—beautiful and loving but ultimately insubstantial, a collection of traits that seemed to reflect more about Rutherford's longings than they described a flesh-and-blood human being. But Mr. Schmitz didn't dwell on this—they spoke as if no time had passed, and he was excited to see that Rutherford still valued their friend-ship. When Rutherford asked him to visit, Mr. Schmitz agreed right away.

Mr. Schmitz alerted Agnes of his plans and left on a steamer for Southampton that week, with promises to write regularly. But once he was in Europe, Mr. Schmitz received Agnes's letters with a mixture of relief and irritation. He felt that even now, while he was abroad, Agnes pursued him as if he were her hus-band. When his responses dwindled, and his stay lengthened, Agnes's letters grew increasingly shrill. And her reach was long, extending as far as a wine cellar in the small grape-growing vil-lage of Langueville, just outside of Avignon. The cellar was not without historical significance—the vintner's family had safely hidden there during the raids of the Luftwaffe, drinking their stores to keep warm and insulated against their fear. Now Ruth-erford, Carlita, and Mr. Schmitz were helping them finish the wine that still remained.

It was while touring this wine cellar that Mr. Schmitz read the last letter he would receive from Agnes. He found the envelope folded in half in his jacket pocket. He had stuffed it there without reading it, and he had to look at the postmark to remind himself that he had picked it up at the post office in Ventimiglia ten days earlier.

The letter began with Agnes's usual account of her ordeals as a secretary in the office of a Newark congressman. She mentioned that her sister had left for her honeymoon—she gave him the address of their hotel in London, in case he happened to be in the area—and reported on the difficulties her mother was having with her varicose veins, which seemed ready to burst out of her calves. One page into the letter, however, Agnes broke off mid-sentence. She had skipped to the next line, where she wrote:

Oh Schmitz, I can't go on like this. It isn't fair. I don't know where you are and what you are doing. And if I don't know that, then how can we even pretend to carry on any kind of meaningful correspondence? You must let me know when you'll come back. If not, I will be forced to withdraw from this conversation. Indefinitely.

When I think about our relationship, in its current state, a funny thing happens. I start punching the wall. That's how I feel. So now you know.

The only kind of punch Mr. Schmitz had ever seen her make was a playful hand curl when she pretended to be mad—like when he teased her lightly and she would make a clown's frown, and press her little fists against his ribs, a disguised caress. The thought of her punching the wall, alone in her room at Miss Margaret's Boarding House for Women, disturbed him. Mr.

Schmitz decided he would drive to Marseilles and fly home immediately.

He excused himself from the wine cellar and stood outside near the vineyard for several minutes, under a short cherry tree, trying to decide how he would break the news to Rutherford. The sky began to pale and yellow, and soon the mosquitoes were on him, raising bumps on his ankles and forearms. This more than anything else motivated him to return to the cellar and announce his decision.

But his path was blocked by Rutherford and Carlita, who had come up the stairs in a kind of blissful fog. Carlita was stunning in the dusk light—her skin olive and her hair hung flat and low to her shoulders like the drapes of an elegant house. When silent, she lapsed into forceful gazes that seemed to offer a challenge, but physically she was fragile, with small porcelain hips and long, wispy legs. She barely spoke, and whenever she did, it seemed as if she had been prompted by Rutherford. His arm was draped around her neck now, and they swayed into each other. Mr. Schmitz assumed they were drunk.

"Mr. Schmitz," said Rutherford, "Carlita and I have decided to be married."

Mr. Schmitz swatted at a mosquito that had perched on the bridge of his nose.

"Gliel'hai detto?" asked Carlita of her beau, for she could not speak a lick of English.

"Sì," responded Rutherford, with an uncomfortable smile. "Lui è troppo contento di parlare."

Rutherford grabbed Mr. Schmitz by the shoulder, and shook him.

"Did you hear, man?"

"Congratulations!" shouted Mr. Schmitz, more loudly than he intended. Rutherford and Carlita stepped back simultaneously. "And now?"

"Be our best man," said Rutherford. Mr. Schmitz never forgot how his friend looked in that moment—his chest puffed out, his eyes dazzling diamonds. "The vintner knows a priest in Avignon. And then join us, will you, on our honeymoon?"

"I'm delighted to be asked," said Mr. Schmitz, squeezing his chin. "Da-Dee-Dee-Delighted. But I couldn't impose like that. No, I think I'll take the opportunity to return home. I'm sure Agnes expects me."

"Ha!" said Rutherford. "I wouldn't think of it. Listen, we've talked this through and we can't think of a nicer way to celebrate our marriage than to continue our trip with you—to preserve the same fortuitous conditions that brought about our decision in the first place. Please stay. Besides."

Carlita smiled blankly. Perhaps it was a trick of the sun, but even in the flesh she seemed unreal; as she moved under the cherry tree, she flickered in the shifting light like a hologram.

"What'd you say?" said Mr. Schmitz.

"Ah, besides. You are in no state to go home."

"What do you mean by that?"

"You haven't fully recovered from her yet. She still has you wrapped around her little finger."

Mr. Schmitz thought of her little fingers, curled up into a fist.

"There may be some truth to that," he admitted, "but is that such a bad thing?"

"You haven't begun to enjoy your liberated life. Look what it might lead to," said Rutherford, and he shoved the uncomprehending Carlita at Mr. Schmitz. "We'll find you one too. Better yet—many."

Carlita came closer, so close that Mr. Schmitz could feel her breath on his chin. Smiling, she embraced him, and then kissed him lightly on the lips. A foreign, flickering sensation rose in Mr. Schmitz's stomach and bubbled into his forehead. The odd smell of a new woman, the small brown mole at the corner of her mouth that he had never been near enough to observe, the whiteness of her scalp in the part of her hair. It was as if he had passed briefly into some other realm.

"I thank you," said Carlita. They were the first English words he had ever heard her pronounce. "I thank you, Signor Schmitz. For love."

Mr. Schmitz set furiously after his own chin. A dizzy mirage of romance and wanderlust passed over him, and he realized he could not go home, not yet. Carlita returned to Rutherford's side and he gave her behind a tender pat.

"You see, Signor Schmitz," he said, "there is more to be done before you go back to Agnes. A new world to be explored."

That night Rutherford called the priest in Avignon and booked two adjacent rooms in a honeymoon suite at a Paris hotel.

Now, at night, when Agnes twists in the grip of some indistinct nightmare, Mr. Schmitz looks longingly at her clenched fist. He encloses it in one of his oafish hands (Agnes always called them his mittens), and remembers her as a young woman—what it must have been like for her to wait out a war only to have Mr. Schmitz abandon her again. When he finally returned with

Rutherford to the United States, after Carlita's fatal parturition, Mr. Schmitz was haunted and depressed, victimized by complex, kaleidoscopic nightmares. Agnes comforted him and he was made to swear oaths and flatter her, while showily castigating himself. Over time they gradually reconciled. But Agnes was never as trusting. Or as beautiful. Something in her face had soured and it never came back. So when he thinks now of her sadness he also remembers her beauty, changed by anger and disappointment, and wonders what might have been had he never left her that summer after the war. Sometimes at night—and this gives him great satisfaction—she sleepily moves her fist back and forth in his hand, as if, in her sleep, she is punching him.

It occurs to Mr. Schmitz that beauty, unlike love, doesn't fade. It becomes grotesque. Yellow hair turns to straw. Translucent, pale skin folds up and coarsens like canvas. Bones push out the skin like tent poles. Eyes pinken and distort. Love, on the other hand, enters a desert and dies of thirst. If only love became grotesque too, there would at least be some fascination in its decline. As Mr. Schmitz tries to figure out what it would mean for love to grow grotesque, he finds himself gazing into Agnes's nostrils; they crinkle and sniffle and finally bassoon sleep-mist over her mouth.

She comes to with a sudden sob. Mr. Schmitz takes her into his arms, cradling her against his chest—two bulks joining together under a mass of blanket. Agnes never explains what causes these crying jags, nor does Mr. Schmitz ask. To do so would be a breach of intimacy. He knows that if he inquired, Agnes would turn away; she might leave the room altogether and go write something down in the private journal that she hid from him. It's clear that she does not want to speak with him about her night-time terrors. She allows him to witness her suffering, and to comfort her with his mittens, in exchange for his silence. And so, despite the absence of spoken communication, this is when he feels closest to her.

6

Several mornings later, in the blue hour that precedes dawn, Eugene left Abe's office after a long night of work. A fog had settled low over the street, which was empty, as empty as the street in *Dolman Hardy*. Birds made ugly twirping noises in Riverside Park. Eugene reached the corner at exactly the same time as Sonia, who was nearly knocked over by the collision.

"What are you doing here?"

They stared expectantly at each other—pale Sonia, her hair cinched with an elastic over her lightly freckled neck, and discombobulated Eugene, his sleepy eyes widening as his purple lips narrowed—and they smiled.

"I'm not leaving for a few more hours," said Sonia. "So I thought I should drop by to see my dad one last time, before I go away."

"He's quite asleep," said Eugene. "But I'll unlock the door for you if you like."

"Oh, I don't want to wake him. He'd be grumpy anyway." As soon as her laughter subsided, a melancholy look crept into her eyes.

"If you're not doing anything," she said, "maybe you'd like to take a walk around the block with me? I can let him sleep a little more."

"How about," suggested Eugene, "the park?"

She took his arm in hers. Her fingertips pressed into his bicep, which he instinctively flexed, and then immediately relaxed, embarrassed at the impulse. Something fragile shifted in his chest.

They crossed Riverside Drive and entered the park, the elm trees damp and the long walkway piebald with brown puddles. A stray cat ran in front of them and hid in an adjacent shrub, its tail languorously coiling around the leg of a white stone bench.

"Long night at the office?"

"When your father gets frustrated," said Eugene, "he throws pencils at me."

"He means well."

"It's true. He usually misses."

Eugene did not know what to do with the arm that Sonia was holding. He put his hand into his pocket, closing it around his keys, and made himself stand straight. Her small hands pressed lightly against his skin and he was suddenly aware of the slight variances in the pressure of each of her fingers as they strode from cement to macadam to grass to dirt to stone. A dull pain radiated from his elbow.

"Your father is going to miss you, I'm sure," he said. After which, he cursed himself silently for his mawkishness and resolved not to speak again.

"Dad misses Connie," said Sonia. "That's for sure."

They reached a long rectangular crabapple grove. The brown fruit hung on branches so tangled that it was impossible to tell whether they were many trees or a single one, and in several places the trunks had fused together. At one side of the grove a flock of pigeons surrounded a half-eaten cheeseburger, in its yellow wrapper. The pigeons took turns stepping up to the cheeseburger and pecking at the bun before scattering in retreat.

Sonia let go of Eugene's arm and strayed over to the crabapples. She plucked one from a nearby branch and tossed it to him underhand. He caught it and, in a mock heroic gesture, took a bite. The rancid fruit stung his tongue and he spat it out immediately. Several of the pigeons jumped over and approached the wet chunk of crabapple with great curiosity.

"I'd rather eat the cheeseburger," he said.

"So would they," she said, as the pigeons, after several trial pecks, flew back to the bun.

"Why are you working for my father anyway? If you don't mind my asking."

"I'm just trying to figure out what I want to do."

"You don't know yet?"

"Do you?"

"No," she said, and circled behind a trunk. "I don't. I'd like to keep my father happy before he dies."

Eugene didn't know what to say.

"Do you still have your parents?"

"I just have a father," said Eugene. "He doesn't show much enthusiasm for anything anymore, though. Not even English. He's from Italy, and retired, so he spends a lot of time with other paisans, speaking Italian and reminiscing about the old country. Whenever I talk to him he goes into long stories about obscure ancestors that he never mentioned when I was growing up. But when I ask him for stories about my mother, he doesn't remember anything."

He followed Sonia back toward the street, passing into a grove of elder trees, their flat white flowers heavy with fresh rain. The ground was covered with black berries that bled a bright lilac pulp and smelled like sulfur.

"I sometimes think that my father's lost in another country too," said Sonia. "If you can think of the past as a country."

"The way my father talks about Italy it's like it has no past or present, it's just some other universe. I think that's why I've never gone to visit. I get enough of that world at home with him. I don't need to see it on vacation."

They walked in silence back out of the park, their backs to the Hudson. As they reached Riverside Drive, Sonia took out her wallet and removed from it two yellow tickets. She waved them up in front of Eugene's face, her eyes flashing green-gray.

"For my birthday, my dad gave me two passes for a session at My Name Is Mud. It's a mud sauna. I don't know how the hell he got involved with this place—I'd guess it's because when he was young, Eakins would always take him to mud baths in Slovenia. The place is right around the corner, and this is my last chance to use the passes." She looked at the fine print. "It's seven now, so they've just opened. Want to go?"

"A mud bath? Where do they get the mud?"

"I think it's a mixture of peat moss and volcanic ash."

"From what volcano?"

"It's fine if you don't want to come," she said, putting the tickets back in her wallet.

"Of course I'll come."

As they walked to the sauna, Sonia told Eugene stories about her previous visits to Trieste. She talked about the family-run farms up in the Carso, a region of limestone cliffs surrounding the city, and of the adventures she had there with her Triestine friends—tubby Poldi, dashing Marco, and a butcher's daughter named Kasia, to whom Sonia bore an uncanny resemblance. For two weeks each summer, the farmers in the Carso would set up tables in their vineyards and backyards, and transform their homes into little restaurants called *osmizze*. It was an opportunity for the families to market their farm's bounty—cured meat, cheese, and the local Terrano wine—to local restaurateurs, neighbors, and Triestini in the know. The only way to find one would be to drive up into the Carso and look for olive branches, which the farmers tied to road signs to indicate the way.

"The most fun I had was with Kasia and Marco at an *osmizza* held on the grounds of an abandoned church at the edge of one family's vineyard. They had strung up Christmas lights over the trees, and after drinking several jugs of Terrano, we went dancing and singing on the tables under the stars. Of course, when I told the story to Dad, I replaced my friends' names with Eakins's. It made him so happy to hear that Connie was still spry and full of life."

By this point they had reached My Name Is Mud, which was tucked into a small alley between two apartment buildings, just off of Broadway.

"Maybe this isn't so fancy after all," said Sonia.

They walked into a spare reception room. A round-faced woman, pockmarked and chubby with a high beehive hairdo, sat at the front desk eating a bagel. When Sonia gave her name, the woman jumped up and hugged her.

"So you're Abe Chisholm's daughter? I see the resemblance. I'm an old friend, Stanislava—call me Stanka. He's told me all about you. You and your 'guest' may come along." Eugene and Sonia hardly had time to glance at each other before she hustled them off into their separate dressing rooms, handing each of them a voluminous green towel. In the men's, Eugene stood in front of a wall lit overhead by low-hanging fluorescent coils. He wasn't sure how much of his clothing he should remove, but after some heated debate with himself, he decided just to take off everything and wrap himself in the towel. He stared in the mirror for several minutes, removing sleep from his eyes and squeezing a pimple near his upper lip. He wondered if Sonia knew how much of her clothing to remove. He noticed, against the far wall, a heavy black door that bore two words in large bold print: TO MUD.

He passed through it into a room the size of a basketball court. Spaced apart in even rows were dozens of tubs filled with black mud. Some of the tubs overflowed and black liquid trickled onto the yellow-tiled floor, and then seeped into large drains. An elaborate network of gray pipes, flecked with peeling white paint, hung from the ceiling and dripped hot water into the tubs. The air was thick with a sour-smelling haze. Several fans hung from the ceiling, rotating idly, as if motored by the steam instead of dissipating it. Mud-crusted speakers stood on poles throughout the room, quietly playing a somniferous piano sonata that did little to drown out the sound of the pipes: an arrhythmic percussion of clanks and hisses.

Stanka was standing on the opposite side of the room. She called out to Eugene and gestured him over.

"This is your bath," said Stanka. "Have you been before in the mud?"

"Never," said Eugene. He noticed with a mild sense of alarm that Sonia was already submerged in a bathtub just several feet away from his own. Only her head was above the mud, and her eyes were covered with a damp white hand towel. The rest of the baths were empty.

"You just lie in it and wiggy around, until you sink," said Stanka. "And then you will fully be in the mud. Go on. It won't eat you."

Stanka gestured at him, and then the mud tub; at him, and then the tub.

"I'm not looking," she said, staring right at him. "Go ahead."

"Go on, Eugene," said Sonia. "I know it's kind of odd. But it actually feels good. Sticky and mushy but good."

He slipped off his towel and stepped into the tub. Pebbles and twigs were suspended in the thick, gummy mud, and it barely gave way beneath his body when he sat down. And it was scalding hot.

"Wiggy," said Stanka.

Eugene wiggled his behind and his shoulders, feeling the mud give way and swallow him. His body had never looked such a pasty hue. As he sank, he began to feel a trickle of scalding water against his ribs and the soles of his feet, pumped from hidden undermud jets. He glanced over at Sonia to make sure she wasn't watching him, or perhaps in the hope that she was. As soon as he was fully submerged, Stanka set down on the rim of the tub a plastic cup of ice water with a straw; Eugene sucked in a mouthful, and noticed with distaste that his lips had left a brown smudge on the plastic. Then Stanka pressed a cold, wet hand towel against his eyes. The water dripped down the sides of his face and into the mud. His diaphragm expanded and his bowels shuddered. It was eight in the morning.

After a minute or so he realized that Sonia was watching him. Her hand towel had fallen to the ground, and Stanka was gone.

"Relaxing, huh? Sort of?"

"It's hot," he said. "Too . . . hot."

"Then do this." She raised one leg out of the mud. The skin was pale and dripped black sludge. "It cools down that way."

Eugene lifted his own leg, and the sensation was, in fact, oddly refreshing. The silt clung to his leg hairs. He lowered the leg.

"This will also do it," she added, raising a pale arm. "Just hold it up in the air." Eugene lifted his arm straight up, plops of mud falling on his cheeks and brow. He saw that Sonia's face was perfectly clean. Fearful of smudging his own face any worse, he simply lay there immobile, feeling the dirt coalesce on his nose. She was laughing gently at him.

"Thanks for taking me here," he said. Sonia laughed harder.

"You're very brave," she said, with a wink of her scarred eye.

Sonia lowered her leg, wiggling it down into the mud.

"What do you do when you're not at my father's office?" she asked. "Besides take luxuriant mud baths?"

Eugene had to think for a second.

"I take long subway rides. I go exploring Staten Island. I eat lots of Chinese food. I go canoeing around the pond in Inwood Hill Park with my friend Alvaro. I read books. I sometimes think about trying to write."

"Oh? Like what? You're working on something?"

"It's embarrassing to talk about."

"Short stories?"

"Something longer."

"Really? How much have you written so far?"

"Not a single line," said Eugene. He lowered his arm back into the tub. "The last few months I've been busy translating a friend's novel into English. He's from the Dominican Republic and speaks a rare Spanish dialect called Cibaeño. It's about a surgeon priest named Jacinto, who falls in love with Alsa, a neighbor in his Inwood apartment building."

"What happens to them?"

"I'm not sure yet, I only just finished with the first section. It ends with a scene in which Alsa's father, having found out about Jacinto and Alsa's love affair, throws Alsa out of the house. She's humiliated and dishonored, so she runs away, back to the Dominican Republic."

"So you're able to understand this dialect—Cibaeño?"

"I get the gist of it. I think I understand him pretty well."

"I don't think I understand you very well."

"I'd like you to."

The sonata abruptly cut out of the speakers. After a brief jolt of static, Stanka's voice came on.

"You will please remove yourselves from the baths and exit the mud room. Please do not put on the towels. They must not be muddied. There are showers in the locker rooms."

Sonia, bracing her hands on either side of her tub, pushed herself out. Eugene did the same. It was impossible not to face each other, two Swamp Things caked in peat moss and black sludge. Swamp Sonia was gorgeous. Her hair stuck to her shoulder in a clump, and mud trailed down her neck, her breasts, the slight swell of her tummy, and just below, filing into thin stringy clusters. This elegant mud monster regarded Mud Eugene with a sideways expression, and extended a small mud paw to his face. Eugene froze. The thing in his chest had claws now and was racing around.

"You have a little something here," she said, picking a small rock off his shoulder. She was grinning, her face bright and impossibly clean.

"And you too," said Eugene. He pulled a root, dangling tendrils, from her neck.

"Thank you."

"Thank you," he replied, "for taking me here."

They headed to their separate locker rooms, leaving a trail of black footprints behind them on the yellow-tiled floor.

After their showers they met outside. Broadway was painfully bright and hot and filled with dour-faced commuters, diving into the subways and glaring from behind the fogged windows of public buses. Eugene hailed a cab.

"I'll be writing regularly to my dad from Italy," she said, hugging him. "I'll include little jokes that he won't get. Just for you. OK? We'll have our own little code."

A sudden physical longing overcame him like a cloud of black smoke.

"But how can I write you? Can I call?"

"That might be difficult. I'm supposed to go live with a family friend in Trieste named Frank Lang, but I may stay with other friends as well. I'll send an address when I know."

"Is that it? You're just leaving?"

"I hate it, but I have to." She was wearing a brave expression: buttoned-up lips, pinched cheeks. "Now wish me a good trip."

"Have a wonderful trip."

She vanished, smiling, into the dark backseat of the cab. Then, just before the door closed, she said something puzzling:

"You too."

7

It is Saturday again, and Rutherford and Mr. Schmitz are on their weekly walk across the northern edge of Central Park.

"I've made reservations for a nice dinner tonight," says Rutherford. "For all three of us—me, you, and Mrs. Schmitz."

Mr. Schmitz pulls at the flesh of his chin, applying great torque. He exhales smoke out of the side of his mouth, a delicate gesture made absurd by the amount of force he applies to it.

"And Agnes?" he asks. "Why did you do that?"

"Because I have some news I want to tell you both."

"What news?"

"I'd rather wait until tonight."

"Is everything all right?"

"There is no need to worry. Believe me, I wouldn't tell you anything that might upset you."

They don't speak about it again, but when Mr. Schmitz returns from his walk, Agnes can see that he is flustered.

"Are you all right?" she asks. "Dear?"

"There's no need to panic, darling."

"I'm not panicked."

"No need to panic."

That night, Rutherford takes the Schmitzes to an expensive, dimly lit Chinese restaurant near Lincoln Center. A plate of green sesame noodles sits on the table. Neither Rutherford nor Agnes is able to eat, so Mr. Schmitz, with a sigh, pulls the plate in front of him.

"I guess I'll warm us up," he says, reaching for his fork.

"Mr. Schmitz," says Rutherford. He pauses for some moments, recollecting himself. Mr. Schmitz swallows his noodles loudly. "I've just had some news from Rudy Teague."

"That's his editor, Agnes," says Mr. Schmitz. A fresh wave of concern ripples her features.

"At *Food and Pleasure*," says Rutherford, taking his eyes off Mr. Schmitz. "Where I write my column. Wrote, that is. I've been dismissed."

A clump of noodles drops out of Mr. Schmitz's gaping mouth.

"Why, you've been writing that column for, what, fifteen years?" says Agnes.

"Thirty. They've made a decision to replace me with a young woman—a chef—who has a popular television show on the cooking channel."

"Bastard," says Mr. Schmitz. "*That* man is a *bastard*."

"There's good news to come of it, however," says Rutherford, with a thin, synthetic smile. "Do you know that section near the back of the magazine, where they have reviews of new restaurants opening across Europe?"

Mr. Schmitz licks his lips, as if they might taste of vengeance.

"You may have seen, in that section, reviews by a certain Giancarlo Varese, who writes about Milan. Wrote, that is. He died last year. They considered discontinuing the post, since they already have a correspondent in Italy, based in Rome. But in honor of my service to the magazine, they've offered me Varese's job, and his apartment in Milan, which they'll pay for, along with all dining costs."

Mr. Schmitz puzzles this over for several minutes, rubbing his chin and gazing off into the distance.

"So you'll resign, naturally. No other response that I can see." Mr. Schmitz seems pleased with this, and begins to put the noodles into his mouth once more.

"Look, I'd love to. I really would. I like my life here. But as you know, I don't have any income. The residuals from my last collection of culinary criticism stopped accruing five years ago. I have an expensive lifestyle in New York. I can't maintain it any longer."

"But that's not true, is it? Besides—"

"I don't have any other option but to accept," says Rutherford, gritting his teeth.

Mr. Schmitz jolts as though he has been kicked from behind. His eyes marble and his fork begins to tap against his plate of noodles. Agnes puts her hand to her cheek.

"The mind," says Mr. Schmitz, "reels."

"I realize this news has a ring of finality to it, but it's probably only a temporary arrangement."

Mr. Schmitz's fork is hitting against the china so forcefully that a waiter approaches, assuming that he has been summoned. Rutherford waves him off.

"We're both very upset to hear you're leaving," says Agnes, looking pleadingly at her husband. "But given your circumstance, we understand why you have to do this. Don't we? We wish you well. Perhaps we'll come to visit?"

"Of course," says Rutherford. "Anytime. I believe Varese's house has a second bedroom, and when you come I can take you around the city. Dinner will be on me!"

"Bastard," whispers Mr. Schmitz. His gaze is still frozen.

"Darling, did you hear what Rutherford said? We can go on a trip together to see him anytime. I can barely remember when we last went on vacation."

"Mr. Schmitz," says Rutherford, "I don't expect this to disrupt our normal pattern of conversations. I still plan on our speaking every day, at the same time, six o'clock, and I will adjust my sleep schedule accordingly to account for the time difference. Or if phone calls are not convenient, we can mail letters back and forth."

Rutherford moves his head to one side and then the other, to see if that will alert Mr. Schmitz from his catatonic stupor. It does not. Mr. Schmitz continues to stare at Rutherford, his eyes open but unseeing.

"Do you even hear me talking to you?" asks Rutherford, his voice soft with guilt.

Mr. Schmitz does not move but his fork starts chipping specks of his dish across the table. Other diners look over. Agnes smiles and nods at them, as if to offer assurance that her husband is not having a seizure. Rutherford waves his hand in front of Mr. Schmitz's face. A piece of green noodle inches slightly out of one nostril.

"Man, are you blind?" he shouts.

Mr. Schmitz comes to all of a sudden: the noodle is sucked back up his nose and the fork flies across the table and into the wall. He steadies himself and shuts his damp eyes. He buries his chin deep in his chest.

"This," says Mr. Schmitz, "is a blow to end all blows."

"I'm so sorry, friend."

"Bastard," Mr. Schmitz whispers. *"Bastard."*

8

Dear Dad,

Just a note to say that I've arrived in Milan safely. With several hours until my train to Trieste, I decided to have a snack at Piazza San Babila. It's even brighter and busier than the day we were last here together—what, when I was fifteen? The last time you traveled to Italy. They've built a new fountain, very modern, in the middle of the piazza. It's shaped like a pyramid with a large iron ball balanced on its point. The water flows down the sides of the pyramid and collects in a shallow moat, which leads out in a narrow canal, beneath a grating across the piazza—like an underground river. It resurfaces in a diamond-shaped pool.

The people hurry back and forth, speaking a hundred different languages and bouncing off one another in their excitement to get wherever they're going. Everything is charged with life. A young Arab boy just tripped onto me and nearly toppled into the fountain. When his mother made him apologize, he took my hand in his and kissed it.

Traveling alone is nice but I look forward to seeing my friends again, both the old and the new.

All my love,

A

Dear Dad,

Trieste is cloudy and festive: the 70th annual international Esperanto conference is in town this week. I haven't seen Connie yet, but my old friend Poldi, the espresso maestro at Caffè San Marco, heard that he had been spotted with members of Trieste's Esperanto Association at Castello Miramare. The gruff gentleman at the front desk there had not heard of him, but I will continue to search for him along the waterfront and at the conference. I'll find him soon—I'm positive I will.

Daddy, don't you just love this postcard? So "bel paese." Do you see that sullen boy, standing behind the donkey? The one on the right, with the sword in his hand? He reminds me of someone, but I can't think of who—someone I met with you? He cuts a valiant figure but I can't tell whether it's just a pose or whether he's about to embark on some noble quest—to free a band of indentured servants, say, or perhaps to rescue his true love from a castle prison.

I'm staying with Frank, by the way, in case you'd like to send me a letter. He's busy assisting with the conference, but he sends his "dearest, rarest, regards" to you. Che carino! I'll write again soon, I hope with news of Connie.

All my love,

A

9

A tremor stirs the mattress. Agnes sits up abruptly and pulls the chain on the bedside lamp.

"What is it, my dear?" says Agnes.

"Turn off the light," moans Mr. Schmitz.

She turns off the light.

"I'm sad about Rutherford," says Mr. Schmitz.

"Well. You have been friends for so long. I'm sure he'll be back soon."

"I don't think he's ever coming back."

"You may be right," sighs Agnes.

Mr. Schmitz doesn't respond though his face is preoccupied.

"Why do we only talk in the middle of the night?" says Agnes.

Mr. Schmitz reflects on this for a minute in silence.

"I suppose that's so," he finally says, and moves his frame a quarter-revolution, a disturbance that pries a tremulous squeak from the ancient box spring.

"Why don't I heat you up a glass of milk?" asks Agnes. She is already halfway to the kitchen.

"I wouldn't come back," says Mr. Schmitz, "if I were him."

"What's that, darling?" Agnes is in the kitchen, where the electric stove is clanking loudly to life.

"I said, Extra sugar in the milk, Agnes."

"Whatever you like, dear."

10

Eugene had no reason to stay any longer at Abe's apartment except to await news from Sonia. He had already stacked and organized every book in Abe's collection; to the top of each shelf he had affixed little green library lamps that cast meniscus-shaped light down onto the books below; he had even organized Abe's voluminous research files. He had assumed that after Sonia left, Abe would ask him to help with his writing in the same way, but it hadn't happened. There were moments when Abe would look up from his desk in confusion, as if he expected his daughter would run over to assist him with some problem. Then he would see Eugene and, with a quiet groan of resignation, slump back to his work.

Abe was working less, however, and his naps grew longer and deeper. Eugene began to take liberties with his official duties. He would sometimes tiptoe around to the back of Abe's chair where he kept his gray sheepskin slippers, and slip them on. Then he'd curl up on one of the leather chairs and read an Eakins novel in some old edition. One afternoon, when Abe had seemed particularly depressed and entered a deep slumber, Eugene reached above Abe and took from the shelf there his most prized possession: a first edition of Eakins's novella, *Every Man for Himself and God Against All.* He glanced anxiously at Abe, but the weary man was snoring now, the dentures slipping loose from his gums.

Eugene had never read the novella before—it was out of print, and not held in particularly high regard—but from the first page, he was happy to see that it was typical Eakins: a strange reality that bordered on fantasy, an exotic locale, larger-than-life characters. The novella told the story of Turk, a young thief in Ireland at the turn of the century, who breaks out of prison to search for his true love, Alcida. Without food or drink, he wanders in search of friendly civilization. But there is no one, as far as he can tell, for hundreds of miles, and he soon finds himself in the middle of a vast, desolate moor. At dusk he takes shelter in a crumbling monastery, building a fire out of remnants of a splintered priedieu and sleeping between two capsized pews.

Before reading further, Eugene reexamined the postcard from Sonia that he kept in his jacket pocket at all times. It was her most recent correspondence, sent nearly a month earlier from Trieste. Eugene flipped the card over and reread Sonia's lines: "I'm sick of codes," it said. "I miss you." He had fired off three letters in response, but had received nothing in return, not even another postcard. He read through Sonia's postcard again, hoping to decipher some hidden meaning. It was signed "Triste in Trieste." This frightened him but he didn't know what he could do about it.

Back in Eakins's novella, Turk wanders into a forest, lured by a fragrant scent of berries. The brush grows dense, and he soon is lost in a green-shaded darkness. He shivers and hiccups with hunger. He comes across a giant maple tree. The trunk is hollowed out, and glows like a lightbulb, with a sallow luminescence. Inside the hollow there sits a tiny man hunched over a bowl of gruel. He has a white-powdered face, pointy ears, and strawberry lips. (Eugene had seen this before: Eakins was obsessed with wood sprites, they were always cropping up in his stories.)

"My friend," the sprite exclaims, in a warbling soprano, "have I a message for you!"

Turk jumps back. But his hunger emboldens him.

"Do you have, by any chance," asks Turk, "a morsel or a crumb? I'm starving, been wandering for days."

The wood sprite offers his gruel, which looks like watery cottage cheese dyed lavender. Turk takes it gratefully, waving off the man's miniature spoon, and eats the whole thing.

"More where that's come from," says the sprite. "Alcida," he adds.

"Yes?"

"Alcida is far away from this wood."

At that moment in his reading, Eugene heard from across the room an ominous rumbling in Abe's bowels. He stood up, inserting the postcard into Eakins's book, and zipped behind Abe, leaving the slippers on the floor where he had found them.

"Ah yes," said Abe, his eyes opening to find Eugene moving about furtively beside him. "Now, where was I?"

"I believe you were studying these report cards from Eakins's middle school." Eugene handed a sheaf of papers to Abe. Eugene pretended not to notice how little Abe had progressed on the biography since Sonia left for Italy, and made an effort to sound cheerful about the project.

"I see. That's right. Now where were YOU?"

"Just straightening things out on your desk here, Abe."

Abe squinted at him for a moment before directing his attention back to the papers in his hand.

"Oh, Eugene?"

"Still here."

"When did this arrive?"

There was a postcard lying on top of Abe's desk, but Eugene had never seen it before. The image was of a giant, rolling field, framed by a mountain ridge in golden light. The lettering said "Der Karst." Abe turned the postcard over.

Dear Abe,

I've been found. By your daughter no less. What a charming, delightful creature—how dear she has become. We're off to my hidden retreat. We shan't be found anon, begab!

There was no signature.

"It's him all right," said Abe. "That's his handwriting."

"I see." Could Abe possibly mean it was from Eakins? Eugene tried to compare in his mind the handwriting on the card with Sonia's notes. He thought it looked similar but couldn't be certain.

"You see, do you?" said Abe. "Well. It's been over a month now since she's sent a note. I'm worried SICK to my bowels."

"I'm sure she'll write again. Soon."

"No no no no no. No! I haven't heard from her, Frank knows nothing—"

"Frank?"

"Frank Lang. Don't you know him? He's our man in Trieste.

She's meant to check in with him from time to time. He's completely unreliable, so I don't have him do any of the work, but he's a FRIEND, you see, and he would let me know if something happened to Alison. If she needed help. Well I've called him over and over and he says he has not seen her since her first week there."

Abe swiveled in his chair, so that he was facing Eugene. He was bloodshot and breathless, and for the first time since Eugene had met him, Abe spoke in a quiet voice.

"She's gone," he said. "She's gone."

Eugene protested but Abe ignored him.

"Eakins has stolen her away. Where he's going, she won't ever want to leave. She might never return to me. I can't go find her. I'm too damn infirm."

Eugene was having trouble making sense of what Abe was saying. He wondered what the wood sprite knew about Alcida. He thought, "Triste in Trieste."

"You're saying she's off with him—with Constance Eakins—in the mountains?"

"I DON'T SEE WHERE THE HELL ELSE SHE WOULD BE! DO YOU?"

Abe slumped into his chair and swiveled again, so that his back was to Eugene. The old man shook his head, over and over, occasionally mumbling something in confused despair. He held papers in his hand, but he did not read them, and finally he let them fall to the ground. Eugene sat back down on the leather chair. He didn't bother to pretend to work. He paused again over Sonia's last postcard to him, without being able to reach any further conclusions. Then he turned to Eakins's novella and read distractedly. Turk was interrogating the wood sprite about his beloved Alcida:

"Where," says Turk, "is Alcida?"

"You might ask," replies the sprite, "*what* she is. For she is not human."

"Liar. Where is she?"

"She's my sister," says the sprite. "She is a sprite. A sprite like me."

"That's a lie. It's true she is a very small girl. But you are lying to me."

"She loves you just the same," sighs the sprite. "Though I can't for the life of me see why."

"Just tell me where she is," says Turk. He is now spitting with anger. "I have nothing else to live for. I must find her."

"Very well," says the sprite. He gestures for Turk to come closer. Turk kneels and the sprite whispers something into his ear.

"After all," concludes the sprite, "it would be impossible for a sprite to save her from that place."

"My gods," says Turk, shocked by what he had heard. "Impossible!"

"Yes, it's a treacherous mission."

"It doesn't matter," says Turk. "Dear Alcida, I'm coming at last."

"So you'll do it?" asks the sprite.

"I'll do it! I'll find her!"

"HURRAY!" shouted Abe, spinning around in his chair. "Go find my girl!"

1

Rutherford and Mr. Schmitz sit motionless at the airport gate, each of them holding an unlit Parliament. Between Rutherford's knees is a brown leather captain's bag containing that day's international newspapers, a toothbrush, his great-grandfather's cast-iron compass, and for good luck, a head of garlic.

"Your Italian will greatly improve," says Mr. Schmitz.

"I hope so," says Rutherford. "It sure is rusty. Far more than I dared to admit to Rudy."

"And you'll be able to buy those Cuban cigars you love so much."

"Legally," says Rutherford.

"You can visit all the beautiful churches and stuff like that."

"Museums too, I wager."

"Perhaps," says Mr. Schmitz, looking askance, "you'll meet a woman there. An Italian woman."

"I would put the odds of such an occurrence at no better than twenty to one."

"She would have olive skin and beautiful dark brown hair."

"Now that's enough," says Rutherford, "of that."

Mr. Schmitz pulls the bottom edge of his T-shirt down so that it covers his stomach.

"It'll be just like your service days in the war."

"Not exactly," says Rutherford. "For one I won't be doing the cooking. I'll be writing about it. Second, I'll have the full use of my right arm, including all of my digits, and—"

"—and Carlita won't . . . well, you know."

"Exist. No, of course not. She's quite long dead now. Alive only in my mind."

"I'm sorry," says Mr. Schmitz. "I'm having trouble speaking, or thinking, or putting my thoughts into words, or rather not putting them . . . there."

"I want to repeat this one more time, Mr. Schmitz. You're my dearest friend in this world. I feel terrible. My heart is breaking."

Mr. Schmitz nods, rubbing his chin.

"But I must leave. And it's not just the money. Something else is drawing me back to Italy. Something from our past."

"I think I understand."

"And you have Mrs. Schmitz, who—"

"Isn't much comfort, I'm sorry to say."

Rutherford scolds his friend.

"It's so just the same," says Mr. Schmitz, with an impudent thrust of his wrist.

"We'll write each other constantly. That's how it was in the old world. And imagine all the new stories I'll have to tell you."

"All the new cities."

"Every city a story," says Rutherford. "Just think how much I'll have to tell you. And maybe you'll have a thing or two to tell me."

12

The day before Eugene left for Italy, he was sitting with Alvaro in a cul-de-sac on Sutton Place, across the street from his old apartment. Eugene had not seen his father since he left the previous June, saying he was late for his flight to West Palm Beach. Signor Brentani's most recent letter, relayed from the post office box Eugene had registered in Florida, had troubled him. The writing was virtually illegible, muddied by cross-outs and inkblots that soaked right through the page, as if the author had sat with the pen pressed against the paper absentmindedly for minutes at a time. There was only one sentence that Eugene could make out with confidence. It was written in Italian, and was somewhat puzzling: *"I would like to visit you, I will visit you, I would like to visit you, even if I don't leave this house."*

Now Eugene waited for his father to leave the apartment building. He thought he might surprise him. But even if he didn't get up the nerve to speak, Eugene wanted at least to see his father before leaving for Italy—feel some proximity to him, gauge his emotional state, make sure he wasn't having any sort of collapse. He sat on a stoop behind Alvaro, who was wearing a green hooded raincoat, carefully billowed to block Eugene from view.

"Don't you think," asked Alvaro, after some minutes had passed, *"that we might be more suspicious rather than less because of the fact that I'm wearing a raincoat in the middle of a bright summer day?"*

"If you're questioning my plan, don't. He'll be out any minute. I know his routine. Or at least the main gist of it."

"Is it absolutely necessary that I wear the hood?" asked Alvaro, reaching for it. *"It's really hot outside."*

"Could you please leave the hood on? It blocks my face. You're too short otherwise."

The door opened and an old man wheeled his wife out in a wheelchair; she exclaimed in delight when she saw the brightness of the sun over the East River. Later a middle-aged woman, whom Eugene recognized as his childhood babysitter, emerged wearing a business suit, her heels clattering expertly on the concrete. The door opened again and they saw a stumpy maid accompanied by a small boy dressed in a Superman costume.

"I bet your father's asleep," said Alvaro.

"Just keep that damn hood on, please. Please, Alvaro?"

A large truck from a Jewish moving company rolled up, blocking their view for a moment. When it pulled out, Signor Brentani was standing under the awning. He was wearing a long trench coat. He mopped his brow with a handkerchief, and then turned and set off north along Sutton Place. Eugene froze. Then Alvaro stood up to follow him, and Eugene jumped up as well, afraid of being spotted.

"Let's wait until he gets to the esplanade," said Eugene. "Slow down, stay farther behind him."

"Do you know where he's going?" asked Alvaro, without turning his head.

"He always goes to the esplanade for his morning walks. It's quiet there. It'll be a good place to talk."

"It's quiet here. Why don't you just go up to him now?"

"I'm not sure. I'll figure something out. I could say I'm back for a surprise visit."

"What will you say to him?"

"It's true. I am about to leave, after all. Maybe I'll say I'm going away. Going exploring."

Alvaro shrugged and kept following Signor Brentani. After several blocks, Eugene's father turned to the esplanade, which was nearly empty at this early hour. He leaned against the iron railing and looked out over an especially turbulent portion of the East River. There, in the middle of the river before him, was an eyot called Mill Rock Park. A flock of cormorants perched on it. They flapped their wings without ever taking flight, their claws sticking in their own filth. They twittered and squabbled in strident voices that carried, together with their stink, across the water to the Manhattan shore.

Alvaro and Eugene hid in the shrubs that bordered the esplanade. They were less than ten feet from Signor Brentani, but Eugene was not concerned about being noticed. His father had entered some kind of trance. The tails of his coat lifted in the wind, showing his bare legs. It is rare in this city, thought Eugene, that one sees a man outdoors quieted by his own contemplations. New Yorkers get lost in crowds, or in Queens, but seldom in thought.

"Go," whispered Alvaro. He gestured Eugene forward.

"Right," said Eugene. He didn't move. "OK. Right. OK."

"*GO,*" said Alvaro, turning to look at his friend. "*What are you so afraid of?*"

"OK!" said Eugene, more to himself than to Alvaro. "Right!"

Signor Brentani drummed his fingers on the black railing. He watched as a pair of cormorants began to fight, pecking violently at each other. The rest of the birds surrounded them, forming a makeshift boxing ring. They spurted up into the air and dove down, feinting attack, as if to spur the two squabblers into deeper combat. A coarse, husky voice rang out.

"Signor Brentani!"

A large woman swathed in a black floral-print blouse sauntered toward him, with beads swinging on strings from her sweating neck. She wore a large straw hat whose brim was encircled by a wreath of plastic roses, tied with a celadon ribbon.

"My darling!" said Signor Brentani, raising his arms up like a man praising his lord.

"My Jesus!" said Eugene. He dove back into the shrubs with Alvaro.

"*Who's that?*"

"I have no idea."

The woman took off her hat, revealing a bleached bouffant. She inclined herself downward—she was tall as well as thick—and kissed Signor Brentani's forehead. Alvaro, averting his head in the bush, spat into the soil.

The woman and Signor Brentani interlocked arms and headed south, in the direction of the Stanley M. Isaac Houses and Senior Center—two dismal, rusted-white buildings that seemed about to fall together, as if they wanted to lean on each other for support.

Eugene and Alvaro watched them walk away.

"What . . . just happened?" asked Eugene.

"It looks as if your father has fallen in love. Just like you, the way you walk around in a daze. I don't know how you keep your interest, with her gone. My women have to be in the same city as me, if not the same neighborhood."

Eugene nodded absently. He supposed he was relieved that his father was happy, had found someone to share the days with him. Yet he couldn't help but feel disappointed. As he and Alvaro made their way back toward the subway, Eugene realized that, on some lower level, he had desperately wanted to communicate with his father. He had wanted to explain that he was doing good work, was living independently, and was finally going to visit Italy—and he wanted to hear what his father had to say about it all. Eugene might not have coveted, or been able, to have such a conversation six months earlier, but something had changed since he had moved to Inwood.

His train of thought was abruptly derailed at York Avenue, when a lizard-faced man jumped out at them from behind the street corner. He stank of rotten juniper and wore a soiled blue ascot; his tawny chest hair tufted out of an unbuttoned pirate's shirt. Eugene shook his head: I have no money, I'm sorry, have a good day.

"I don't want your money," said the drunk, sweating alcohol from the folds in his loose skin. He hiccupped loudly, and then winked.

"OK," said Eugene, without slowing his gait.

"Don't you recognize me?"

Eugene turned. He noticed that one of the man's legs was made out of wood.

"I don't think so, sorry."

"We'll meet again soon enough," said the drunkard. "Remember me then."

"OK, buddy."

Alvaro gave the man a coin and pulled his friend by the arm.

"Hey," shouted the man behind them, and then he said something in a foreign language: *"This is a Dominican peso."*

Alvaro stopped.

"He speaks Cibaeño!" shouted Alvaro.

"I saw you in Italy," said the man to Eugene, a slight southern lilt in his voice.

"I speak the language," said Eugene, turning to face him, "but I never went to Italy."

"I can see you there right now," said the man, closing his eyes.

"Have you been to Jamao?" asked Alvaro, stunned. *"You have a perfect accent. But you're definitely not a native. I'm from Jamao. What are you asking my friend? I don't understand English."*

"Though I am going to Italy next week," said Eugene. He wanted to keep moving but there was something about the man's drunken glare that exerted some kind of pull on him.

"I'll see you there," said the drunkard. "Not in Italy, but very near to it."

"Whatever you say, man."

"Constance will be there too," said the drunkard, turning away. *"He's been waiting for you."*

"He's too smashed to speak coherently," said Eugene, not recognizing the man's foreign tongue. He forced himself to start walking again, away from the river. Alvaro followed him reluctantly.

Back at the esplanade the one-legged drunk teetered to the cast-iron railing. He passed a mismatched old couple that ignored him completely, so busy were they pawing at each other.

"Love," mumbled the drunk, "cures boredom. But lust—lust cures sorrow."

With a lurch and a chuckle, the drunk hopped over the railing of the esplanade. If the couple had been able to tear themselves away from each other—or if Alvaro and Eugene had turned back toward the river—they would have observed a peculiar sight: the drunk fell end over end into the East River without making a splash, and disappeared.

PART II

TRIESTE—MILAN

1

Several days after Rutherford's departure for Italy, Mr. Schmitz finds himself in an unusual predicament. For the first Saturday in twenty-seven years, he has no place to go. Normally, at nine in the morning, after chugging a warm pot of coffee and crunching on a buttered croissant, Mr. Schmitz would hear Rutherford's cheerful knock at his door. They would stroll north alongside Riverside Park and turn right on 110th Street until they reached the western edge of Central Park. There they would sit on a bench overlooking the park, its sparse thin-branched trees and dirt fields, and trade stories. If their Uzbek friend Augie was at one of the stone chessboard tables, they'd amble over and take turns playing him. Whenever he captured an opponent's piece, the Uzbek master pulled a sleight of hand that made it look like he was inserting the piece into his ear: the reverse of the children's trick where an uncle pulls a coin from his nephew's ear. The Saturday before he left for Italy, Rutherford played Augie one last time, and suffered his final, demoralizing checkmate.

"Where do all the pieces go?" asked Mr. Schmitz, after the match had concluded.

"Up his jacket sleeve," said Rutherford. "Look at his elbows next time you play him. They're clunky with rooks and bishops. Those aren't bone spurs."

But Mr. Schmitz has no desire to play Augie again. When he awakes this Saturday, it is already half past nine. The coffee in the kitchen is tepid and the butter has congealed on his croissant. Agnes is waiting for him at the kitchen table, eyeing him hawkishly over the weekend newspaper. Her glance settles briefly on his hair, ribboned this way and that, and then on his undershirt, yellowed by nocturnal sweat. Mr. Schmitz realizes that he has never seen her read the paper at the kitchen table before. He wonders what else he does not know about his wife. All those missing Saturdays.

"I slept late, dear."

Agnes gives him a watery smile and returns to her paper.

As he nibbles on the croissant and politely sips the coffee, Mr. Schmitz looks around the kitchen as if for the first time. New details, previously unnoted, emerge. A brass fish mold, hanging decoratively over the oven; a photograph of unidentifiable family members in an oversize wooden frame; a wok. Has Agnes ever cooked him Chinese food?

"What do you say we go to the park today?" asks Mr. Schmitz.

Agnes does not look up from the paper. "Did it ever occur to you that I might have my own plans of a Saturday?"

"I'm sorry," says Mr. Schmitz, wounded. He takes a large bite of his croissant. Its flakes cling to his undershirt.

Agnes puts the paper down, creasing the spine in a deliberate fashion. Her face fills with something tender: affection, perhaps, or remorse.

"I would be happy to accompany you on your walk to the park," she says, like a half-asleep mother trying to calm a son who has awoken from a nightmare.

Mr. Schmitz grins and swallows the rest of his croissant.

At the edge of the park Augie is enthroned at his normal stone table, playing chess with a female Columbia student with long bangs and thick sunglasses. Mr. Schmitz points the man out to his wife.

"Whenever he takes a piece, he slips it into his ear. See?"

"That's not so bad," admits Agnes. "But really, where does he put the pieces?"

"It's actually quite clever," says Mr. Schmitz. He leans back with the pride of a man revealing a valuable secret. "He puts them up his sleeve."

He looks at his wife to catch her reaction. But instead of smiling in wonderment, she crinkles her nose as if something smells raw.

"His elbows are clunky with rooks and bishops," says Mr. Schmitz, to clarify.

"But he's wearing a T-shirt."

"Ah. So he is."

"He seems to have terrible bone spurs in his elbows," says Agnes. "He should see a doctor."

Their conversation lapses into a profound stretch of silence. Mr. Schmitz stares at the trees lining the park's perimeter, which shimmer a living green and yellow. He is used to smoking on his walks through the park, because Agnes forbids him to do so in the apartment. But with her there beside him, he can't just take out a cigarette. It is likely, he realizes, that she doesn't even know he still smokes.

When he and Rutherford fell quiet during these Saturday walks, the silences seemed tonic and comfortable. Not so with Agnes. He is not accustomed to talking at length with his wife. They eat, read, and do housework together, but these activities leave little time for meaningful conversation. Mr. Schmitz spends his days in an office he rents out at his life insurance firm, from which he retired five years earlier. He is cut off from Agnes, since the office does not have a telephone—he sliced the wire as soon as he moved in. In the evening, he reads in his study, a Beethoven symphony playing so loud that even its composer would have heard it, while Agnes putters about the kitchen, organizing coupon clippings, paying bills, and shouting (so as to be heard over the strings) to Mrs. Louhon or Mrs. Ramses on the telephone. He often spies her in the kitchen, her bottom turtlenecking through the splintering bast seat of one chair, her bulbous knees hung, like onion domes, over the back of another. When Mr. Schmitz hobbles into bed (earlier in their marriage, Agnes likened his skulking approach to the hunting ritual of the Abominable Snowman), she is already asleep. Before turning out her bedside light, he takes care to remove the crossword puzzle from under her chin, which is inevitably smudged with newspaper ink. Sometimes he grazes the edge of his forefinger against the side of her cheek, a vestigial habit that has survived the passage of decades—like his occasional stutter, his tendency to click his heels while standing in one place for any extended length of time, and his poor command of mastication. Other times, he remembers her little fingers, curled up into a fist, and he closes his eyes until sleep comes.

2

Eugene ambled half-awake from his ramshackle hotel onto Via San Lazzaro like a man reborn. Via San Lazzaro was a narrow side street lined with shuttered storefronts: a cramped haberdashery, a Chinese restaurant, and a chandlery bursting over with plastic incubators, encyclopedia sets, and silver espresso canisters. Despite all the clutter, none of the stores looked as if they had been opened, let alone visited, in a long time. Everything was faded and dusty. It was so quiet that Eugene could hear the muted sounds of families preparing to eat—the tinker of a pot and a tired man's appreciative mumble—from the open windows above the street. He looked again at the two pieces of paper he was holding in his hands: a city map supplied by the tourist office at the train station, and a scrap of envelope on which Abe had written, in his wobbly chicken-scrawl cursive:

Frank Lang,
A Friend
Libreria Antiquaria Constantino Eakins

30b via San Nicolò
A nice man
FIND ALISON!

There was a sudden patter on the cobblestones. A pair of young girls in frilly white tulle dresses raced around the street corner and shuttled wordlessly into a nearby doorway. Eugene waited for the sound of a shutting door but heard nothing. Finally, one of the girls poked her head out of the doorway, her large brown eyes fixing right on Eugene.

"Ciao ciao," he said, waving awkwardly. The girl bristled but stood her ground. On the corner behind her, a large clumsy insect flew into a white streetlamp, exploding in a loud buzz and bright flicker. The girl said, "Xe el cinciut?"

"Mi scusi, cara?" he replied, squinting.

"Aio!" she squealed, and disappeared again. A few moments later, a small parcel flew from the doorway and landed in the middle of the street. From a distance it appeared to be some kind of purple fruit strung with feathers. A breeze sent the parcel slowly cartwheeling up the alley, tripping on a raised cobblestone before settling near his feet, against the base of the streetlamp. He looked closely and saw a crushed beak, matted feathers, a twisted wing. A door slammed shut loudly behind him and, in a panic, he started running.

After several minutes he turned onto Via San Nicolò, and found the single unlit window of Frank Lang's bookstore. There were several browned volumes on display, including a tattered edition of poems written by a Triestine author in the local dialect with a translation into Florentine Italian on facing pages, and a green leather Slovenian hardcover whose cover sketch depicted two old men sitting on the edge of a cliff. Cupping his hands over his eyes and leaning against the glass, Eugene could make out enormous bookshelves, standing nearly two stories high. They hemorrhaged their contents into piles of varying size and bulk scattered about the floor. It reminded Eugene of Abe's office, only it was twice as big, and filled with four times as many books. A ladder on casters leaned against one shelf, and a red mahogany rolltop desk was just visible in the back of the room, where it seemed to sag under a pyramidal stack of art books and over-stuffed string-bound manuscripts.

Eugene gently rapped on the door, waited several minutes for a response, then rapped again, harder. A group of emaciated stray cats stirred in an alley behind him, their white felt ears tensing in expectation. It occurred to Eugene that, in his fugue of travel, he was unsure whether it was dawn or dusk. Just as he turned to set back to his ratty two-star motel, a heavy volume fell from the wobbling pile at the edge of the desk, and landed with a loud smack on the floor. A hairless head butted into view and recoiled. There was some shifting and grumbling and the crash of more books before the man appeared again, right behind the glass door. He was short, almost miniature—his thin blond mustache was even with Eugene's collar—and his delicate spectacles rimmed hungry, staring eyes. He rapped on the glass right back at Eugene.

"Ma chi sei? Che cosa vuoi?"

"Mi scusi, sono Eugenio. Lavoro per Signor Abe Chisholm."

"So you're the American," replied the man loudly, in a clean New York accent. He pinched his cheeks to wake himself up. They turned pink.

"I hope I'm not disturbing you," said Eugene.

"Sorry?"

"I HOPE I'M—"

"Hold on," said the man. He opened the door, which had not been locked.

"I hope I'm not disturbing you," Eugene repeated. The fusty air of the bookstore wafted over his face like a warm exhalation; he was reminded of Abe's breath.

"You were sent by Abe?" said Lang. His voice was a high, laughing trill. "Abe is a friend. A nice man. Ah yes, so you're the boy? And what a darling boy you are. Tell me, would you like some coffee? Is Abe in good health?"

"Mr. Frank Lang?"

"That's me. But here they call me Signor Lingua." Lang grinned like a jackal, and something in his jaw clicked like the second hand of a watch: *ticktock, ticktock.*

Lang turned a knob on the wall and little electric candles, mounted in frosted green glass on the columns between bookshelves, flared up, soaking the room in a queasy Adriatic hue. Tens of thousands of books sprang into existence all around Eugene. As he followed Lang across the room, the creaky floorboards caused the nearby stacks to teeter slightly, so that they seemed to exhale dust.

"I was just sitting in my chair, preparing some notes for a conference I've been asked to organize, and I must have dozed off," said Lang. "I am so absentminded. It's a good thing you woke me, otherwise I surely would be . . ." And here he paused for comic effect, brushing his mustache down with his forefinger and smiling mischievously. ". . . Still sleeping."

Lang cleared off a stool next to his desk and invited Eugene

to sit. When the little man moved behind his desk, Eugene could
see that he walked with a pronounced bowleg.

"You arrived . . . ?"

"Oh, today. Or yesterday. I'm not quite sure. I was so exhausted
that I fell asleep in my clothes. When I woke up, I came straight
over here."

"Watch out for sleep. It can be a dangerous thing, you know."

"Mmm?"

Lang turned solemn. He adjusted his spectacles and swept his
wispy blond hair off the bald center of his scalp.

"I have," he confided in a stage whisper, "a sleeping dis-
order."

"I'm very sorry to hear that."

Lang nodded gravely. "I've had it for nearly ten years. A
sleeping *sickness*. You see, I just can't seem to keep myself
from sleeping at times."

"Narcolepsy?"

"No, no, no. I don't just drift off in the middle of a sentence
or fall headfirst into a bowl of spaghetti. I have some self-control.
But take just now. I was sitting at my desk, at that quiet time of
day I normally reserve for studying and updating my journals. I
hadn't slept for many hours, and suddenly—you are knocking on
the door. You see, I had fallen asleep. Just like that. It's as if I had
been . . . enchanted."

"That doesn't seem too unusual," said Eugene. "When you're
tired, you're tired."

"No, no, no. I come from a long line of people—cliff dwellers we
are—who do not sleep. Up in the morning and up late at night,
always busy. An industrious people," said Lang, busily ticktocking.

"Farmers?"

"Some, I suppose. But there are many others of us who could easily blend in in any major cosmopolitan city. We're a highly adaptable group. Sleeplessness is really a fine quality to possess. But ever since I left the village about a decade ago, I've had terrible trouble sleeping. The feeling alone disturbs me, that sensation of drifting, helpless and mindless, off to oblivion. It's not like eating, for instance, which one can do quickly and in conjunction with other, more useful activities."

It didn't appear, however, that Lang had done much eating either. His throat was as tight as a newt's, and the shapes of his ivory-white teeth were imprinted on his lips when he closed his mouth, so thin was his skin. Still, in the warm knowingness of his jackal smiles—which ended in a mock-serious, self-deprecatory curl at the corners of his mouth—and in the fluttery movements of his slender, tapering hands, he reminded Eugene of somebody he had once met.

Lang's jaw started to ticktock.

"You must be here for something tremendously important, since everything that Abe does is tremendously important. I assume it's something about Constantino. But quiet one second," he said, with false severity. "We'll have plenty of time for research and all that bunk. I want to know, first of all, who *you* are."

"I work for Abe Chisholm . . ."

"Yes and your name is Eugenio: like the great Genovese poet." In the queasy light his eyes appeared the same dusted blue as the sky above Trieste. "I mean to ask, what are you *doing* here? Besides going on some kind of fantastic mission for Abe, who I know can be a tiresome old geezer when it comes down to it. But don't dare tell him I said that." He winked and pursed his lips. "Now, tell me. Who are you? I know you're an American."

"Well, I grew up in New York, but my father is Italian, from Milan. A retired businessman. My mother was beautiful, an American singer for the musical revues. They met while she was on a European tour in college. She never learned how to speak Italian and he can barely speak English even now."

"Che romantico."

Eugene eyed the man curiously and then summed up the rest of his existence in approximately one minute. He skipped the part about his father's descent into remoteness and old world reverie following his mother's death. He realized that the only person he felt comfortable talking about this with was Sonia.

Lang asked him about the ream of papers that were threatening to spill forth from his shoulder bag.

"I have a friend named Alvaro from the Dominican Republic whose first novel I've brought with me to Italy. I'm translating it from a rare Spanish dialect. It's about a Dominican priest named Jacinto who moves to New York and falls in love with a girl named Alsa. She runs away from home and he has to go find her."

"What happens next?"

"I'm not sure, I'm only partway through the second section. The last thing I know is that Alsa has gone back to the island, where she's been kidnapped by a tribe of cannibals. But tell me: where is Alison?"

"You mean Alice? I call her Alice, or Alicia in Italian. She is a beautiful girl, isn't she?"

"Yes, she is."

"I see. You love her. That's why you came."

"No," said Eugene, taken aback. "Or—yes."

"Alice is with Eakins."

"You mean Eakins is . . . alive?"

"Oh yes, quite. Robust, even."

"Is he here? In Trieste?"

"Or hereabouts."

"Hereabouts?"

"About."

Eugene closed his eyes and opened them again.

"Where's Eakins?"

"Funny you ask. I just saw him. Both of them in fact. Couldn't have been a week ago. They came to my store."

Lang shaped his pink lips into a thin, citric grin.

"Where does he live?"

"Up there." He flung an arm in the direction of one of the bookshelves.

"In the hills?" Eugene wondered whether Lang was intentionally deceiving him.

"In the Carso. There are a number of villages clustered above the cliffs on curly roads and pockmarked hillsides and grottoes hidden deep in the rock face. He lives up there. Most of my friends do—that's where I'm from. Very rarely does he come down to the city. I had told him that Alice was coming to town, so he stopped to pay her a visit. That's when it happened."

"Now when you say 'happened' . . ."

"The girl was charmed," began Lang. "Do you know what it is to be charmed?"

As Lang made them coffee in a mini-kitchen in the back of the store, he explained to Eugene what transpired after he met Alice at the Aeroporto Friuli–Venezia Giulia. Lang could tell right away that she had been crying. He didn't see it in her face, which was as delicately translucent as ever, or in her dry gray eyes. But there was something moving within her, a flutter and a shiver that sent her fingers grasping in disjointed gestures and her knees buckling; she interrupted herself often with misplaced smiles and wary pauses. She seemed stricken with a secret sadness.

Driving back from the airport in his Fiat Cinquecento, Lang took the long, scenic route home, thinking that the view might divert her. They snaked along the ridge of the cliffs at twilight. The Adriatic sparkled purple behind murky, decrepit castles and scattered groves of Austrian pine trees; tunnels lit with dim yellow bulbs conveyed them through the mountainside. Chalky, moss-covered rock formations abutted the road, seeping rust-colored fluid. Soon they reached the urban limits, careening above the city's low tawny roofs and its narrow, lifeless streets. Lang asked Alice to read the signs to him, since he couldn't see them until they were right over him—his eyes barely peered over the steering wheel. Cologna é qui a destra, she said. Montefiasco. Dieci chilometri al centro storico. Alice asked Lang if he would take her to his family's village in the Carso during her visit. Maybe, said Lang. If necessary.

Lang took Eugene downstairs to show him the basement, where Alice had slept on a thin foam mattress in a room crowded with books and papers. The air was cool and smelled of orange peels and clothing detergent. A rickety bookshelf blocked the only window—a high, horizontal pane—so that strips of thin lavender light slotted into the room through the gaps above the books.

Alice had told Lang that upon waking in this place, she didn't know where she was or how she had gotten there. She had the odd sensation of having misplaced something of little significance—a hairpin, say, or an earring, though she didn't wear earrings. She took a single volume off the bookshelf and a rectangle of light fell across her chest. She removed, at random, a second book, then a third and fourth. A pattern like piano keys lit across her, from shoulder to shoulder. When she had moved the whole shelf's contents onto the floor, sunlight filled the room and she began to feel like herself again. The window gave onto a side street, just above the level of the sidewalk; a patch of orange gardenias sprouted from a narrow fissure in the dewy pavement.

She found Lang upstairs, bowed over his desk. He was preparing his keynote speech for the annual World Esperanto Congress, which was held in Trieste that summer. Lang was the chairman of Trieste's Esperanto Association and had worked for the past several years to bring the annual meeting of the Congress to Trieste.

At last, said Lang, hearing her bare feet patter on the warped wooden floor. You're awake.

Lang took Alice to the Civico Museo di Storia ed Arte, where they spent time in front of Lang's favorite exhibits: a diorama devoted to Freud's one-year stay in Trieste, in 1875, as a university zoologist student charged with dissecting male eels to determine whether they possessed gonads; a room devoted to James Joyce, dressed in a shabby suit and lugging a fat manuscript along the Canal Grande, and his English student, the doting, limping Italo Svevo, pictured with a cigarette burned nearly down to his fingers; and the papyrus scrolls and sarcophagi of the Egyptian collection. The guards saw that Alice was a tourist, and they flirted with her. She came alive, bursting into the full, giddy laughter she had inherited from her father. She looked happy.

"She didn't mention you, if that's what you're wondering," said Lang, frowning.

"I was, actually," said Eugene.

"Then again, she didn't mention anyone else either."

On the way home, Alice talked excitedly about all the old friends she would visit in Trieste—Poldi, Marco, and Kasia—and they walked through the sun-dazzled Piazza Unità d'Italia to the old Jewish ghetto. It was a maze of cramped, veering streets lined with secondhand stores, many owned by friends of Lang's. He wanted Alice to meet one of these friends, but his store was locked up, and two lugubrious, dirt-stained children were taking turns tossing a red ragball against the window.

Children! he chirped. *Children!* he chirped louder, this time in the Triestine dialect. The urchins turned and regarded Lang with mute apprehension: a man no larger than them, bumbling and trembling, with a puckered neck quivering pink beneath his mustached mouth. A voice that sounded like a deflating balloon. The boy kicked his feet together; the girl stuck out her tongue and put a grimy hand on her hip. Alice, giggling, tried to lead Lang past the children before he got himself hurt.

When the children noticed Alice they jumped as if they had seen a corpse. The ragball dropped with a squish from the boy's hand.

"Xe el cinciut," said the girl, pointing at Alice. The boy's eyes grew blurry with tears.

"El cinciut," they said. "El cinciut!"

And they ran away. Alice was mortified.

"Don't be upset," said Lang. He explained:

"It's an old Triestine superstition that dates back to the medieval age. Many young Triestini still go for it. They believe in a demon they call a 'cinciut' that lives in the Carso and descends upon the city when the bora wind blows with its nightmarish gusts. The cinciut is a kind of incubus, who feasts on any children playing out at night. In February, during the high-wind season, the cinciuts rush down from the Carso, rattling through the forests above the city. It's a nursery tale told to children to make them stay inside during the bora, so they don't get hurt outside.

"The only talisman against the cinciut is a dead sparrow. There's a line in Proverbs that reads: Like a fluttering sparrow, an undeserved curse does not come to rest. So if you throw a sparrow at a cinciut, you're protected. It's just a children's game, nothing to take seriously."

But this absurd encounter seemed to return Alice to her previous melancholy state. She pitter-pattered up the cellar stairs earlier and earlier every morning. It was clear she wasn't sleeping. Her hair, that gorgeous russet hair, coiled together, scraggly and dry. She moved with uncertainty, and declined Lang's invitations to explore the city, or even accompany him on his errands. When he asked what was wrong, she admitted she felt unsettled and preoccupied, though she didn't know why. But she'd see her old friends most days, and she never allowed herself to be anything but her old glimmering self around them. She would jump on the back of Marco's Vespa and they would plow out of Via San Nicolò, sending the pigeons aloft and the miserable stray cats limping back into their alleys. She grotto-hopped with sly Kasia, the butcher's black-eyed daughter: they went to the nightclubs down the coastline and swam off the rock beaches. With Poldi, the coffeemaker, she picked olives on a sunny hillside just over the Slovenian border. Yet every afternoon, when she came home for a nap, her face collapsed, her color drained. She would tell Lang briefly about her day in a tone of false cheerfulness and then slink down to her room.

"What do you think was upsetting her?" asked Eugene, afraid of how Lang might respond.

"I think she might have been worried about her father's health and fragile condition. Other times I felt that she resented having to take care of him, and didn't know what she wanted to do with herself, now that she was an adult. But I was never certain. One day, I decided to approach her about it and have a conversation. But before I could, she got better."

"What happened?" asked Eugene, suddenly hopeful. "Did she . . . did she get one of my letters?"

"No," said Lang. "Connie showed up."

Alice, said Lang, had been walking across the wide graphite spread of Piazza Unità, toward the sea. At the edge of the piazza, past the boardwalk, a quartz-white stairway led down right into the water, so that the sea seemed one vast swimming pool. Above the horizon before her, a slim crescent moon sliced apart the pink sky. She liked to sit on the third step, so the water could tickle her ankles. To her left extended a long pier, the Molo Audace, lined with tinselly bronze streetlamps. By dusk the water level rose so high that the assembled crowd of horizon-watchers on the pier seemed to be standing on nothing more substantial than the sea itself. The far end of the pier was tacitly reserved for couples, who lingered in the day's final light, outlasting the sun by slow, wondrous minutes.

But on this midsummer afternoon it was not quite dusk. The children, free from school and hungry for dinner, their mouths like coin slots, wandered in grubby, querulous packs. Alice told Lang that she had immediately noticed among these boys the one who had yelled at her in the ghetto a week earlier. She watched helplessly as he spotted her, and then called out to his friends. The children ran over, forming a cautious semicircle around her—though not too close, fearing, perhaps, that she might jump after them with gnashing teeth.

Something splashed into the water just in front of her and then floated up, bobbing lifelessly in the tide. Gradually, herky-jerky, the tide pulled it toward her, until she could make out what it was. The sparrow's head had been twisted down into its breast, its neck secreting an oily iridescent film. There was a spurt of high-pitched laughter and the scampering of two dozen little feet. She felt a crackling in the small of her back and began to grow faint. El cinciut, the children whispered. El cinciut. It was a chant. They shuffled closer, their confidence surging, until they were nearly upon her, a midget mob of squirrelly faces and small angry hands with chewed fingernails.

A slow roar rent the sky. One of the girls, a blond tomboy wearing corduroys, fell to her knees in preemptive surrender. A boy grabbed his mouth with both hands and screamed hoarsely into them, and another boy promptly lay down in a fetal position.

A man—or something resembling a man, only much larger—

stood planted on the boardwalk between Alice and the children. His piston legs, themselves like two small children, supported a mighty torso heaving with rage and adrenaline. Arms shot out like distended pythons, waving heavy red fists. He had a warrior's face: a sharp, muscular jaw thick with a grizzled beard; a broken nose shaped like a scythe; hawkish, cavernous eyes; and a sun-bronzed forehead that, like a rampart, supported a mountainous skull, from which there dangled a rich thicket of curly orange-white locks—for he was, despite his ferocious vitality, an elderly man. As he spoke to the children, he swept his arm across the horizon, a gesture that implicated them all, and had the incidental effect of making them shudder in unison. They seemed too terrified to respond, run away, or stand still; several of them shivered uncontrollably.

"She is not a cinciut," shouted the man, in thick Triestine dialect. He unleashed another booming, stentorian roar. *"It's ME! I'm the demon you fear. I am the commander of the cinciuts, and I will send them down to devour your malnourished skulls. Now, run off, or I will tear off your heads and force-feed them to your destitute whorish mothers."*

The children sprinted off hysterical in every direction, tripping and falling. One boy ran straight into the fence that surrounded the Piazza Unità's fountain, fell on his back, and lay motionless for a moment. Then he stood up and, grasping one crooked arm, slithered off in the opposite direction. Another boy jumped into the sea and began dog-paddling in the direction of Venice. The great man turned to face Alice.

"I'm so sorry, little darling. I hope I haven't disturbed you." He spoke in English, and in a genteel tone, unrecognizable from his previous tirade. He smiled courteously as he spoke. "I hate to see people act cruelly to young, innocent women, especially those traveling abroad. You are American, aren't you?"

Alice nodded, her gray eyes gaping in amazement at the physical oddity before her. The man helped her up, nearly lifting her off the ground entirely.

"Thank you," she said, "for saving me from those awful children. But I hope you didn't scare them too badly." As she said this she noticed several small puddles on the boardwalk where the children had been standing moments earlier.

"I'm just gratified to be able to help you out, Ms. . . . Have we met, by any chance?"

"Ms. Chisholm. I don't think so. I'm pretty sure I would have remembered."

The man raised a platinum eyebrow. He gave her a wide feline smile and, somewhat abashed, relaxed his grip on her hand. The lopsided pair strolled along the boardwalk together. The sky was growing dark, and the vast piazza was already lit for night, illuminated by oval spotlights embedded in the pavement, and by the extraordinary tall bronze streetlamps, from which frosty globes hung like poisonous fruit. The expensive cafés lining the piazza thrummed with the crowds of vacationers and bankers just off from work at the stock exchange, conversing in languid, sardonic tones. A group of elderly men stood in a semicircle, their hands clasped behind them, speaking with pinched, declamatory gestures; a few feet away, a group of elderly women gossiped in their ankle-length housecoats.

"Of course, you don't need to call me Ms. Chisholm."

"That's fine! How about Agata? You see, I once knew someone named Agata, and you bear an uncanny resemblance to her.

The same graceful, high cheekbones, the red-gold hair . . . She was a frank, sophisticated woman."

Alice later told Lang that she was overcome by a vague, hazy calm. The excitement of the wharf drained from her like a dream upon awakening. "Agata," she said to herself.

"She was named after agate," said the giant. "The striped gem. The ancient Persian magicians used it to protect against fevers. I happen to succumb myself, from time to time, to the most savage fevers. You wouldn't believe. Fevers of the brain. Now, I'm not one to put a whole lot of stock in ancient Persian wizardry. But dear sweet Agata did cure a few of my fevers. I don't mean anything vulgar by that, of course. But suffice it to say, she was a good woman to me. A strong woman." Spidery creases worried at his temples and it seemed to Alice that he might weep.

"I love the name, Agata," said Alice. "I'd be *honored* if you called me that." She smiled, wanting to reassure the nice old man.

"What a dear child. Now, would you permit this old fellow to make sure you get wherever you're going safely?"

"It's a bit out of the way—a little antiquarian bookstore on a backstreet. It's called the Libreria Antiquaria—"

"Constantino Eakins."

"You know it?"

"Just follow me. You see," he said, "Agata. You see, Agata, I know this city pretty well."

His murderous outburst seemed distant, as if it belonged to some previous era of her life. She blamed her earlier anxiety on her dazed, melancholy state. When he had shown up on the boardwalk, that mood had vanished, replaced by a feeling that something strange and new had entered her life.

———

Y ou can imagine what I thought when they showed up together at the bookstore," said Lang. "Through the window I
spotted them. Their arms were linked and she was laughing.
Positively *twinkling*. And her hair that day, I'll never forget! It
was a fantasy. I swear: it glowed red and gold. Meet my savior,
she said, in her best dame-in-distress voice. Connie just grinned
at me, and I admit there was something in that grin that gave me
the chills."

Lang's jaw ticktocked uncomfortably. Eugene was beside himself—he had finished his coffee, and was jittery in his seat.

"On the way back from the piazza Eakins finally came out and
told Alice who he was. She wasn't shocked at all, but only said,
'Oh, somewhere deep down I think I knew that.' Then the three
of us sat around for several hours or so, Connie captivating Alice
with stories about her father. In the sixties Abe was a passionate,
virile man—though Alice laughed at the use of the word 'virile'
to describe her father—zealous for adventure in obscure lands.
Connie talked about a yearlong journey he took with Abe around
the Adriatic Sea—interrupted by brief jaunts in Bari, Vlorë, and
Corfu—aboard a dilapidated Slavic schooner. Abe was like a
younger brother to Connie. He told how they once skirmished
with a small band of nomadic mountain bandits outside of Ti-
ranë, disputing the sacrifice of a terrified, bleating doe. How they
once smuggled burlap sacks of silver ore over the Yugoslavian
border with a band of Gypsies, who melted the metal for use in
a religious healing ritual. How a victorious fight in a Dubrovnic
bar led to the dismemberment of a Greek sailor.

"Miraculously, Connie emerged almost entirely unscathed and

Abe suffered only a cut on his jaw. The fight had broken out after Abe asked the young girlfriend of one of the sailors to dance. Connie said she was beautiful: she wore a red polka-dotted bonnet and had a bright, heart-shaped face with eyes as round as the sun that was then rising, for it was dawn by the time the fight was over. This girl took pity on Abe. When they stumbled out into the port she left with them, and traveled with them all the way back to Trieste. Abe and she were married under an orange beech tree in a small town in the Carso, in a cliffside mansion overlooking the sea.

"Connie admitted that he recognized Alice on the boardwalk because she resembled her mother so closely.

"Alice was transfixed. It must have been difficult for her to imagine her dusty old father young and boisterous, let alone shattering a beer bottle over the head of a Greek sailor. But Abe rarely discussed Alice's mother, and she had certainly never heard the story of her parents' meeting. She begged Connie to stay and tell her more. He said, I wish I could talk to you further, and I will soon, but not now—I have to make it back up the Carso before morning. My friends expect me, he said.

"When Connie left, Alice slumped downstairs. She reminded me of her father then—the first flicker of disappointment and he takes to bed like an invalid. Her sadness was gone, but it had been replaced by something else, something shapeless: not melancholy so much as restlessness. When she came upstairs that night, she wanted to talk with me about her parents' love affair. She spoke about the pain of losing a great love too early—her mother had died when she was just a toddler. She told me that she had once fallen in love herself, but she was torn away so abruptly that her love remained just a wish, apparitional and feeble, attenuating with time. And she wondered whether maybe that was the best kind of love. The one that is snatched away before it can breathe and settle.

"On the way to dinner that night, Alice barely spoke. When we passed under a streetlamp, a tress of her hair, which had fallen loose from her forehead, appeared to have turned white. When I mentioned this to her, she complained that she didn't feel well and ran back in the direction of the bookstore. When I came home from dinner, she was gone. I never saw her again.

"I don't know what she's doing now, or why she ran off. But I'm certain I know where she is."

3

Around the time Rutherford left for Italy, Agnes began collecting seahorses. It strikes Mr. Schmitz as a peculiar development—his wife has never had a fish tank before, or any pet after the death of her childhood dog. She does, however, have a mania for reading the science section of the Sunday newspaper, and he supposes she has gotten the idea from an article on seahorses that ran the weekend of Rutherford's departure.

The piece, called "Seahorse Attitudes," profiled the world's leading authority on seahorses, the marine biologist Mollie Owen. Owen had opened, in New London, the first center for seahorse preservation, and had made several major discoveries so far. For instance, she said, many people know that seahorses are monogamous and that the male, not the female, gives birth. But she was the first to discover the method by which a seahorse chooses its partner, that a male seahorse eats a different diet when it is pregnant, and that a seahorse's death shortens the lifespan of its mate.

Most recently, Owen had begun testing the creature's often

promoted medicinal properties. For centuries, seahorses have been prescribed by folk doctors on the Asian continent to treat fever, baldness, rabies, sore throat, asthma, bone fractures, menstrual cramps, insanity, incontinence, impotence, delayed childbirth, and fatigue. Owen was the first Western scientist to examine the seahorse's genetic sequence, and her research had explained the science behind many of these curative powers. To aid in the protection of the threatened species, her organization had sponsored a number of programs to encourage responsible seahorse farming.

Owen hoped to increase awareness of her cause by encouraging home aquarium stores to sell the animal. Her foundation was working to create an incentive program that would encourage private seahorse owners to donate whatever offspring their tanks produced, so that after several generations, the pet seahorse industry might make a significant contribution to the growth of the world's endangered seahorse population.

Agnes explains all this to her chin-rubbing husband as she dumps a plastic baggy of live brine shrimp into her new temperature-controlled aquarium. She has placed the aquarium, much to Mr. Schmitz's consternation, in the middle of the kitchen table.

"It's the only flat surface I have to work with" is Agnes's excuse.

Opaque partitions divide the thirty-gallon tank vertically into four different columns. Each segment contains a pair of mating seahorses, a plastic fern, and a miniature pagoda.

"Why are there Oriental figurines in the water?" asks Mr. Schmitz.

"Those are five-story pagodas of Nanjing," replies Agnes, admiring her creation. She removes the napkin holder and salt and pepper shakers from the table, so as not to distract attention away from the tank.

"I thought it would be in keeping with the spirit of the thing. Isn't it fun?"

Mr. Schmitz frowns and, tucking the newspaper under his arm, heads to his favorite reading chair.

He finds himself staring at a sidebar to the Mollie Owen piece. It explains that the seahorse's largest problem is not that its populations are too concentrated, but that they are spread across great distances. Of all the ocean's small creatures, the seahorse has the lowest population density. When a male gives birth, his fry swim off to whatever crevice they can hide in, usually quite far from home. And when they grow older, they lose their mobility. As a result, lost partners are not quickly replaced. So if a seahorse is caught, its partner is doomed.

With the night settling in outside, and Agnes having tucked herself into bed, Mr. Schmitz plods back to the kitchen to prepare his postdinner snack. A bluish glow spills down the hallway from the darkened kitchen, waves of light playing gently on the walls. Mr. Schmitz feels as though he has walked into an underwater cave.

In the refrigerator, propped on top of a carton of egg salad, is the baggie of brine shrimp, sealed at the top. The white diaphanous creatures writhe their exoskeletons and paddle their leafy legs through the saline solution, hairy caterpillars of the sea. Mr. Schmitz grabs the baggie and turns to the tank, his eyes brimming with turquoise light.

He sees a yellow seahorse nestling its dorsal fin against the top ridge of its pagoda, like a bear rubbing its back against an oak tree. Mr. Schmitz lifts off the top of the tank and dips the bottom of the bag into the water. The seahorse, seeing the brine shrimp, curls and uncurls its tail, puffs out its snout, and wiggles its coronet. Soon its partner emerges from the ground floor of the pagoda to investigate the source of this commotion. The two creatures begin to engage in an elaborate dance. The larger one—the male—circles around the female, wrapping his tail around hers as a man might embrace his partner in a waltz. The male's spine turns darker, its bright yellow seething into apricot, while his torso grows pale. The female seems to show little interest: she floats still in the water, occasionally breaking her concentration to nudge with her snout the plastic baggie containing the shrimp.

Mr. Schmitz cannot take it anymore. With a single flourish, he opens the bag and tilts it so that the hundreds of brine shrimp spill into the tank. To Mr. Schmitz's surprise, the seahorses do not interrupt their dance, but only raise their heads. Whenever a shrimp passes nearby, the seahorse snorts it up whole. The shrimp slides down the tube behind the seahorse's gills, illuminating it with a bright spectral hue, before disappearing into the digestive tract.

All night Mr. Schmitz sits in the kitchen, watching the waltz of the seahorses. The shrimp cling to the pagoda like Christmas lights, and flash like star clusters around the dancing pairs.

Mr. Schmitz wakes up the next morning with his jowl pressed against the side of the tank. Agnes is rubbing his shoulder under his nightshirt, and their miniature ocean is swarming with seahorse fry.

4   Agata sat on her
duffel bag at the tram stop in
the empty Piazza Scorcola, her foot tapping erratically against a jagged split of concrete.
After some time a young woman roughly Agata's age, with
plaited brown hair and a drawn, restless face, started walking
back and forth beside her. Agata smiled, and the woman returned
the smile gratefully, opening her mouth as if she had something
to say, but never actually saying it. Still the tram did not come.
A Greek navy ship was docked in Trieste for the week, and as the
night progressed, more and more of the sailors returned with
local women to a pensione near the tram stop. Upstairs the windows would illuminate and then, several minutes later, darken,
and deep laughter would echo through the square. Every few
minutes squat Italian cars, rusted and voracious, would accelerate
to the curb and then slow into a creep. Each time, Agata politely
shook her head and the car sped up a hill, toward the Carso.
Agata sensed that there were people in the black windows above
the street peering down at her and her brunette counterpart in
hungry expectation of some event she could not anticipate. But

maybe it was just a feeling, an understandable case of the heebie-jeebies in this nowhere city where everyone seemed to speak a different language.

Agata palpated her temples with her fingers—an old habit of her father's—and wondered what had happened to her that afternoon. She felt like the woman beside her, careening lightly back and forth, unsure and probably a little bit drunk. It was a soft, airy sensation, as if her brain was slowly floating around inside her head, gently bouncing against the walls of her skull like some cranial version of Pong.

"*I know how you feel,*" said Agata, addressing the young woman in Italian. The woman stopped in her tracks so abruptly that her brown loafers planted to the sidewalk with a small squeaking sound.

"*Me?*" she said, and then laughed. "*Of course you mean me. Who else is there? It's so nice to finally meet you. You speak Italian very well.*" Agata gingerly pushed herself up off her bag and lightly shook hands with the woman, who introduced herself as Stasia, flapping a nervous wave when she said her name. The city had grown quiet and dark. The streetlamp held them in its spotlight.

"*Do you know when the tram is supposed to come?*" asked Agata. "*It's been a long time now.*"

"*Where are you going?*" asked Stasia. She was attractive, Agata decided, though she did bear a certain likeness to a small bird: her nose was slender and beakish, and there was very little skin between her nose and her lips, which gave the whole face a pleasing, pinched quality. Her eyes flickered emerald.

"*Up to the top of the Carso,*" said Agata. "*Opicina, Trebiciano, Padriciano . . . all those roly-poly-sounding names. I'm looking for an old friend. He lives in one of the villages there. I know it's a long trip. I'm in no rush."*

"I come from a town up there myself. But it's very small, you wouldn't have heard of it," said Stasia, with a laughing voice. *"Hey, I'm looking for someone too. He's a young man, about my age. He looks like a local who spends all his time on his parents' boat deck: skinny like a mountain goat, funny little ears, black curly hair, and big squishy cheeks. Have you seen anyone like that on the streets tonight? I've been wanting to ask you this."*

Agata didn't think she had seen him. Judging from her acquaintance's reaction, she thought it best to change the subject. *"I wonder when this tram will come."*

"Oh it won't," said Stasia, rubbing her arms as if they had been bruised.

"Sorry?"

"The tram won't come. This line doesn't run during the summer. See?" She pointed to a cardboard sign that hung by a string from the streetlamp. Someone had scrawled in red marker the number of the bus line and the words "fuori servizio," underlined twice.

"I thought you just wanted to talk to somebody," said Stasia, by way of explanation.

Agata wasn't sure she was telling the truth. There was no other tramway in Trieste that went up the Carso. Was it possible that no trams ran up to the mountains all summer?

"Can I show you something you want to see?" said Stasia. Agata nodded absently.

The woman walked into the street, several yards from the curb, and pointed down at a black patch on the road that Agata could not quite make out through the darkness.

"Help me lift this."

Agata approached like a sleepwalker, leaving her duffel bag on the curb by the streetlamp. When her eyes adjusted she saw that the woman had her fingers curled around the bars of an iron grate, and was straining to lift it out of the ground. The grate appeared to cover a sewage pipe.

Agata put her fingers through the grating, which was slick with a greasy, levigate guck that stained her hands black. They pried it off and it dropped to the pavement with a loud clang.

"*Boom bang!*" said Stasia.

Agata looked around, but not a single light came on in any of the windows above the piazza. Stasia wiped her soiled hands on the lap of her skirt. The two women squatted down by the hole and peered into it. It was a deep well, with glistening walls that slanted outward, so that it grew wider and wider as it went down. Some twenty feet below, a pool shone silver in the starlight.

"*Sometimes I think I hear my friend down there.*" said Stasia. "*Maybe yours will be there too.*"

Several round objects bobbed and floated in the glimmering pool. Agata hunched over farther to try to get a better glimpse. Her silhouette passed over the pool's surface. But Stasia's silhouette was gone. Agata looked up in time to see her rush around the corner. Agata ran in pursuit, but when she reached the end of the block, Stasia had disappeared.

Agata nudged the heavy grate back into place with her shoe and wiped her hands off on the streetlamp as best she could. Why, she wondered, had that odd girl wanted to show her the inside of the Trieste sewer system?

She peered up to the Carso, where lights flickered intermittently behind screens of plane trees, and realized the lunacy of her plan. Looking at her mud-stained sneakers and hands and jeans, she remembered how she had been covered in mud before, only one week earlier, with Eugene. Though he had managed to get covered even more completely. Somehow, he had sealed his ears with the gunk. She was surprised to feel a sudden, painful stab of homesickness.

Out of the murk behind her there came a breathless scampering. It was Stasia. She was winded and her face was flushed the color of violets.

"I'm sorry," she said, huffing. "I thought I heard him— My boy. I didn't mean to abandon you like that."

"That's fine. I think I'm just going to go home now."

"No, wait, I'll take you. I know how to go. Besides, these cliffs are powerful. You can't go up alone. We're each looking for someone. It's better we go together. Maybe they'll be in the same place."

Agata picked up her bag and, without thought or calculation, followed Stasia. Soon the road tilted upward toward the barren Carso. The plane trees engulfed them and they lost sight of the Adriatic gaping behind them. Agata was cold and disoriented. To distract herself, she tried to make conversation with Stasia, asking her where she was from.

"I'd love to tell you," said Stasia. "But some of the facts are fuzzy."

"Oh, you don't have to get every detail right." Agata realized that even if she wanted to turn back now, she wouldn't know how.

"Well, I'm pretty sure my parents were farmers in the foothills of the Alps," said Stasia, wincing as if the memory pained her. "But my early life with them was so dull that I can hardly remember it. I know we had a cow I had to milk and that, one day when it got fat, I slaughtered it . . . or perhaps my mother did. And my father, he was happy and friendly. But blank. I can't make out his face anymore. I might have had a brother or two, or a sister perhaps. It's all so vague *until the day I met— Ooh! You can't see it but I'm blushing just to say his name. It's funny, but—I can't!"*

"Whisper it."

She said it fast, with a thrill.

"*What a nice name,*" said Agata. "*Very Italian. A happy little name.*"

"*My whole life began that day. Everything before that was wiped right away, swept off a table, and in its place there he was. I had to fight over him with this other girl, a real witch, but he took to me. And the remarkable thing was, we never even had to speak.*"

"*You never spoke? But you won him over anyway?*"

"*Actually, we still haven't spoken,*" replied Stasia nonchalantly. "*I haven't seen him after that day, you see. But I've been looking for him ever since.*"

"*Where did he go?*"

"*He just disappeared. Just as neatly as he appeared. Boom bang.*"

"*How did that happen exactly?*"

"*We were walking away, down the street, and just as I was being filled with this incredible happiness, a darkness like death swooped over me. I didn't remember, I didn't think, I didn't feel a thing. It was like I had entered a coma. When I woke up, sprawled on the floor of an unfamiliar empty room, I sensed that a long period of time had passed. Though when I saw myself in a mirror, I didn't look any different at all. I still had on the same ugly gray dress I had been wearing when I met him. My hair was still plaited and the sweat from his palm was still damp on mine.*"

Agata noted that Stasia's hair was still plaited and she still seemed to be wearing the dress—a lopsided, thin, yellow-gray affair.

"*I realized that I was not in a hospital or a homeless ward but a small ramshackle house in a town I'd never seen before. The town was filled with shacks like this one, painted red with yellow windowsills and high gables. There was a single rocking chair on the porch, and a little plot of dirt in the back—a yard—surrounded by a wire fence. The houses stood along a single main street. The air in the town had a faint anesthetic quality to it—it smelled like turpentine."*

At this point the two girls had wound their way up a rocky path through the shrubs and to a limestone cliff that towered over the city. Their trail ended at a two-lane highway, which boomeranged out of a tunnel and bent around the cliff several hundred yards farther down the road. The yellow lane-divider hash marks, spaced at regular intervals, jigged like a trail of fireflies.

"Don't worry," whispered Stasia, which only worried Agata more—who could be listening that she had to whisper? Stasia extended her tiny, clammy hand and Agata squeezed tight as they skipped over the hash marks and darted into the woods beyond the highway. After some stumbling through high brush, they reached an overgrown dirt path that ran parallel to the highway, around the side of the cliff. The diminishing city below them grew indistinct and the streetlamps grouped together into blurry pockets of light.

"There were many people in the town's main street. I didn't recognize any of them, but they looked familiar, like distant relations. We had something in common, a wariness perhaps, only they were comfortable in this town and seemed to have lived there for a long time. I asked them where my boy was, and the people smiled at me with pity but said nothing. I started to panic.

"Their only suggestion was that I go see the Mayor. The Mayor was the only person in town who didn't live in those strange little red houses. He lived in a three-story mansion with bright white walls,

*stained-glass windows, and a tower that was topped by jagged battle-
ments like bad teeth. To get to this mansion, you had to walk to the
end of the town's single avenue, where there is a black iron gate. Once
you pass through the gate, you walk down a long brick lane shaded by
spruce trees. The mansion stands at the end of this lane, on top of the
cliffs, and is usually cloaked in a streaming sea mist. When I approached, the only part of the house that was visible to me was a
single window at the top of the tower. I had the feeling that someone
was spying me from within. I remember holding my shawl close
around me and wishing it was my boy's embrace."*

Agata hugged herself tightly; far above the sweaty harbor the
air in the lower Carso was flat and cool.

"As I got closer," said Stasia, *"I heard a waltz, and the ground floor
windows were moist and bright with golden light. The door swung
open and there appeared an elderly butler with drooping features,
wearing a starched tuxedo and swinging a gold-knobbed cane. There
was a tea party under way, with many colorful characters seated in a
tall, red-velvet-walled hall, around a long table piled with cookies
and jams and scones and small steaks too—all sorts of things I had
never seen before. A young maid scooted about with a kettle, refilling
the teapots. A waltz was playing and several people danced. I studied
each person's face for a sign of my love, but he was not there. The rev-
elers were dressed as if for a costume party. There was one young man
in a ratty pirate's shirt and torn slacks, who looked as if he had just
rolled down a mountain, while another, wearing a natty pinstriped
business suit and top hat, seemed to have come straight from the stock
exchange. There was also an elephant hunter, a Turkish prostitute, and
a young soldier with an eye patch. At the end of the table, there sat the
host, the Mayor.*

"He was a gigantic, frightening man built like a mountain, but *everyone there seemed to adore him. He cracked jokes nonstop in a deep, gravelly voice and roared with drunken laughter. At one point, he took the businessman onto his lap and bounced him like a baby. The businessman didn't mind it all—in fact, he giggled and raised his hands like he was on a roller coaster."*

Agata had lost herself in Stasia's story, and had ceased to worry about where she was being led, or what might be lurking within the darkness of the Carso. She just listened and tried to avoid tripping over the roots that knotted the steep mountain path. She tried to visualize the Mayor, but couldn't do better than a wide, blurry face.

"The butler tapped his cane on the floor, quieting the room. He introduced me by my name, which I do not remember telling him. The Mayor paused mid-bite, a piece of silverware immersed deep inside his mouth. Then a look of recognition came over him and he took me by the shoulders—I must not have stood much higher than his waist— and led me around the room, introducing me to the people there. They had incredible stories. At each introduction, the Mayor would say something like, 'This is George, an accomplished elephant hunter, who pined after a princess in a faraway land and embarked on a journey through terrible kingdoms and unfriendly landscapes to save her. George is one of my best friends.' Or, 'This woman of bewitching beauty is Afet, who caught the eye of a crippled American army lieu-tenant, suffering from blood poisoning after a botched surgery in a Budapest hospital shortly after the War. Her loving gaze gave the lieutenant hope, even in the final throes of his disease. She is one of my dearest, truest, friends. The lieutenant is as well.' Everyone there was one of his 'best,' 'oldest,' or 'most constant' friends. It was a happy gang all right, getting plastered together.

"After the introductions he said that he wanted to see me alone. He

took me to a private study. As soon as we entered the room I began to cry. It was not the excitement or the newness of the place, or even my disorientation. No, I genuinely yearned for my boy, and my frustration was so great at not finding him that I couldn't behave myself anymore. When I had been with him, as briefly as it was, there had been a feeling of complete understanding. Everything had made sense, as if the universe had been shrunk down to a single pebble that could fit in my hand and be felt and measured and swallowed. Now I was floating debris, zigging through space, ignorant and blind."

Agata nodded sympathetically in the dark. The two girls had reached a clearing in the woods by a shivering, lily-blotted pond. Plane trees leaned into the water at uneven angles, silhouetted by the moonlight. The bushes droned with the nervous movements of dormice and hedgehogs. Stasia went over to the black pond and, with a deep sigh, leaned over and began to sip the cold water.

"Wait—" said Agata, *"I have a water bottle."*

"That's fine," replied Stasia. *"I'm used to this. It doesn't get me sick one bit. No water ever does."*

Agata took a cautious sip from her bottle and laughed quietly to herself at her situation. She realized she was exhausted. Stasia sat next to her, wiping her mouth with the back of her hand, the tips of her braids dangling wet. She helped Agata to her feet, and they set off again.

"I begged the Mayor to tell me, if he knew, where my boy was. He smiled and there was something like pride in his face. He said that the boy had left town, and that I was free to leave as well. The Mayor asked only that I stay for a week to see how I liked it. Most people, he said, enjoyed living in town and couldn't imagine anything worse than leaving and entering civilization. Then he put his arm around my shoulder, a bear paw that weighed me down. I was afraid not only

of what might happen if I lost my boy, but also what might happen to me if I stayed there any longer. I did not want to find out anything more about the Mayor. His presence made me queasy.

"Outside the window of his mansion, at the bottom of the cliffs below, I saw a large city. I figured that's where my boy must have gone. I left in the middle of the night for the city, and I haven't been back to the Mayor's town since."

Agata and Stasia had arrived at a broad grassy hillside, terraced and hatched with vine-entangled trellises. The sky was already growing light to the east over Slovenia. Above them, at the top of the hill, was a wooden A-frame cabin. Its front wall was a single triangular window that overlooked the vineyard, the sparse woods, and the glossy bay beyond.

"If you're hungry like I am," said Stasia, *"come with me."* She tucked her body between the horizontal rails of the fence. Agata followed. They crouched low among the young vines, and when they believed themselves to be out of view of the cabin's triangular eye, they plopped down in the damp clover. They plucked clusters of underripe grapes, small and acrid, and ate them by the bunch, spitting out bits of pedicel. In the predawn dimness Stasia looked wan and unfocused. As she popped the grapes with her pointy teeth, flecks of juice appeared at the corners of her mouth.

Agata asked if they might rest for a minute before it got light again. Stasia seemed irritated, but assented. She did not move from where she was sitting, just mechanically leaned back into a supine position. Agata stretched out next to her, using her duffel bag as a pillow. She offered to share it, and Stasia scooted over, so that the two girls were lying side by side in the narrow clover between the rows of vines.

"*Why, if you're so afraid of the Mayor, are you going back now?*" asked Agata, staring up at the moon.

"*It's not about wanting to go back,*" said Stasia. "*It's just that I have nowhere else to go. And I feel it pulling me.*"

Agata asked further questions, but Stasia could not explain her reasoning, and finally Agata gave up. She drifted off into an uneasy sleep, harassed by persistent thoughts of Eugene and of Eakins. The cold moisture of the soil soaked into her shirt and jeans and the two girls drew together, very gradually, until finally they were hugging, runny nose to runny nose. The Carso's nocturnal cracklings and shiftings stirred Agata every so often, and whenever it did she saw that Stasia was staring back with her restless emerald fish eyes wide open. This alarmed Agata at first, but she fell asleep feeling reassured that someone was looking out for her.

Someone else was awake nearby too. From the triangular window of the cabin, a dark form peered at the girls, its mouth breathing a small circle of moisture on the pane.

5

Caro Sig. Schmitz,
I write you from the Cas-
tello Sforzesco in Milan, where I've just
seen the sculpture collection. One of them made
me think of you: a bust of a woman's head, from the seventh
century B.C. Lean and narrow, with hair like a monk's and a
broken nose in the shape of an attenuated triangle. Her eyes
are closed—no pupils, just blankness. Melancholy captured in
stone form. Her name is Teodolinda. She was a blind queen of
Lombardy, the last of the Monza dynasty.

Do you remember when you tried to return to Agnes, after
our European jaunt, and you found her in the kitchen with a
dozen freshly picked plum tomatoes drying on paper towels?
She said, "I will feel sorry to eat these."

When you asked why, she replied, "Because they have scars."

And you noticed that they all had minuscule scars and
stitch marks, here and there. You told her that it was normal,
that all tomatoes have blemishes and that she wouldn't get
sick. To demonstrate you took a bite out of one of them. But
as your teeth broke through the tomato skin, pricks of tears

appeared in the corner of her eyes. And you realized—I remember you telling me this vividly, we were playing chess with Augie at the park—you realized that she did not mean to say that she was worried about food poisoning. No, she was simply sad for the tomatoes. She sympathized with them. She felt guilty at the prospect of eating the ripe little things.

How we laughed at her! But I apologize now. Sitting here outside the ancient castle I'm seeing more clearly my deficiencies as a friend to you. I hope you don't mind a string of apologies, delivered in letter form, or perhaps by postcard.

It is fine to be back after so many years. I'm looking forward to finding my favorite old trattorie and exploring the outdoor food fairs. Most of all, however, I'm looking forward to mastering Italian. I realized that I've barely spoken a lick ever since Carlita's death. But now I'm immersed in it, so we'll see where that gets me. My restaurant Italian is already back in form. Watch: "Il conto, per favore!"

abbracci,

Rutherford

6

In a rising, incautious voice, Eugene asked Frank Lang why he hadn't bothered to look for Sonia after her disappearance. Lang's answers were alternately defensive, fearful, indifferent, childish, guilty, ponderous, and befuddled. He had tried asking around at her favorite bars and cafés, he said, but no one remembered seeing her. Eugene asked him which bars and cafés. Lang stuttered and wheezed. He insisted that he really had tried. Then he added that he didn't have many friends and found it difficult to talk with strangers. Besides, he asked Eugene, why should her disappearance be his concern? She was no longer a child. She could make decisions for herself. Lang then sat mute while Eugene repeated the same questions to him over and over.

"How could you let her run away? When did you notice she was gone? Where could she have traveled in the middle of the night?" Eugene suffered none of the inhibitions he felt around Abe, and Lang's timidity was wearing on him. The anger felt good—clear, strong, as if he was in control.

"She's in better hands than mine," said Lang at last, glancing at his own knobby, maculated claws. "Who are you to question me in this manner, anyway?" he shouted suddenly. He looked at Eugene directly for the first time, with a fierce, empurpled glare. Eugene held the stare, and Lang lowered his head again, muttering to himself.

"What's that?" asked Eugene.

"I'm afraid to go back up there," said Lang loudly, in a skirling falsetto voice. "It's been so long. Ten years."

"From the way you've described it, I'm not sure she really wanted to go up there anyway. She clearly wanted something, but I don't think Connie is it."

"And you are?"

"I don't know. But she's in danger, and I have to find her. I *need* to find her. You've got to take me up there, to the Carso. It doesn't sound like there are any maps that show all the tiny towns up there."

But Lang would not leave his desk. He shook his head and gestured like a blind man, terrified and uncertain. There was something internally violent about his refusal, as if his human interests and sympathies had been pitted against a more profound, constitutional code. He seemed a much older man on this side of the conversation.

Eugene wondered what Jacinto would do, in his position. Would he go home, back to New York? Of course not—Alsa's honor would be worth any effort, any adventure, and with that, Eugene ventured out of the bookstore alone, in search of Sonia's few friends in the city. He began at the meat market on Piazza Ponterosso, where Lang had said he could find her friend Kasia.

At this early hour the square was busy with handsome women in high starched collars and dark woolen jackets too hot for the weather. Many held wooden baskets piled up with raw meat and swarmed by insects. They wandered between carts painted the colors of their nation of origin, offering samples of sausage and cheese with cups of mustard for tasting. Walking among these carts was like taking an olfactory tour of Mitteleuropa, where smells of saure Blunzen, Quargel, and Verhackerts mingled with prosciutto, pancetta, and speck, all trafficked with hairsweat and the pigeon musk rising from the brackish Canal Grande. Around the perimeter of the market, a gang of stray cats circled with calculating eyes and scabbed flanks.

After much confused pointing and shrugging by a Hungarian butcher, Eugene spotted Kasia. Her resemblance to Sonia stunned him. Although she was dark-eyed and black-haired, she had the same lissome movements, the same dallying, sultry pose.

"*I have a freshly stuffed sheep's belly,*" she said.

Eugene rubbed his ear.

"*Also lean pork sausage from a farm in Colludruzza. What are you looking for?*"

"*I'm looking for a girl named Sonia. I think you know her.*"

Kasia laughed softly to herself, covering her mouth.

"*Ah, Sonja, you say? I recognize you from her description. You work for her father. Eugenio, the Italian Jew from New York.*"

Kasia hadn't heard anything about Sonia in a month, and was concerned when Eugene told her that Sonia was missing. But when he said that Sonia had run off with Eakins, Kasia removed her hand from her mouth and laughed loudly in his face.

"We always said that Signor Eakins was the ideal boyfriend," she said. "*He brought her to Italy on an expense-paid trip, encouraged her to explore the city and the countryside and consort with other boys. And she didn't have to sleep with him—or even see him for that mat-*

ter. You know," she said, cutting off her laughter and taking a serious, confiding tone, "*he's been dead for very many years. He was a great writer but not since before we were born.*"

"*He's not alive?*"

"*Are you a dreamer? Not even Sonja believed he was. Now I must get back to selling my meats. But maybe we could have some wine later?*" She sucked in her cheeks and winked at Eugene.

On a strip of butcher's paper she wrote out her number, as well as the address of a café in the old Jewish ghetto where Sonia's friend Poldi worked as a bartender.

"*She was always fond of older men,*" said Poldi, who looked about fifty himself. He wore a short white bib splattered with coffee and crystallized milk foam, under which was visible a white fleshy paunch that ribbed over the elastic of his underwear. He spoke with deep heaving motions, as if the burdens of advancing age had consolidated deep within him and ached to come out in a cascading display of sighs and mutters and other gestures of regret. The subject of Sonia's disappearance seemed to have put him over for good. As he spoke he yanked at his hair in such a violent manner that it seemed he might pull his whole clever face off with it.

"*It was not so long ago that I was with her in the hills above Tartini Square, picking pendolini. We were having so much fun. But I never heard from her again. I am sure she is with an older man now.*"

When Eugene told him that she had been abducted by Constance Eakins, Poldi scoffed, flapping his bib at him. It was lunch now, and university students had begun to enter the café in jittery, loquacious groups.

"*Constantino Eakins? The writer?*" asked Poldi. He turned

away from Eugene to line up espresso cups for the students. *"What are you talking about? He's been dead forever."*

Poldi wouldn't say anything else on the subject, but he did mention that Marco, another friend of Sonia's, would soon stop by. Several minutes later, the screeching uproar of a braking Vespa filled the café, followed by the sputter and cough of its tailpipe. Poldi was smiling at Eugene.

"The fanciulle *love this guy,"* he said, flapping a coffee-dampened towel over his shoulder. Marco appeared in the doorway, wearing a bomber jacket and platinum sunglasses, with a green scarf swung around his neck—a flamboyant Italian simulation of James Dean cool. The tables of female students flittered and flustered, while the adolescent boys shook their heads in what was evidently a daily expression of disgust and resignation.

"Ciao, Poldi! Avanti!" said the bedecked bomber pilot, swaying over to the counter. "Tre," he ordered, holding up three long splayed fingers.

Poldi grinningly placed three coffees on the mahogany bar. Marco swigged the first and then scanned the café with a lady-killing smirk. He found a suitable, blushing victim at a nearby table, and was about to make straight for her with the two remaining saucers when Eugene grabbed his wrist. Marco turned to him, his smirk fading into a perturbed grimace. He yelled a couple of syllables of indecipherable Triestino but calmed when Eugene spoke Sonia's name.

"Ah, Alicia," sighed Marco, and downed another coffee. The image of Sonia on the back of Marco's bike passed through Eugene's head and he wondered, again, what girl he was searching for.

"She ran off with an older man," offered Poldi from behind the bar.

Marco slumped over. *"I figured,"* he said. *"Sonababic."* Then, with sudden merriment, he looked up again at Poldi: *"But what ass! Can't blame the old pig."*

"It was some ass!" said Poldi, immoderately loud. Eugene suffered his horrors silently.

In a patient voice, Marco described to Eugene the last time he had seen her. He had been riding at night along the coast, past Miramare, to a nightclub with an American name—Enjoy—that played American hip-hop, Italian disco, and Slovenian pop, which sounded like polka with a drum machine. On his way out of the city he spotted Sonia, standing by herself in Piazza Scorcola at an out-of-service tram stop. She was slumped over her duffel bag and seemed dazed when he woke her up; she said she didn't want to go to the nightclub. When he told her that the tram would never come, she shrugged, and said she'd walk. But she refused to say where she was headed. He returned to the piazza several hours later, but she wasn't there. He had assumed she had gone off with another man.

"Another man?" asked Eugene, stunned. *"Maybe someone attacked her, left alone on the street at night like that. Or something worse!"*

"Pish-posh," said Marco. *"Our city is safe. Only thing our women need to fear are—"* and he said a number of vulgar words in Triestine dialect. Poldi snorted and made wild humping motions against the espresso machine. To make him stop Eugene overturned what was left of his coffee on the bar. Poldi rushed over with his towel.

"This kind of thing happens every day," said Marco. *"Find your-*

self another girl. There are plenty here, for example," he said, making a sweeping gesture over the room. The girls in the café looked up, following the path of his hand as if it was holding the Rod of Aaron. *"Did you say Eakins?"* Marco asked, turning back to Eugene. *"I love Eakins. Have you read* Songs for Agata? *Fantastic poems. But you must be confused. He's long dead. We Triestini have known it for years. He often came to the city—we'd see him in Piazza Unità by the boardwalk, staring at the sea. When he died, we all knew it. Even if no one else in the world believed it until now. It was like the weather had suddenly changed and his influence on our city would be no more."*

And with that, Marco downed his third coffee.

Eugene didn't have any ideas but to walk to Piazza Scorcola. The piazza was like a bicycle wheel crushed by a car, with street spokes flying off in several directions. The tram line curved through the center of it, before turning up toward the mountains north of the city.

Eugene wasn't sure what he expected to find there. A group of commuters yawned and harrumphed at the slow trams: a circle of Italian bankers in three-pieces and black polished spats holding quartered copies of Trieste's daily newspaper, *Il Poliglotto*; secretaries in checkered rayon blouses speaking rapidly in their after-work slang; a bonbon of a woman halfheartedly trying to prevent her two tussling grandchildren from spilling over into the road; and a teenage couple engaged in an argument with angry, declamatory hand gestures, exaggerated pouts, and bulging eyes. Eugene looked at the bankers, and realized that he had been trying to find one who resembled his father. A black sadness tumbled through his body, and he vowed to write his father a letter as soon as he returned to Lang's. He would talk about the glories of Floridian life, he supposed, and would promise to visit soon. But he knew that was a lie. It would only hurt his father worse when he found out.

A young man, roughly Eugene's age, stood apart from the crowd. He wore a black double-breasted blazer over a wrinkled, untucked shirt, and slumped around like someone who had recently suffered a great loss. Despite his mild-mannered appearance—tidy brown schoolboy's hair and a stringy build—he had an odd intensity of gesture that made him seemed capable of wildness or, perhaps, violence. He rubbed his face with gnarled hands and walked in a circle, skidding the soles of his feet against the ground. He had been crying. No one in the commuting crowd besides Eugene seemed to notice him.

The teenagers' bickering turned into a screaming match and the boyfriend threw up his hands and walked away. The girlfriend took a step toward him, faltered, and then stood still, her anger crumpling in on itself. Immediately the weeping man in the double-breasted blazer sped over to her. His arms were thrown apart wide in an awkward gesture of consolation, but more than anything he resembled an eagle swooping in on his prey with outstretched wings. He started to holler at the stunned girl through his sobs:

"I know! It's so sad! It's so sad to lose the one you love. Let's mourn together. Life is the saddest. We are kindred souls," and more to that effect, in a screaming mania of empathy. Although Eugene believed the young man was acting with sincerity, the girl, upon seeing the rapidly advancing stranger, did not. She cursed at him

and ran off, causing the man to recoil in a whole new series of injured sobs.

The two tussling grandchildren grew alarmed, abruptly stopped fighting, and in chorus began to bawl. When the man saw them, a faint shadow of hope glided across his face. Swooping, hunched, he ran over.

"Children! My poor children, you sad, innocent, lonely creatures!" And then he burst into a high yelp, since the children's nanny had begun to clock him with her handbag. He crumpled to the ground holding his neck, crawled a few feet, and then curled into a fetal position. Eugene couldn't watch anymore. He approached the man cautiously and stood him up by his shoulders, leading him out of the piazza to the closest side street.

"What's wrong with you, man?" said Eugene. *"Get yourself together."*

The man rubbed his face with his wrists, and his convulsions slowed. Eugene got his first good look at him. His eyes were rimmed with tears and his thin nose was muddied, but he had a romantic, swaggering mouth and a concentration to his glare that unsettled Eugene. He was tall, thin, and nimble; his suit, despite being creased and speckled with street dirt and other bits of scum, fit tight and flattering. Eugene was jolted by a feeling that he recognized him from some earlier period of his life.

"Have you seen . . . a girl . . . around here?" Eugene was stunned—the man spoke perfect English.

"Who?" asked Eugene. A new exasperation started to build up in him. "Are you looking for Sonia?"

"Well, I don't know her name, but I love her I'm sure."

Eugene patiently described Sonia in the most straightforward terms he could muster: longish brown-red hair, crescent-shaped scar beneath one eye, wide mouth, lucent pale skin, excitable and headstrong, yea high.

"No, I don't think that's her," said the man, stifling a whimper. He called himself Enzo and explained that although he was not English, he was "naturally adept at foreign languages." He was from a city in northern Italy and couldn't remember how he had gotten to Trieste. The only thing he was certain of was that he had last seen his girlfriend at a bus stop. Ever since then he had wandered around the city, visiting every bus and tram stop, searching for her.

"I don't know what else to do," he said, and again gave in to his mounting despair. Eugene sympathized. Like Enzo, Eugene was looking all over Trieste for a girl who had fled for reasons unknown. But at least he knew Sonia's name. And then a sick, green panic roiled his belly and slunk up his spine. It told him that Enzo was holding out on him—maybe he was after Sonia too.

As Enzo bent over on the curb, hacking through sobs, Eugene silently backed away and peeled around the corner. Enzo didn't bother to give chase. Soon Eugene was back in Piazza Unità, among the sunglassed tourists heading out to the Molo Audace for the sunset, the briskly walking bankers, and the North African peddlers, who blocked his way with arms full of slippers and women's purses. He pushed through their outstretched arms and walked along the water, looking for a familiar face. He sat by the staircase that led into the sea, exactly where Sonia had been sitting when she claimed to have met Eakins. In the afternoon light, the Adriatic was blue-black and lazy, washing against the seawalls with such indifference that it seemed as if the tide were as exhausted by the summer sun as Eugene was. He removed his sneakers and sweaty socks and dipped his ankles in the cool water. He needed to think, and rest. Maybe, if he was quiet enough, Sonia would be able to reach him somehow.

A taunting voice whispered loudly in his ear.

"Xe el cinciut!"

He turned, and saw the two little girls he had met his first morning in the city. They had brought their friends.

Eugene jumped onto the pavement, his feet dripping seawater. *"I am not the fucking cinciut. I'm just a tourist."*

The children—there were at least a dozen of them—stood impassive and silent, staring blankly at his forehead like it was a television set. The leader couldn't have been older than twelve, but his eyes were sunken and his yellow teeth were jagged in his dark mouth. He held a dead sparrow against his jacket.

"You look like you might be a cinciut," said the boy, solicitous and hoarse.

"Well, I'm not. I'm from New York." This aroused a groundswell of murmured interest among the children. They conferred secretly among one another with cupped hands and wide-eyed stares.

"Listen," said Eugene. *"There was a girl here once, a friend of mine, sitting right here, whom you harassed. Do you remember her? She had reddish hair, pale skin, gray eyes . . ."*

"With a little scar under the eye?"

"Yes! That's her."

"Ah, the cinciut. We sent her away. Don't worry about her."

"Where?"

"Up in the Carso, where the cinciuts live. There's a small wicked town there. It's our job to protect the city from their kind. Otherwise they'd come down and choke us in our sleep."

One of the children, a skinny little runt who resembled one of Trieste's stray cats, his movements quick with some disease, blew a snot rocket onto the pavement.

"What about the man that was with her?" said Eugene. *"Elderly, strong, low voice, very tall—"*

"What do you want with her anyway?" said the leader. *"If you are really a tourist you should go visit Miramare or the Rivoltella or throw breadcrumbs in the Canal. Buy a whore at La Chiave d'Oro. But leave our demons alone."*

"Do you know where I can find the man that was with her?"

"There was no man. Just the girl."

"I heard that a man scared you away."

The children took a step toward him. Eugene took one back toward the seawall, so that his heel was just inches from the water.

"We don't back down from anyone," said the leader, chewing the inside of his cheek. *"Especially not touristics."*

Eugene decided, after briefly weighing his options, not to fight the ragtag group of gangly, muddied children. Children at that age don't fear getting banged up, so they can be dangerous and unpredictable in a skirmish. They have nothing to lose. That's what Eugene told himself anyway. But just then a high, reedy voice rang out from behind the urchin gang. At first, Eugene couldn't see who it was, since the owner of the voice was shorter than the children.

Frank Lang pushed through the children's ranks, waving his cane like a hatchet, and turned to face them in a trembling rage. The kids spat at Eugene and then, unhurriedly, began to retreat, laughing at the odd little man, sticking out their tongues and lifting up their unscrubbed chins in the Italian gesture of mockery. Just before the children left the piazza, their hoarse-voiced leader spoke one last time to Eugene:

"*Be careful, touristic,*" he said. "*I hope you realize: your little friend here might be one of them too.*"

7

Mr. Schmitz finds Rutherford's second letter as soon as he gets home from his monthly meeting of the Committee of Retired Insurance Workers. He immediately sticks it in his pocket to hide it from his wife, even though she undoubtedly must have noticed it when she brought in the mail: it was lying flat on top of the bills, AARP pamphlets, and coupons. Mr. Schmitz walks through the living room and finds Agnes in the bathroom, on her knees beside a bucket of bleach water, the bath faucet running.

But he needs to read the letter in isolation: he can't have Agnes craning over his shoulder to see what Rutherford has written. And he doesn't want her to find out what he has written to Rutherford either. Without saying a word, he takes the bedroom hamper and walks right back out of the apartment. Agnes doesn't even look up.

He takes the elevator to the apartment building's laundry room, where he stuffs the soiled bedsheets into a washing machine. Then he leans over the folding table and opens Rutherford's letter. He removes several pages of yellow handmade paper and, before reading them, holds the parcel up to his nostrils. Closing his eyes, he smells a sleepy aroma of Mediterranean sunshine, crushed garlic, and perhaps, very faintly, the bergamot tang of Rutherford's acqua di colonia.

"My friend," Mr. Schmitz says. He smiles. And then he opens his eyes.

After Rutherford's normal salutation, "Caro Sig. Schmitz," he has written:

"Thanks be to God! What beautiful day."

Mr. Schmitz crinkles his nose at this opening line. The letter proceeds rationally from there, so he attributes Rutherford's holy exuberance and his uncharacteristic ellipsis to the fuzzying effects of the Italian air. But there are other infelicitous phrasings. Rutherford writes from a piazza in the "city center." He sits by a fountain that he describes as "a pyramid topped by a red and brown ball." He goes on:

A thin sheet of water falls down the pyramid's four sides, at which point the stream is conducted through a narrow channel under a grate on the ground, where it then flows into a diamond-shaped reflecting pool. Couples sit around this pool on their lunch hour, nuzzling and tossing coins. Although Babila, a fourth-century saint of little distinction, has nothing to do with the tower of Babel, the Milanese refer to this statue—a popular meeting point due to its central location and proximity to a Metro stop—as "La Torre di Babele." An innocent but fitting solecism.

Except for the ancient Basilica di San Babila, the piazza

is surrounded by expensive department stores and an enormous British record emporium, whose jumbo television
screens flash American music videos. It was here, staring up
at one of those screens, that I first saw him.

At this development, Mr. Schmitz begins to pet his chin.

Rutherford explains that "him" was a skinny oily-faced boy of
about fourteen, with long brown hair, a hoop earring in one ear,
and ankles no thicker than a three-iron. The boy paraded about
without a shirt, his sun-yellowed chest bare and hairless. Granted,
writes Rutherford, the Milanese summer is equatorial and filthy,
but the shirtless boy made a peculiar sight amid all the suited
"men of affairs," window-shopping tourists, and models clinging
to their portfolios.

The absentminded boy ambled around the piazza, backing
into racing pedestrians without seeming to notice. He leaned
over the diamond-shaped pool and stared at his own reflection.
Then he dipped his hands in the pool and splashed himself
with the water. "What my countrymen call 'la benedizione
dell'Acqua Santa,'" writes Rutherford. Afterward, the boy
peered slowly around the piazza until his gaze fell on Rutherford, who was staring back at him, a single stationary figure in
the febrile crowd.

Mr. Schmitz looks up from the letter, disturbed for a second
time. Behind the glass portal of the washing machine the bedsheets churn in a bath of strawberry-colored bubbles.

Since then I've been feeling a strange sensation in the left
side of my head. It's nothing painful, mind you—just the
feeling that something is *off*. A floating. Like nausea of the

brain. I don't know how else to describe it. I doubt it's connected to the appearance of the strange boy, though I have no other explanation.

I'm sure it will pass, but it has been two days now and I'm considering seeing a doctor. Yet I'm afraid my command of the language isn't up to the task. What do I complain of, "una nausea del cervello"? He'll laugh me out of the hospital. A stupid American who can't tell his head from his stomach.

Rutherford goes on to explain that he has settled in a clean furnished apartment near the Porta Romana, which he calls a "beautiful quarter." The apartment is simple: a dining room, a study, and a bedroom, all of which "communicate." Rutherford was shocked to see the same shirtless boy one day later, this time in his own neighborhood. The kid was wearing exactly the same outfit—no shirt, black jeans, dirty red sneakers—and walked by the café where Rutherford took his morning coffee. As at San Babila, the urchin seemed ignorant of his surroundings, stalking behind a pair of fannypacked British women who were too absorbed in their guidebooks to notice him. If Rutherford could detect any single difference in the boy since the first sighting, it was that he was dirtier. His chest was smeared with a flaky rustlike substance, and his hair had wilted into a damp mop that hung down over his brow. Every so often he broke his languorous skulk for a beat and started skipping; after one such skip he disappeared behind the great Roman column. He never reappeared.

"I would have followed him, out of curiosity," writes Rutherford. "Only I was feeling quite fatigued on account of my head just then and had to retire to my bed." Here Rutherford ends his letter. As an afterthought, he adds a postscript saying that he is sorry to hear about Mrs. Schmitz's recent health problems. He hopes she is feeling better by the time Mr. Schmitz reads this.

After reading the letter through again, Mr. Schmitz carefully stuffs it back into the envelope. He takes the elevator upstairs, leaving the laundry to spin. When he enters the apartment, he sees that a plate of meatloaf and mashed potatoes has been left cooling for him at the kitchen table. He calls for his wife, but she has already gone to bed.

8

Eugene watched from the passenger seat, his fist white from squeezing the window handle, as Lang fidgeted with the clutch and kept peeking over the wheel so that he could see the road ahead. Lang was navigating his Cinquecento up a hill so steep that it seemed the car would peel back from the asphalt and backflip down the Carso. He explained in his loud, animated falsetto how guilty he felt for not agreeing sooner to help find poor Sonia, but Eugene wasn't mollified—he was worried they might be too late. Every time Lang fixed his beady gnat eyes on Eugene, Eugene would manically gesture ahead, causing Lang to snort and roll his eyes up into his head so that he couldn't see either passenger or road. He wore a teeny green plaid beret that made him look like a wood sprite.

It was at this juncture that Eugene noticed himself forming a new habit, one that might have alarmed him in the past but which he now accepted as a natural corollary to the unusual circumstances in which he found himself. He began talking to himself. With Lang around, he had sense enough to avoid speaking out loud, but he could imagine that a time would come when this would no longer be the case. How, he wondered, had he ended up at the foot of the Julian Alps, in a small city that had been forgotten not only by the world but also by its own country? He had read in a guidebook that most Italians didn't even realize Trieste was a part of Italy.

"*Easily answered,*" said a meek voice just inside his left ear. "*Duty. You were hired for this job. You have a duty to Abe, as well as to his daughter. Besides, it's better than picking up boxes, walking with them, and setting them down again.*"

"*Easily answered,*" said a second voice, which seemed to be sitting in the base of his neck and spoke with some kind of ethnic accent—Yiddish perhaps. "*You go along with whatever inane pursuits come your way, in the name of 'adventure'; you don't care about the girl—you barely know her—nor Abe, nor do you care if Eakins exists or doesn't. You're excited by peril, exploit, risk, rescue. For what cause, you don't care. This is your weakness. Basically, you got bored sitting at home with your babbo.*"

"*Easily answered,*" said a third voice, perched behind his temple and speaking in an immediate, righteous tone. "*Love brought you here. You fell in love with Sonia, and now she's been kidnapped. She is beautiful and brilliant, and you two have an animal attraction to each other—remember the mud bath? Plus, she is a redhead. This is your great strength: you will travel the lengths of the world for the love of a woman.*"

"*But which woman is she?*" added the first voice, in a soft, daring trill.

"*My God,*" interrupted the second voice. "*Can you imagine what liberties Eakins might take with that poor, helpless girl? If we're*" *to trust his own memoirs, he's one violent animal. He's also needy, treacherous, and all-wise."*

"Did you read about his conquest of the goatherd's daughter in Mallorca, when he was just out of the army? She was barely twelve and he told her how to do it all right."

"I wouldn't let my daughter so much as read a sentence out of one of the ugly bastard's books lest she get the right idea."

"In matters of romance he is a sexual cannibal."

"He is a well-oiled bilker of women even if he is about a century old—talk about one hundred years of Sodom, yessir. And nary a complaint on the part of his mistresses, even the goatherd's daughter, bless her overtaxed heart."

"Is there something wrong with your mouth? It is twitching mightily," said Lang.

"The road!" shouted Eugene.

A white boulder stood several feet ahead of them, nearly as wide as the car. Lang braked and swerved in the direction of the sea. The Cinquecento's front bumper nudged several pebbles over the cliff, into the silent abyss below. Eugene and Lang jumped out and backed against the stony cliffside, as far away from the edge as possible. Beyond the boulder was another one just as big, and another, and then the road ahead disappeared under thousands of white rocks.

"Landslide," said Lang, chuckling nervously and pulling down on his mustache. He sounded like a broken windup clock. "There's very little infrastructure money here. It takes a long time for them to clean these things up. Especially in August."

Eugene tiptoed back to the car and after grabbing the book bag containing Alvaro's manuscript and his translation from the backseat, he reached inside the driver's-side window, putting the gearshift into reverse. With a groan the car slid back, lengthwise across the road, until its bumper slid against the rock face with a quiet crumple. They knelt behind it and pushed, but it wouldn't budge. The chipped limestone rock wall scrabbled against their backs.

"I'm a weak man," said Lang, sweat leaking from his forehead into his eyes. Eugene noticed Lang's arms for the first time: they were stringy and blanched, and now scratched from the limestone.

"I'm a weak man."

"We can do it," said Eugene. "Once we budge it, it'll start to roll, and we can get back in."

He stared at Lang, and his stomach fell. The man was on the verge of tears. A gust licked off the cliffside and smacked him in the face.

"I can't!" said Lang, in a loud falsetto.

Since they hadn't passed a house, or a car, for over an hour, they decided to walk farther up the hill in search of help. In the ravine below, yellow moss-covered rocks peeped out from clearings among the juniper shrubs, and near the bottom of his view a thin brook squiggled between plane trees like an artist's signature. And farther off, the calm olivaceous water of the sea and the city's needle spires and terra-cotta roofs.

Eugene paused every few minutes so that the short-legged Lang could keep up—it took two of Lang's paces to equal every one of Eugene's. Eugene could tell that Lang was growing increasingly anxious, and not just because of the abandoned car. The higher up into the alpine air they walked, the more rambling his speech became. He engrossed himself for many minutes with an excited monologue on the history of the Esperanto language; did Eugene know that there were regions in inner China where people spoke a dialect of the language so evolved that it was incomprehensible to other Esperanto speakers? Halfway into his monologue, Lang shifted from English to Esperanto without seeming to notice. Lang took Eugene's bewildered expression as encouragement and patiently attempted to clarify his points in greater detail. Eugene did not bother to disrupt this chatter, but wondered how far they would have to walk before they saw another person.

The road turned into the cliffs, and entered a thick forest. On one side a narrow dirt path led down in the direction of the ravine.

"Could this be a path to someone's house?" asked Eugene. Lang looked up, surprised, and stopped talking, even though his jaw kept ticking for several seconds longer.

"You know what this is?" said Lang, speaking in English again. He didn't wait for a response, but headed down the path straight into the brush. Eugene followed along, ducking and dodging, happy at the thought that a friend of Lang's might be living at the end of the trail. Soon they saw a large white rock formation running parallel with the trail. As they reached the bottom of the path, Eugene saw that the formation was the mouth of a natural tunnel. A river burst from the tunnel into a large pool, making a churning noise like a washing machine. The water gleamed an enchanted blue-green, and was surrounded by a sparkling ring of travertine.

"Isn't this a beautiful spot?" said Lang. He removed his boots and socks and dipped his feet at the edge of the waterfall. Looking up, Eugene saw that the cavernous rock tunnel ran up the hill in the direction of the road, like a fallen column. There was no house—or other person—to be seen.

"The Timavo," said Lang. He cocked his beret and peered off into the distance. "The hidden river. It begins on Mount Nevoso, the Slovenian Carso's highest peak, where seven streams merge into one. It disappears into the grottoes of San Canziano, flowing down the Italian Carso in hidden caves as many as three hundred meters underground. It doesn't reemerge until it reaches the city gates of Tuba, where it springs up near the apse of the Chiesa di San Giovanni. Simply put, it's marvelous. A real marvelous adventure!"

"Good. So we're near the town of Tuba."

"No, no, that's miles up. This surfacing of the Timavo is not on any maps. But trust me, the river is navigable from here. It's the fastest way up the mountain. Faster than any road or path."

Eugene peered into the mouth of the tunnel. It looked like a gigantic sewer pipe, roughly ten feet tall, with stalactites hanging from the rock ceiling. The river itself seemed, at this point at least, only three feet deep, but it was nearly ten times as wide; it galloped over the rocks, spurting foam. It was difficult to make out much else, because the tunnel admitted no sunlight. The turbulent water made a ferocious, gnashing roar. The way did not, to Eugene, seem passable.

Lang whistled jubilantly to himself, a high-pitched sound like a popped bicycle tire. He shouted into the tunnel, cupping his hand to his mouth in a theatrical gesture.

"We're coming, Alice!"

He bounded, childlike into the cave.

"Francesco," called Eugene, reaching out to the tiny man. "What about the car?"

"Oh leeeeeave it," shouted Lang over his shoulder. His voice was barely audible under the sound of the river. "Don't worry— no one lives anywhere near here! Hey, look at this—it's just the *strangest* thing . . ."

And Lang's voice, together with his body, vanished into the obscurity of the cave. Eugene looked back at the pool, gave a final sorry glance up to the heavens, and stepped onto a rock at the foot of the tunnel. He stepped to another rock, and then another, and then it was very loud and very dark.

9

Mr. Schmitz spots the next envelope from Rutherford during a brief turn at home from the hospital. He has come to shower, change his clothes, and collect new reading material. Glancing through the heap of mail sitting on his doormat, he sees a thick manila envelope bearing the Poste Italiane sticker. When he picks it up, a heavy scent of bergamot plumes into the air.

Mr. Schmitz scans the letter and finds it difficult to understand. Rutherford's command of language appears to have deteriorated. At times he seems to be writing in koans, elsewhere in code. Mr. Schmitz wonders what he could possibly be trying to say.

In the letter, Rutherford explains—as far as Mr. Schmitz can tell—that his head malady has indeed healed. The doctor understood Rutherford's ailments and recommended an MRI. But it no longer mattered. For as soon as Rutherford entered the doctor's office and began speaking to the receptionist, his head cleared. What's more, Rutherford had surprised himself by speaking perfect Italian. The pain never returned. He prays that Mrs. Schmitz will experience the same kind of rapid recovery.

Despite Rutherford's strange diction, Mr. Schmitz is relieved to receive Rutherford's sympathy. He has not been able to discuss his wife's condition with anyone besides her doctors.

Rutherford does not mention the shirtless street urchin again. Mr. Schmitz assumes the boy has vanished. When he finishes reading the letter, he grabs a couple of novels and magazines, a pillow, a blanket, a thermos, and a plastic bag containing the contents of the top shelf of the medicine cabinet, and leaves again for the hospital.

In the following weeks, Rutherford does not send any more letters, but instead a train of postcards, bearing views of Lake Como, Milan's Duomo, and a piazza in Monza. Rutherford does not respond to the questions posed by Mr. Schmitz in his increasingly frequent, and increasingly anxious, letters. Most upsetting, Rutherford ceases to acknowledge Mr. Schmitz's forlorn reports from the hospital, where Agnes lies in mute agony. Rutherford's notes are instead filled with obscure doodles, jokes that rely on Italian puns that make no sense to Mr. Schmitz, and short passages—descriptions of place and cryptic snippets of dialogue—that seem, in their formalized style, to be quotations from English novels and history books. On the back of one postcard, Rutherford has written simply:

Schmitz!
I cannot liberate my malady of the head. And that, I say, is the humor of it.

The next postcard reads:

Schmitz!

In sum I feel that this opaque seaport of my vision, so full of sweet melancholy, illustrates not just my adolescent emotions of the past, but my lifelong preoccupations too. The Trieste effect, I call it. It is as though I have been taken, for a brief sententious glimpse, out of time to nowhere.

Beneath Mr. Schmitz's address is a hastily sketched doodle of a little boy waving.

A month later another note arrives:

Schmitz!

Hello da Monza. Ho visto oggi la mia fidanzata. Si, la mia fidanzata. Non lo dico per scherzo. Quando l'ho vista, sono svenuto. Ma anche lei è svenuta. Tutti e due di noi stavamo sdraiati per terra. Molto di più da dirti nella mia prossima lettera.

Mr. Schmitz puzzles over this letter for several minutes. Finally, with the aid of his worn Italian dictionary, he tries to decipher it. In his translation, it reads:

Hello from Monza. I saw today my girl. Yes, my girl. I'm not joking. When I saw her, I fainted. But she fainted too. Both of us were lying on the ground. Much more to tell in my next letter.

Mr. Schmitz has no idea who the girl is, and can only marvel that Rutherford has not bothered to mention Agnes. Despite the fact that, in his last letter, Mr. Schmitz explained that her ovaries had been removed. She hasn't opened her eyes for three weeks, except for when the nurse stretched the lids back to administer saline drops. In response, from his closest friend in the world, he receives only nonsense and obscurity. After that, there are no more letters, and only one more postcard. "Schmitz!" it says.

And that is all.

1o

"Oooooh," said Lang, giggling to himself. "My feet are wet. They tickle."

In the dark tunnel, the river had calmed. Eugene and Lang were walking on the rockbed along the side, where the footing was more stable.

"Do you think we're near?" asked Eugene. He was breathing heavily now and, not for the first time, genuinely concerned for his physical safety. "Don't tell me if we're not."

There was no response, only the steady rush of water. The air felt close and thick and smelled like iron. Far behind him, at the opening of the tunnel, the oval of light grew dim, until it finally disappeared. Once in a while one of them would slip on a slick stone or get smacked in the forehead by a protuberant rock shelf. When this happened to Lang, he would snort and exclaim, "What fun!" Eugene would gasp and curse himself.

A region of light began to appear ahead of them. In it they could see the river tumbling over the submerged boulders, spotted with slimy growths; the jagged stalactites that hung like frozen rain; and the cavern walls, densely beaded with condensation. A light mist coiled lazily over the river.

"Here the rock gets extremely thin; it's almost like paper," said Lang, pointing to the tunnel's ceiling. And Eugene could see it for himself—the calcite overhead was translucent, so that the sunlight filtered through, between fissures snaked like green veins. So while it was still dark, the underground river was now lit by a spectral glow, the outside world seeping in from above. Eugene pressed his book bag close to his chest, and his thoughts turned to Sonia. He somehow expected to see her around each bend, reclining on a boulder, perhaps, or washing her hair in the river, sirenlike.

After they had walked for more than an hour, the tunnel opened into a clearing surrounded by dense juniper. Above the clearing there rose a vineyard terraced on a hill, and beyond that, the limestone mountains. The woods rattled with unseen life. Eugene had never been anywhere like it. He sensed that he was close to something—to Sonia, perhaps, but maybe something even bigger.

There was a man on the hill above the clearing. He chopped vigorously at a stump of wood with an enormous blunt ax. He couldn't have been more than forty years old, though his round features were disguised by a bushy mustache and triangular goatee, and the Carso climate had given his skin a leathery, forlorn quality.

Lang clapped his hands with pleasure.

"GorAN!" shouted Lang. His voice scared a flock of sparrows into flight. The mountain man looked up from his ax to see the two dirt-caked men—one tall and young, the other tiny and shriveled—standing at the bottom of his property.

"Do you know him?" whispered Eugene. Lang did not reply but waved his arms excitedly.

The man approached, ax in hand. A horrified look of recognition slowly spread across his face. He hollered a greeting in a Slavic tongue, to which Lang responded, in his perfect Italian,

"Speak in Italian for the boy. His name is Eugenio."

"Eugenio," said Goran, becoming animated. *"You look like a goat shit!"*

"He's a funny man," whispered Lang to Eugene. "You'll never guess what he will think of next."

Eugene followed Lang up a stone path, through several plateaus where tangled vines and clusters of full black grapes hung from white trellises.

"What are you chopping?" asked Lang when they had reached the top of the hill.

"Tree stump," replied Goran. *"It's good exercise and also beneficial for relaxation of the nerves. I need to be in top condition for the harvest next month."*

Goran led the men to his house, a hulking A-frame built of dark pine. There was an outdoor shower stall in the back. Goran told them to remove their dirty clothes. Eugene thought he might have misheard him, but Lang began stripping to his underwear, so he went along with it. Goran threw the clothes into a wine cask. With a garden hose, he filled the barrel most of the way with water, and then squeezed in half a bottle of clothing detergent. Using a vine cutter, he plunged the clothes in and out of the barrel, till the water turned muddy. Then he tipped the barrel so that the dirty water ran off into the vineyard and seeped into the red soil.

"Good for fertilization," said Goran, smoothing down the hair over his forehead. He resembled a religious figure—a holy fool, Eugene decided—with his girlish bangs, ponderous earlobes,

gaunt cheeks, and long hanging arms. His speech was garbled, as though he were chewing something, but there was nothing in his mouth except for an excess of saliva and a long crimson tongue.

Lang stripped off his underwear and danced into the shower stall, his nude body hairless and petite as a child's. This left Eugene standing on the grass with Goran, his chest and legs banded with hardened striae of dirt. The vintner filled the barrel again and plunged the clothing with all his might.

"Don't you want clean underwear too?" asked Goran. He seemed offended.

Eugene grimaced, looked around, and then stripped naked. Once Goran had taken his underwear, Eugene realized he still had to wait for Lang to come out of the shower; he covered himself with his hands out of modesty.

To make conversation he explained to Goran the reason for their expedition. Goran mumbled in response every few minutes, seeming to pay more attention to the washing barrel, but when Eugene started to describe Sonia, Goran stopped mid-plunge. His flat brown eyebrows raised up so high that they touched his bangs.

"I was woken by a girl's laughter one night when I was lying asleep in my house. It was coming from the vineyard," said Goran. *"When I walked outside I saw, hiding between the trellises, a pale-faced girl with reddish-brown hair."*

"That's her!"

"She was not alone. There was another girl there too, silent but not sleeping. I recognized this other girl at once. She often comes to my vineyard at night, and eats my grapes. She eats more of my grapes than even the deer."

"Who is that girl? Where does she live?"

"She is a spirit of the mountain. I don't know why she bothers me, when there are so many other vineyards around here."

Goran smiled at him for a long time, until Eugene surmised that the mountain man had been joking. Eugene returned a frozen grin. Goran plunged the clothes into the barrel again.

"I've heard her called Staja," said Goran. *"She haunts these hills. I think she's been wandering lost for some time. I had said to myself that if I see her again lying in my clover, she's going to catch it. And she did."*

"I don't understand." That is, he desperately hoped he understood wrong.

"I waited for a long time until they were quiet and the human girl—"

"Sonia," said Eugene. *"Sonia is her name."*

"Sonia was asleep. When I walked up to them in the vineyard I made sure to be quiet, since Staja never sleeps and also knows a strange running style that makes her very fast. I didn't know then that your friend—Sonia—was not a fellow spirit. How could I have known?"

Eugene felt something slippery move in his gut.

"I took with me the ax," said Goran, pointing to it where it was stuck in the battered stump.

"Dear God."

"Sonia was sleeping. She was beautiful, peaceful, and curled up like a child. I could tell that she was dreaming of love. I hope for your sake that she was dreaming of you. Right away I realized that she was human. Staja did not see me. She was staring at the sleeping human girl."

There passed several silent moments as Goran resumed his study of the wine barrel, which dripped gray suds and gave off a smell not dissimilar to chestnuts. Goran bowed his head and Eugene saw for the first time his bald spot, pale and puckered, like a monk's tonsure. When Goran spoke, his voice was hurried and he didn't make eye contact with Eugene.

"If your love is halfhearted, you might turn back now."

"Who said I was in love—"

"Otherwise it's not worth it."

Eugene felt a weight plunge through him, like he was in an elevator that had come to an abrupt stop.

"Did you say something about LOVE?" Lang had come out of the shower and was dripping and prancing across the soil without a towel, pale-skinned as a newborn and just as pink. "Get in, Eugenio, the water's warm."

Eugene felt uneasy about continuing his conversation with Goran in front of Lang, so he hurried through his shower. When he came out, he found Goran and Lang exactly where he had left them. Goran was staring down at the damp soil beneath his feet, the garden hose dangling from his hand over the clothing barrel. Lang was still naked and damp, though he had put on his green beret. He cocked his head at Eugene and grinned, as if he were struggling not to disclose some deeply comical news.

"Would you like a towel, Francesco?" asked Eugene. "There's an extra one in the stall."

Lang waved him off. "I believe that Goran has something to say to you," he said.

Goran cleared his throat.

"I think I must have been confused about what I said to you earlier, Eugenio. You see, the mountain air plays foolish games on my mind sometimes." Goran looked at Lang, who ignored him. Lang was giving Eugene his jackal smile.

"I think it was a pair of deer that I saw in my vineyard that night I was telling you about. These woods are not haunted by anything except the forms taken by my imagination. I scared the animals off by waving my ax, and they haven't come back ever since." He stared at Eugene from under his bangs. *"I'm sure they have found a more friendly home elsewhere on the Karst."*

"In any case," said Lang, *"I know where Alice is. You need only to follow me. She went to the town where I was born. Even if she met someone along the way, she would only have needed to ask for Eakins on this slope and she would have been told where to go. We don't need changelings or mountain sylphs or any other made-up creatures to show us the way."*

Goran laughed uneasily and, after glancing again at Lang, invited his guests to stay the night.

The house was just a single open room with blond wood-paneled walls and several pieces of haphazardly arranged furniture, but it felt genial and calm. Two rocking chairs sat opposite a fireplace and, in a nook next to the kitchen, a thin mattress lay crooked on top of a box spring. The floor was covered by a patchwork of dusty, irregularly shaped rugs and several tall wine racks, which tilted like towers and cast monolithic shadows in the firelight. The kitchen area was empty except for a mini-fridge and a two-burner hotplate.

Eugene sat in a rocking chair by the fire while Lang, having refused the other chair, squatted on his haunches like a chimpanzee. As night fell, they wrapped themselves up in wool blankets that smelled faintly of sweat. Goran stood by the hotplate, preparing a pot of meat broth. He did not speak except to mutter to himself in some Slovenian dialect. He ladled the broth into large earthenware bowls and brought the bubbling liquid to his guests. Goran had the pitiful look of a foreigner in his own home.

"How did you meet Francesco, Goran?"

"Well, it's a funny story. . . ." He saw Lang and his voice trailed off.

"Yes, go on, tell it, Goran. Eugenio is my good friend now." Lang grinned broadly.

"Well, it started when . . . I'll just say it started when I was sitting right here, in that rocking chair."

"Just like us now!" shouted Lang.

"Yes, just like us now," said Goran. He stared into the blushing coals, petting his bangs.

"Is that it?" asked Eugene.

"Oh," said Goran, coming to. *"Not at all. I was looking out at my vineyard, as I have a habit of doing at night. You see, there are deer and other, ah, animals that come at night to eat my grapes. And sure enough I hear a rustling in the trellis, that trellis right over there."*

Eugene followed Goran's pointed finger out of the giant triangular window. Through a gap between two fig trees at the foot of the hill, he could spot a patch of violet sea.

"As I always do, I took out my ax and rushed outside. But there, squatting in the clover between the two vineyard rows, was not a deer or animal at all. Just a very, very small man."

"It was the silliest thing, you see, I was—"

Goran ignored him. The story seemed to have imbued the mountain man with newfound confidence.

"He was wearing a funny little costume. Tiny reading glasses that pinched his nose, plaid baggy pants, and a tweed professor's jacket. A

full, bushy head of brown hair, and cheeks that, even in the moonlight, shone as red as apples. He was shivering."

"Ha ha," said Lang. *"That was many years ago. Fashion was unsophisticated in those days."*

"I noticed that the man was not wearing hiking boots. His loafers had been ripped up by the rocks and his feet were bleeding. You see, he had been hiking down the Karst."

Goran pointed behind Eugene, toward the back wall of the kitchen, behind which loomed the mountains and the buzzing forest.

"My Italian was very poor then," said Goran. *"I had only moved from Sovjak, my village, a year earlier. I addressed him in the Istrian dialect first, not thinking, and then in my cleanest Slovene. He responded twice, speaking in both tongues. I was shocked."*

"Languages just come naturally to me," explained Lang.

"In Sovjak we speak a variation of the Istrian dialect that not even Slovenians living in the peninsula can understand. He spoke it fluently. I invited him to join me by the fire. He was brave but anxious. Nothing like this savvy man you see here today!"

"I'll never forget his kindness," said Lang, frowning solemnly. Goran patted him on his shoulder—a little too hard. Lang coughed several times, then continued, *"He was the first real person I met. After the village. He took me in when I was young and afraid and knew nothing about the world below."*

"I'll tell you what was funny. He wouldn't say anything about where he came from but he was desperate to hear about Trieste. He must have been exhausted from his trip, but he refused to go to sleep and would easily have stayed up all night listening to me talk about the city."

"*I was quite naïve then,*" said Lang. He giggled. "*Oh yes.*"

"*Finally I had to rest, since the sky was turning purple, so I made him a bed with these blankets by the fire. But he never even lay down.*

"*When I woke up the next morning, he was standing next to my bed, just staring at me. I was frightened and reached for my ax, which I keep under the mattress, but he looked so peaceful that I did not wallop him. I asked him what he was doing. I'll never forget what he said: 'I only wanted to watch you sleep.'*"

"*Sleep is a strange thing,*" said Lang, after spooning in the last of his meat broth. "*I try to do as little of it as possible. Though I admit that as the years pass I need more and more rest. In fact, perhaps we should all have a rest now. It's getting late.*"

"*But where were you coming from?*" asked Eugene. "*And why had you left?*"

"*I think we've had enough stories tonight,*" said Lang. "*Besides, we have a long hike ahead of us tomorrow.*" Lang rose abruptly out of his squat and made Eugene a bed with the blankets by the fire. Goran went to the kitchen to clean the bowls. When everything was put in order, Lang announced that he would take a brief night walk before he retired. On the way out, he turned off the lights. Eugene and Goran were left in darkness, lit only by the fading fire. Goran collapsed onto his mattress.

Lang's whistle could be heard from outside as he wandered through the lanes of the vineyard. After a few minutes his chirping tune grew distant, so that it seemed he had entered the woods. Eugene rose from his mass of blankets and felt his way through the room, careful not to overturn any of the wine racks, until he reached the bed.

"*Goran. Are you awake?*"

Outside the wind carried the echo of Lang's whistle against the trees, sweeping it under the door and through the house like a phantom.

"I'm awake, Eugenio."

"Tell me, Goran. What did Lang say to you earlier, when I was in the shower? You did see Sonia, didn't you?"

Goran exhaled uneasily. *"No,"* he said. *"I saw a pair of elk."*

"You said deer."

"This is what I said."

Eugene sat down at the foot of the bed. He tried not to let his frustration creep into his voice. *"Then I suppose you're not going to tell me the rest of your story about how you met Lang. Where was he coming from? What is it about his town? Why is it so secluded?"*

"I'd better leave that to Francesco. He's a good storyteller, don't you think?"

"Listen, Goran, I'm not going to repeat to him anything you tell me. Why has he aged so much since then?"

"Oh, I've aged too! Believe me. I'm even starting to gray. It was ten years ago, for godsakes. That's an eternity on this mountain. Well, I'm starting to feel my age now! Time for bed, eh?"

Eugene didn't move.

"OK, fine. I'll tell you a story, if that's what you want to hear."

"Tell one about the people who live in that town above. Where Eakins lives, and where Lang is from. Where Sonia is."

"You read Eakins?"

"Of course."

"Me too. See?" He gestured at a pile of books on the floor by his bed. Sure enough, in the flickering firelight, Eugene could make out Eakins's name repeated on the spine of each paperback. They appeared to be Slovenian translations.

"He is very popular in these parts," Goran said. "He is said to live in that town above."

"Have you seen him recently?"

"Eakins? Why, he's been dead for decades! No one's seen Italo Svevo either, for that matter, but people still love him too. Of course, no one claims that Svevo still summers in Opicina. But I'll tell you quickly, before our friend returns."

"You've never seen Eakins?"

"I hope not. For then I would have seen a ghost. And that would probably mean that I wasn't long for this world. But others say they've seen him. Not only our little Francesco."

The monkish man propped his pillows behind his tonsured head and sat up in bed. His eyes were closed, his face illegible.

"They see him in different forms. Snjezana, the wife of a vintner I know in Colludrozza, claimed to have seen him about ten years ago, shortly after her daughter's fourteenth birthday. The two women were barefoot in a wine barrel, stomping grapes. Their property was on the edge of a grotto, a large cave that shelters the underground river that flows down the Karst—"

"The Timavo."

"That's the one. When the daughter was born, they built a little protective fence along the chasm. So here they are, stomping on the grapes and exchanging gossip or womanly advice, and they see a hand gripping the fence. Then another hand. But these hands, they are not ordinary—they are thick with brown curls, and the palms are streaked with dried blood. They hoist up a man from over the edge of the chasm. Slowly he rises behind the security fence, tall, taller, tallest, and finally, giant."

"Yes, I've heard it said that he is quite tall, well over six feet."

"He was eight and a half feet. That's what Snjezana said."

"I see."

"He had climbed out of this deep pit, using no tools but the power of his muscles. After he pulled himself up, he stepped over the fence as if it were a twig lying in his path. That is, he did not seem to notice it AT ALL."

"So he was quite tall." Eugene was getting anxious for Goran to get to the point. He couldn't hear Lang's whistling anymore, but that didn't mean he wasn't close by.

"He was a sight to be seen all right. He wore a three-piece suit made of fine sheep's wool, and he had a yellow neckerchief tied around his neck in the dandy style once popular in Trieste. He wore a silk pocket square on which his initials were embroidered in gold thread. Snjezana thought they read C.E., but it's true that she is half-illiterate.

"At the sight of the giant, she wrapped her arms around her daughter. They crouched down in the barrel to hide from him, and they kissed the identical white gold crosses that hung around their necks. The sound of the man's footsteps on the pasture was a dark ominous noise like this: squelsh, squelsh, squelsh."

"That would be the sound of his boots pressing into the earth?"

"This is so. Soon the man reached the barrel, and looked down into it from a distant height above, casting the women in an unnatural darkness. His shadow was so total, and so black, that they shivered from the sudden cold. Here was a mighty man. What he did next you will not barely guess."

"Did he try to kill them?"

"He did not. He spoke to them—"

"A curse? A threat?"

"Neither. He recited a stave of poetry. And it was the most beautiful thing Snjezana had ever heard. She did not recall the exact words,

but I later found it in one of Eakins's early collections of poems, Songs for Agata. *The poem was called 'The Mender of Canoes.' Do you know it?"*

"I know his fiction and his essays much better than the poetry."

"Well, it contains a passage of such beauty that to describe it would beggar imagination and put a lie to the transparency of language."

"What does he say?"

"I haven't memorized it," said Goran, somewhat abashed. *"I'm afraid to. After all, when the giant recited it to Snjezana and her daughter, stomping the grapes in their vineyard, it charmed them."*

"Charmed?"

"Unable to move. The giant reached into the barrel and wrapped the daughter up in his arms. He carried her over the fence and disappeared into the chasm. The girl was never seen again. You can imagine Snjezana's shock when she came to, face down in the grape mash, and her daughter gone.

"There are other stories too. A blind Bulgarian pensioner from Plavia claimed that his wife was spirited away by a wild-haired satyr, with horns and a tail. The monster had leapt down from the mountaintop, the pensioner claimed. No one, of course, believed him. The woman's parents brought up the pensioner on murder charges, but since no body was ever found, he got off.

"A similar story was told by a young boy from San Dorligo della Valle. While he and his teenage sister were picnicking by the top of the waterfall after school, a demon appeared at the side of the river. The demon did not say a word, but the sister, mesmerized, followed him into the current. They sank into a swirling eddy and disappeared. By the time the boy wandered back into town, it was night. His arms were scratched from running through the woods. At first, he couldn't remember anything that happened. He walked to his sister's room, and

collapsed on her bed. He slept for two full days, while the villagers searched the woods for his sister. They found the tablecloth floating in the river—but no girl. On the third day, as the members of the search party began to despair, the sleeping boy began to turn and shudder in his sister's bed. He chanted the same word over and over again until his chants turned into a scream: Cinciut! Cinciut! Cinciut!"

Lang's whistle pierced the air outside the cabin.

"Get back into bed!" whispered Goran, and he fell to his mattress, pulling the blankets over his head. He began to fake a snore—a shuddering, mucoid noise that no sleeping person had ever made. Eugene scampered back into his blankets by the fire. But he felt silly for doing this when he saw Lang's tiny silhouette on the opened door, looking less like a man than a doll on a cupboard shelf. Much to Eugene's surprise, Lang did not seem to question Goran's suspicious manner of respiration. He squatted down by the hearth.

Eugene did not speak and must have fallen asleep shortly thereafter, for when he next observed the fire, it was an oven of embers. He glanced out the A-frame window. It was now the blue hour, when the air chilled and stretched thin like starched cotton. Outside, a sparrow's coloratura rang through the creaking woods. Nuzzling his toes back under the covers, Eugene turned slowly toward the room. Lang, still fully dressed, was standing by the head of Goran's bed. He was staring at the mountain man, who was silent and genuinely asleep. Lang noticed Eugene with a start.

"I'm glad you're awake," he whispered. "Let's get going, we have a big day ahead. I've packed us lunch, see?"

Sure enough, a paper sack sat by the door.

"What time is it?" asked Eugene.

"Shhh. Go outside."

Eugene grabbed his book bag, and patted it to make sure he still had Alvaro's manuscript, and his translation—he had a slightly irrational fear that Lang might steal it from him, but it was still there. As Eugene reached the front door, Goran coughed and stirred. Lang turned back, but Goran let out a shudder through his nostrils, and started snoring loudly.

"Oh good," said Lang. "I thought he might have woken up."

"Oh?"

"Yes, but you see, he's snoring again. After you."

Eugene regretted that he would not be able to say a proper good-bye to Goran, but it was clear that the mountain monk was happy to let them leave without further interference. Eugene knew he had to go on, but seeing Goran there, lying secure in his bed, Eugene couldn't help but envy him.

They entered the woods through an inconspicuously marked path behind the vineyard. As they climbed higher, the blueness dissipated and a white glare sank through the leaves, warming their skin.

"This is the path that first took me to Goran's house," said Lang. "The way is steep but it leads straight up the mountain. I made it myself, thrashing through the cashew shrubs. I've never been back since the day I made this track. It doesn't seem to have been traveled much since."

Eugene had to agree, since he couldn't make out any path at all. They hurdled rocks and fallen pine logs and were raked by brambles as high as Eugene's chest (and Lang's spectacles). Lang's speech grew excited; he constantly adjusted his beret and occasionally lapsed into Esperanto or his singsong whistle, sometimes in the middle of a sentence.

Eugene tried to tell himself that Lang, despite his evident pathologies, had a powerful instinct of self-preservation and would not lead them to any harm. If Lang was growing increasingly nervous, then they must be approaching their destination. The only thing that made Eugene uneasy was the whooshing sound that filled the dense woods around them. The leaves of the poplar trees soughed and crackled and wailed, as if some flock of manic creatures were racing through them. Lang noticed Eugene's unease.

"Boars," suggested Lang, smiling as if in pain. "Or perhaps badgers."

But Eugene knew that he was lying.

1

Agnes's funeral is held in Elmont, Queens, at the bustling necropolis of the Bloom Memorial Gardens. The cemetery is dense with towering stone obelisks that compete for sunlight like emergent trees in a rain forest. To reach his wife, Mr. Schmitz has to step on the dewy grass sprouting from the graves of other deceased Jews. The service is quick and small. Mr. Schmitz doesn't speak. When it ends, Mr. Schmitz decides he will walk home.

But first he waits for everyone else to leave. He shakes hands with his furry-haired neighbor, the old clockmaker Moishe Zohar, whose lower lip droops sympathetically, like a beaver's; Moishe wipes away his tears with a white paper doily. Mr. Schmitz also thanks the Liza twins, Ellie and Elsa, who came over every Saturday to knit with Agnes. Mr. Schmitz had met them only once before, probably five years earlier, when he came home early from his weekly park walk with Rutherford. The twins frown at Mr. Schmitz and offer to drive him back to their apartment, but he silently declines. Just when he thinks everyone has left, a pale young girl steps out from behind an ivy-covered mausoleum, a backpack swinging from her shoulder. Though less than ten people attended the service, Mr. Schmitz did not notice her. She comes right up to him. Her thin tapering eyebrows are even with his hip. Mr. Schmitz figures she isn't more than twelve years old.

"Your wife was a beautiful lady," says the girl. Her voice is thin and piping and pauses over the long vowel sounds. "A beautiful LAY-dy," she repeats. Orange freckles dot her nose and sweat brims above her eyebrows; the tips of her long, light brown hair clump together and slowly rotate in the white sunlight.

"Thank you, dear," says Mr. Schmitz. "I'm sorry, but how did you know my wife?"

"She tutored me in arithmetic." She picks at a ragged fingernail. "I live beLOW you. In 2A. Kate."

"Agnes tutored you in arithmetic? Mhmph. I didn't think she had touched that stuff for years. Though it's true she was a whiz at mathematics, when we were young. In high school, she'd wear a protractor around her wrist like a bracelet."

Mr. Schmitz's eyes wander upward.

"Every day after the lesson she read me a chapter from my book." The child pulls a large hardcover from her backpack.

"*Heidi*? The girl in the Alps? With the sheep and the old man?"

"The German girl," says Kate. "I wanted to show you the last thing she read to me from it. Just before she went to the hospital." She opens the book and finds the spot. It reads:

> The happiest of all things is when an old friend comes and greets us as in former times; the heart is comforted with the assurance that some day every thing that we have loved will be given back to us.

Mr. Schmitz studies the girl's face. She is sweating badly now in the heat. She wipes her forehead and, with a flick of her hand, casts the line of sweat to the ground.

"Please read it again."

As Kate reads the passage again, an expression of dire concentration clouds Mr. Schmitz's eyes.

"Could you read that one more time?"

And she does.

"It was nice of you to come and talk to me," says Mr. Schmitz. "You see . . . I'm in trouble."

"That's my mother." A black sedan inches up the road beside the graveyard, its opaque windows reflecting the sunshot tombstones.

"I'm in trouble," says Mr. Schmitz, pulling at his chin like a hyperactive child. "Would you like to walk with me for a bit? We can walk home together."

"It was nice to meet you, Mr. Schmitz. But my mom is waiting. Sorry."

Mr. Schmitz reaches out toward the girl's face. She doesn't move. He puts her head in his hand, softly, and then lets her go.

A moment later he is alone in front of his wife's grave. Adjacent is the plot reserved for Mr. Schmitz himself. The grass over it is neatly manicured; there's no tombstone, but otherwise it looks the same as all the other graves.

Mr. Schmitz looks up to the sky again. He registers the position of the sun and, estimating its arc, begins walking west.

The air is thick enough to chew. Mr. Schmitz proceeds down what locals call cemetery row (past Odd Fellows, Evergreen, Zion, Glenwood, and Mount Hope) to the pristine macadam of Elmont's Main Street. He feels his toes perspire. He is not paying attention, and when he crosses the street, several church-leaving cars are heading right for him. They brake abruptly and honk, but when they see the dazed, humble look on the elderly gentleman's face, they relent. It's evident what part of town he is coming from. Mr. Schmitz walks on, as though in a dream. He's dreaming of Rutherford.

He marvels that Rutherford did not come to his wedding either. Rutherford was away from New York at the time, gallivanting in Sweden—he had booked a flight to Stockholm immediately after reading in the Israeli travel magazine *Gonif!* that Jewish men had fallen into vogue in Scandinavia. Sure enough, Rutherford found an albino woman and ran off with her on a six-month tour of Scandinavian spas. As a result he did not receive Mr. Schmitz's wedding invitation until the week after the event had taken place (or so Rutherford later claimed, bowler in hand, to his friend). Mr. Schmitz did not forgive him, even after Rutherford sent impressive gifts—a large set of bronze pots and pans as well as a two-volume Garzanti Italian dictionary. It was clear to Mr. Schmitz that Rutherford, even though he would never admit it, disapproved of the wedding, believing that men of their age (they were both twenty-six at the time) should stay unattached. Carlita's death had left him defiant and disapproving. She had come as a fantasy but lingered on as a nightmare; she clung to him like an apparition, her shape shifting in his mind depending on his mood or fortune or engagement with the outside world.

Main Street tapers into a quiet residential lane of lawns and compact Victorian houses, which dead-ends a half mile later at a brick wall. The wall supports a freeway. Mr. Schmitz touches the brick. It is so hot that its chalk seems to stick to his fingers.

A narrow pedestrian road leads off on one side, and he follows it into an asphalt no-man's-land under the highway. The area is strewn with plastic bags, soiled clothing, and a baby's crib filled with soda cans.

Mr. Schmitz finds his way through a broken wooden fence into a patch of high, bristly grass, thrumming with insect life and, he suspects, furiously mating rodents. The highway overpass gives way to a milky gray sky. His socks grow slushy from the mud, and his shins chafe against the knee-high brush. Ahead, in the distance, he can make out several buildings clustered around a large open space, and as he stands on his toes to get a better look, his loafers sink into the ground. There is no other person within sight to observe the unusual expression that constricts the old wanderer's face. It is a mixture of contentment, confusion, and bloat—the look of a man who has just swallowed, with some remorse, an extra serving of a sumptuous meal.

He wades into a brown creek, the tails of his jacket floating like lily pads behind him. A plane flies overhead, close to the ground, and he freezes. He wonders what he looks like from that height. What would someone see, up in the sky there, when they peered down at this marshland? Would they see a man? A speck? A fat turtle, drifting down a stream?

Mr. Schmitz climbs up a small hill, crosses a dirt field, and reaches the tarmac, at which point he starts to jog. Airplanes taxi several hundred feet away on either side of him, though their engine roars are mute to him; several passengers point out their window at the strange old man jogging along the runway. Is he going to fly too? one child asks his mother.

An air traffic controller jumps when Mr. Schmitz grabs his shoulder. Mr. Schmitz asks him how to get inside the terminal.

This is before squad cars and airport police and federal agents are entrusted with supervising the runway at all times, and the air traffic controller doesn't know how to handle the situation. With his semaphore he gestures to Mr. Schmitz to sit down on the ground—another plane is approaching. After the plane lands, the air traffic controller leads the confused old man into the terminal building through a service door. Once inside, Mr. Schmitz follows the signs to Alitalia airlines and walks up to the counter, wallet in hand. Weeping softly now, Mr. Schmitz marvels at how full his married life had been of solitary walks just like this one.

12

Eugene was growing uneasy. The Carso's alpine air stifled his lungs. Pine needles raked over his chest and face and fell into his book bag. They had passed the tree line that morning and now the light was cool and too bright.

"Hardly there!" shouted Lang. "Not even close!"

"But we're near the top of the slope, I can see it myself." And it was true, the last visible ridge now appeared in sharp detail above them. Its rough limestone gave off jagged sparkles.

"Ha! Shows what you know!" Lang gave his jackal smile and stopped to examine his beret. "We'll freeze if we have to sleep in the woods tonight. Of course, we could always go back to Goran's."

Eugene thought about that for several minutes before responding. He decided Lang was trying to scare him. There was something up the mountain that terrified Lang.

"I'm not going back now."

Lang's eyes whisked around like flies in his head and he couldn't keep his knees still.

"Well then, so that's how it is. You're quite headstrong for someone with nothing to gain."

"What are you afraid of anyway?"

Lang shook his head and eased down into his squat. He picked up a pine cone and, scrutinizing it, began to peel off its scales. He put one in his mouth and chewed absentmindedly.

Eugene wondered how bad conditions could get on the Carso. Could it really be so harsh that he would die? His thoughts turned to his translation of Alvaro's novel, which, along with the assorted hiking snacks Lang had made him carry, weighed down his bag. There was no other copy of the manuscript—Alvaro had entrusted him with the only one—and he was anxious about losing it. In his room in Trieste he had finished translating the second section, in which Jacinto saves beautiful Alsa from a tribe of cannibals, only to have her contract a horrible disease. She is bitten by a deadly shinefish while swimming through a swamp to escape the cannibals, and Jacinto begins to fear for her life.

Lang spat out the pine scale. His jaw started excitedly to ticktock.

"I have to admit something. I told you I was born in this town where we're going. That's not exactly true. I remember being born elsewhere. Glimpses: a mother's smile, a breakfast of strawberry scones and chamomile tea, a schoolteacher who paddled me with aluminum metric rulers when I skipped class, the dusk-light slanting through the leaves of a Joshua tree under which I would sit and read my favorite authors—well, I really can only recall reading Eakins but surely there must have been others. And of course, very vividly, the bookstore where I worked."

"Where was this? Where did you grow up?"

"A town in the American West, on the edge of the Mojave

Desert. You wouldn't have heard of it. One day there was a murder in the town—it's a long story, but I played a small part in the investigation. Suffice it to say it was a difficult affair and it exhausted me so to think about it that I passed into some kind of sleep. The next thing I knew, I was waking up in a bed in this village in the Carso. Quite far away from my sad, no-name town on the edge of the Mojave!"

"But how did you get there?"

"The Carso plays tricks with one's memory," said Lang. Since that morning Eugene had played along with whatever Lang had said. He didn't want to risk upsetting the man, and being stranded in the woods. After all of their weaving, Eugene had no idea where they were. But now he feared for Lang's mind.

"I never would have thought you grew up in America."

"I wonder myself now if I did," said Lang. "If I ever saw a Joshua tree. Or helped solve a murder mystery. The memories have faded quickly these last ten years. But let me ask you: have you noticed any effect on your memory since being here?"

"Not exactly. But I keep seeing strangers who look oddly familiar—a man weeping on the street in Trieste, or Sonia's friend Kasia."

Lang winced.

"I have to leave you here, Eugene. I'm sorry."

"What? You can't! Why?"

"Don't worry, there's a town right around that bend. And the other town, the town you're looking for, is only a half-day's hike farther. That's where I'll forward your father's mail. But I can't go on. You might not understand this now, but you will soon. I've gone this far for Abe, for Alice, and for you. But I have to stop here. For me."

A loud warbling wail rang out ahead of them, as if in protest of Lang's proclamation.

"A birthing roe deer," said Lang, by way of explanation. He rubbed the hair under his beret with an air of irritated preoccupation. "Or possibly a hare snared in a boar trap."

The sound was close by, so Eugene went to investigate. He walked around the next twist in the trail and saw a man's body. It was lying prostrate, half on and half off the path. His head hung down into the abyss.

"Don't jump!" shouted Eugene, running over. He grabbed the man, who was trembling, and pulled him back. The jacket swung over his head and Eugene recognized him at once.

"Enzo?"

Disconsolate, the boy rubbed his wet face, streaking it with mud.

"Do you know this man?" asked Lang, scurrying over. Enzo's hands began to claw at the gravel and moss. The noise made Eugene shiver.

"I think he's like this all the time," said Eugene. "I saw him in Piazza Scorcola the other day—I was just telling you about him. He was sobbing then too."

"Money trouble?" asked Lang. "Or a woman. It's one or the other. Always is."

"Una donna bellississima!" said Enzo. His linen shirt was tattered and smudged with grass stains.

"He's been climbing too," said Lang. "But without a guide."

"What's wrong?" asked Eugene.

"I—I—I—"

"Yes?" asked Lang, in a steaming falsetto.

"It's so sad," said Enzo. "It's so very, very, very, very—"

"Sad?" asked Lang.

"You understand me!" said Enzo, gratified. "You understand me completely!"

"It's not so hard," said Lang. "What's her name?"

"She is my true love," said Enzo. His voice dropped. "And she has vanished, as far as I can tell. Vanished into nothing at all."

"Maybe I know her. What's her name?"

"Does it really matter? As if she were of this world! Can you paint an angel? What colors would you use? What colors!"

Lang pressed his lips together until they turned white.

"Were I even to whisper her name," continued Enzo, "it would crumble this mountain and crack open the sky. On our very heads!"

"You don't know her name, do you?"

Enzo's eyes began to well up with tears again.

"It's fine if you don't know her name," said Eugene in a calming voice. He was alarmed by Lang's sudden anger. Eugene credited it to whatever other anxiety was bothering him.

"I know your type," continued Lang. "You don't even know what love is."

"Oh yes!" exclaimed Enzo. "Oh yes, I do. I have spent my life in search of it."

"Bah!" said Lang, thrusting his arms in the air. "Crap! I'll tell you what love is. It's better you learn it now before you go all the way up there. You are going up the mountain, aren't you?"

"Oh yes. Yes, I am. It is the only place left for me to go," said Enzo. "I figured—"

"Figured nothing," piped Lang. "Love. Love is that."

He pointed to a tree.

"A fig tree?"

"Yes. A fig tree. Love is a rock. Love is around every corner and in the garbage cans overflowing in every alley in Trieste. It is the open air above us. And it's below, down there."

Lang pointed off the trail, into the abyss. Eugene followed his finger and saw, at a depth of about two hundred feet, a thin current falling down the rocky ravine and disappearing into a cave.

"A river?" said Enzo.

"Not any river. The Timavo. If you follow it down the mountain, you'll find your love there."

"She's in Trieste?"

"I don't know where your girlfriend is. I imagine she might be up there. But I warn you. Don't return. If you go back up to Idaville, you'll never leave again. Safer to go back to Trieste. That's where I'm headed.

"What you're after is unsubstantial, the creation of a human mind. And not your mind, I might add. Your thoughts are not even your own."

Enzo collapsed again, sobbing.

"Well, you may be right," he said. "I'm not myself. I'm not anyone really."

"What's Idaville?" asked Eugene.

"It's the town where you're headed," said Lang. "But don't use that name in any of the villages around here. No one will understand you."

"My love is there," said Enzo. "So I have to go."

Eugene thought of Sonia. She was still strange to him, but he was getting closer, he felt it. He wondered who he would find with her in Idaville. He knew Eakins wasn't there—but who was?

Enzo was making a mess of his trousers, rolling about in the dust and rocks. Eugene grabbed him by his wide, fanciful lapels, and shook hard. Enzo sat up straight and looked at Eugene directly for the first time.

"It's you! But why did you leave me in the street?"

"I thought we were after the same girl."

"It's not Alice he's after," said Lang. "Don't worry about that."

Lang spoke with a degree of certainty that seemed to indicate he knew more than he let on. Eugene had an idea.

"Do you know how to get there?" he asked the boy. He had to shake Enzo again to get an answer out of him. "How to get to Idaville?"

"Yes," he gulped. "I lived there once."

"Can you take me there?"

"We'll go together? Please! I think we have something in common."

"That solves it," said Eugene.

He turned to Lang, but the little man was gone. The pine branches rustled and the rocky trail beneath them was silent. Eugene peered over the precipice of the gorge, fearing the worst. But all that he saw below were fiery thickets of juniper shrubs; the quiet Timavo, winding and tumbling down the Carso; the orange roofs of the changeling city and the purple sea beyond.

13

In the airport bathroom Mr. Schmitz checks his pockets and finds: a postcard from the Bloom Memorial Gardens ("Welcome to the Rest of Your Afterlife"), a money clip, a boarding pass, a white silk yarmulke, a passport—and a torn envelope, containing a letter from Rutherford. He holds the paper up to the fluorescent glare of the public bathroom's tubular light fixture, and studies the return address with a squinty, watery eye.

Outside a red sun inflames the morning haze. Mr. Schmitz, unburdened by baggage, runs into the traffic and seizes a vacant cab. He hands Rutherford's envelope to the driver.

"Capito," says the driver. He jags out of the station, his engine snorting loudly and the chassis bucking.

"I only have dollars," says Mr. Schmitz.

"Sta be'," the driver replies, with a toss of his hand. "Cinquanta."

Mr. Schmitz nods his assent. The driver sniffs the air, and his hand flies up to his nose.

"Sessanta."

Mr. Schmitz agrees, and the driver rolls open the windows. An indistinguishable landscape stretches out on both sides of the road—co-ops with laundry strung up on the balconies, dirt fields, industrial parks, and bulky, windowless buildings painted beige, with large black antennae poking up like porcupine spikes.

"Listen," says Mr. Schmitz, leaning forward. "I need information."

After waiting for a few seconds, he tries his Italian for the first time:

"Io ho bisogno d'informazione."

"*Who doesn't?*" grunts the taxi driver, as they swing into Milan.

T he taxi drops Mr. Schmitz in an alley not far from the central train terminal, in front of a dark wooden door three times his height. Mr. Schmitz rubs his yarmulke in the pocket of his suit. It is dirty, like the suit. Between his transborough hike and his trans-Atlantic flight, his jacket and shirt have accumulated a twig (tucked into his shirt, between buttons, as a conscientious diner might tuck his tie), a tuft of yellow moss (protruding from his breast pocket like a handkerchief), stains of swamp water and airplane ragout about his belly and legs, and a luggage sticker on his behind that says "OVER 70 POUNDS."

He searches the listing by the intercom at the front door, but does not see Rutherford's name. He walks to the curb and gazes up at the building, a simple four-story affair with tall windows and green wooden shutters. Across the street, a grocer stands in front of his store, staring at Mr. Schmitz, with his fingers in the shape of a crucifix and his apron pulled up over his nose. Schmitz waves.

"Ciao," he says.

"Porca miseria!" yells the grocer. He raises higher his crossed fingers.

Something occurs to Mr. Schmitz. He goes back to the list of names and traces down the list with his finger until he hits upon one he recognizes from the past: "#3B: Carlita Passamonte." Memories of black dancing eyes, a small brown mole, and a lingering kiss.

He hits the buzzer several times but there's no answer. A few minutes pass before a smaller door within the larger front door creaks open. A dirty, shirtless teenage boy appears. He glares at Mr. Schmitz with disgust, spits on the sidewalk, and hastens past, his fingers pinching his nostrils. Mr. Schmitz catches the door behind him and walks into a warm, damp courtyard. With a loud harrumph, a burly woman with a bandanna tied around her head throws a rotten tomato at Mr. Schmitz from her second-floor apartment. When he looks up at her she makes an obscene gesture and slams shut her windows so forcefully that their panes vibrate. Mr. Schmitz makes for a staircase in the opposite corner of the yard, tomato juice dripping from his shoulders.

The door to apartment 3B opens when he nudges it, and he lets himself into a shadow-darkened apartment. What he sees stops him. Nothing is particularly unusual about the decor; it is rather clean, if lived-in and redolent of tuna and onions (a reassuring scent, since this is one of Rutherford's favorite culinary combinations). Sunlight filters through gossamer yellow curtains. It illuminates a slice of the living room, exposing the armrest of a dark flame mahogany chair and the corner of a coffee table overlaid by clouded glass. The kitchen is to the right. A shelf above the oven is weighed down by unruly stacks of cookbooks;

several dirty plates clog the sink, and shake slightly when a Vespa's engine ignites with a roar downstairs. The hallway is lined with amateur paintings of food dishes, like one would see at a cheap pizzeria.

It is not too different from what Mr. Schmitz anticipated when he pictured Rutherford's Milanese apartment. A bit more modest, perhaps, and darker, but not unlike Rutherford's New York apartment. Mr. Schmitz might have even felt reassured about his friend's well-being, were it not for the Post-it notes.

They're everywhere: yellow sticky-notes, the kind available in any office-supply store. There is a note posted on every visible flat surface in the apartment. On each note, Rutherford has written, in his round, womanly handwriting, the name of the object to which it's stuck.

Mr. Schmitz laughs to himself—of course! This is how one studies a foreign language. He has heard of the method: the student writes the foreign word for the object on the Post-it, and is reminded of the word every time he sees it, until it is memorized.

Yet here in Rutherford's apartment, something's different. The words are written in English. Mr. Schmitz quickly glances around the house again, this time focusing on the sticky paper. He reads them aloud to himself: "door," "curtain," "bookcase," "oven," "cookbook," "ashtray," "rug," and "floor" (this one is written over a hundred times, the paper scattered all over the parquet and sticking to Mr. Schmitz's feet). On the hall paintings he reads: "pizza pie," "Coke," "sandwich," "a bottle of wine," and "shrimps." Mr. Schmitz lingers by that last one for a while.

At the other end of the hall, next to a spotless white marble bathroom ("toilet," "flusher," "sink," "hot," "cold"), there is a door, which Mr. Schmitz nudges open. Inside he sees tasteful, replaceable furniture: an oak "chest of drawers" that stands on legs resembling claws, curling upward; a white-framed plastic "chair"; a blond wood "bookshelf" built into a wall, sporadically and untidily stocked. An ancient cast-iron "compass," pointing northeast. A four-poster "bed" high off the ground, draped by a bright green "blanket" whose frilly trim brushes the parquet "floor" (covered, as in the hallway, with the yellow paper). Clackety green wooden "blinds" tap lightly with the breeze against the open "window."

And there on the bed is Rutherford. Or perhaps, Mr. Schmitz thinks, "Rutherford." He is lying flat on his back in a silk, pastel blue bathrobe cinched so tight that the collar seems to chafe against his neck. Almost imperceptibly, at irregular intervals of about ten seconds, his stomach rises and falls, his breath faint enough that the silk of his bathrobe does not even crinkle. Yet it seems to Mr. Schmitz that except for the dandyish robe, which he does not recognize, Rutherford hasn't changed much after all. This observation does not prevent Mr. Schmitz from feeling a sudden, impossible desire to run out of the house and back to the airport.

"Rutherford?"

The body on the bed is still for several moments. Then he stirs, so gradually that Mr. Schmitz must examine the contours of Rutherford's bathrobe to register the movement.

"You look charming," says Mr. Schmitz.

The man on the bed still does not make any significant movements, but shuts and opens his eyes several times. His wrinkles tense and his mustache quivers in a dumb show of consciousness. But now, with a shock, he recognizes Mr. Schmitz.

"Rutherford," says Mr. Schmitz. "It's me."

Rutherford sits up in bed and gasps. His cheeks are plump and unnatural under his wide-open eyes, and he points at Mr. Schmitz with a shaky forefinger. Then, as if a switch has been triggered in his brain, Rutherford falls back against his pillows and passes out again.

Mr. Schmitz's grief is like a foreign language, inchoate and strange in his mouth. He races over to his friend with a mounting sense of alarm. His feet shuffle Post-it notes; many of them stick to his soles.

He now can see, creeping down one side of his friend's face, a purple mark, two inches wide and four inches long. The blemish is rounded at the lower end, so that it resembles a tongue. It runs from Rutherford's temple to his jaw, and a light down grows on it that does not match the salt-and-pepper of his mustache but is a clean, pure white. The purple-black skin is puckered like gooseflesh and tightly stretched. A breeze pricks Mr. Schmitz's perspiring neck. The blinds float up and then fall flat against the window with a loud clack and chatter.

Rutherford again comes to. He regards Mr. Schmitz with bleary, frightened eyes that have withdrawn deep into his head. His dry lips mouth a word.

"Yes, Rutherford?"

Rutherford repeats the word, which Mr. Schmitz makes out to be his own name.

"What's happened to you, Rutherford? Are you sick?"

"Schmitz," says Rutherford, in a distant, garbled voice.

"I decided to visit you. I'm angry at you, you know. You have not been writing. Not decent letters at least."

"Schmitz!" yells Rutherford. And with that he jumps out of bed to hug his friend.

"Oh, Rutherford!"

"Schmitz."

The two men embrace for some time. The blinds shudder against the window frame. Rutherford begins to grow heavy in Mr. Schmitz's arms, and Mr. Schmitz pulls back.

"What is that on your face?" he asks. "Some kind of chloasma, I think. My aunt Frida once got one on her neck."

"Schmitz! Come stai, amico?" says Rutherford. His Italian seems perfect, but as he speaks he constricts his face so that his chin dips unnaturally into his collarbone. Mr. Schmitz is chilled.

"Are you ill? And"—for he can't help himself—"why haven't you written to me? Agnes . . . Agnes is dead. Haven't you received my letters?"

Rutherford smiles benignly and gives his friend a little wink.

"Schmitz," he says, trailing off. Panic begins to distort his gaze.

Rutherford is saved from further discussion by the sound of the front door opening. There is a scuffling noise on the floorboards and the crinkle of paper. Rutherford shows no sign of alarm at the intruder. Only relief.

The bedroom door opens on the shirtless, olive-skinned boy. He has long, sweaty brown hair that catches on his neck and shoulders. A round Mediterranean face, with deeply set eyes and a pug nose. He has a gaunt, ribby chest, surprisingly tendinous and hairless arms, and wears jeans cut off at the knees and red sneakers without socks. He stares at Mr. Schmitz with a look of disbelief—tempered, perhaps, by ridicule.

"Chi è?" He addresses Rutherford but keeps his eyes fixed on

Mr. Schmitz, a heaving, chubby man of sixty dressed in a ragged suit mottled with filth.

"È un gran'amico di New York," says Rutherford. "È appena arrivato. Sii gentile!"

Mr. Schmitz is surprised to hear such an animated tone from Rutherford; he seems to have regained his former self.

"He stinks della Madonna, come cazzo e pesce e merda," says the boy.

"Why do you speak to him but not me?" Mr. Schmitz asks Rutherford. "We haven't talked for so long."

"Che cosa di'?" asks the boy.

"Non lo so," says Rutherford. And Schmitz finally understands. For the first time since his wife died, he begins to cry.

"Che sfigato," says the boy.

"OK," says Schmitz, raising his hands. *"I try . . . to speak with you . . . in Italian."*

"Grazie," says Rutherford.

"What is happening on the face?"

"This tongue here," replies Rutherford, pointing to the mark along his jaw. *"It has begun to grow. Down my cheek. It's so good to talk to you again, old boy. Welcome to Italy. Oh, the meals we'll have!"*

"But who is this boy?"

"My name is Daniel," says the boy, defiant.

"It's Daniel," says Rutherford, his voice wobbling. *"The shirtless boy I described in my letters."*

"Why can't you speak English?"

"I'm very ill, Mr. Schmitz."

"But why?"

"I can't speak English because . . . I forgot it. My control of the language faded and faded until I woke up one day and I had com-

pletely forgotten it. But," he says, gesturing to the sticky notes all around him, *"I'm trying to learn it again."*

"I need to take you to a doctor. Now."

"Don't worry about me. Daniel here takes care of me. We have a close relationship, you see. Do you know who he is?"

"You need to see a doctor."

"I'm his son," says Daniel.

"Are you mad?" shouts Mr. Schmitz.

"What did he say?" asks Daniel.

Both Daniel and Mr. Schmitz turn to Rutherford, awaiting his response. The old man grins with half of his mouth, and Mr. Schmitz realizes that the left half of his face—the side with the purple tongue-shaped mark down the jaw—is frozen. His left eye droops, his lips sag into a half-frown, his hairline angles down to the one side, and his cheek droops into a jowl. Meanwhile the right side of his face works furiously, as if to compensate—his eye blinking rapidly, his nostril flaring, his lips grinning, and his ear tweaking this way and that.

"The tongue," chokes Rutherford, out of half of his mouth, *"the tongue is taking over."*

He coughs, raises one frail arm like a broken wing, and after executing a desultory pirouette, falls face-first onto the floor. A hoarse scream echoes down the hallway and into the courtyard. Sticky notes float and feather in the air above the body as Mr. Schmitz kneels down to check for a pulse.

14

The ridge at the top of the limestone mountain was a chain of loose rocks that crumbled at the faintest pressure—a human step, the scurry of a dormouse, a lick of breeze. The high air felt light and ill, difficult to breathe. Behind them the Adriatic was a blue crab's outstretched claw, pinching the furry Istrian peninsula. In front of them, on the other side of the ridge, lay a richly verdant valley: a large lush pocket surrounded by a ring of mountains, like a green satin napkin tucked into the mouth of a wineglass. It was the most vibrant landscape Eugene had seen in days, a scratch of life in what up to then had been a craggy, scarred terrain. He laughed with the happiness of an explorer who, stripped and destitute, has finally reached a land that only he believed existed. He was John Wesley Powell on Longs Peak, Zebulon Pike at Royal Gorge.

Beside him, Enzo wept the tears of a young maid.

"What the hell is wrong with you?" Eugene clapped him on the back. Enzo shuffled his feet and several stones tumbled hundreds of yards down the escarpment.

"It's down there," said Enzo. "Idaville."

"Idaville? Down in the valley?"

"That's where my love is. And yours. And him."

"Eakins?"

"The Mayor," said Enzo. He refused to make eye contact. "I hope he has not taken her already. I might be too late. Do you have any tissues?"

Eugene did not. Enzo shrugged and, reaching into his jacket, found a wad of fig leaves. He rubbed them against his runny nose and then stuffed them back into his pocket.

"I don't see any town," said Eugene. He absentmindedly patted the book bag under his arm, feeling the weight of Alvaro's manuscript. He hadn't found much time to work on it, but he'd gotten far enough to determine that Jacinto had sucked the shinefish venom from Alsa's neck, and saved her life, only to discover that her father had shown up in Cibao, with vengeance on his mind.

"Don't worry," said Enzo, "the town is in the valley. There's a good reason no one can see it from up here. Who wouldn't want to visit a town down there, if you knew it existed?"

"No one in the Carso visits the town?"

"Of course they don't. My goodness. Imagine what might happen then!"

Eugene followed Enzo over the ridge and down a narrow muddy path hemmed in by a line of short heath bushes that sprouted urn-shaped flowers. The path curled around misshapen mounds covered with odd leafless shrubs, their branches white like bones left to dry in the sun. The landscape reminded Eugene of the scene from Eakins's novella, in which a young thief tracks his true love across a desolate Irish moor.

"Have you read Eakins's *Every Man for Himself and God Against All*?"

"Fantastic!" said Enzo, stumbling over a root. "Do you remember the wood sprite?"

Eugene nodded.

"You know, he's quite a good guy once you get to know him. Once you get past his wicked mouth. He swears at children."

"I don't remember that."

"There's no need to remember anything. I'm telling you how he is."

Eugene was looking forward to having Sonia join him as a partner in sanity.

When they finally reached the floor of the valley, they came upon a clear, shallow brook. Enzo bent down to drink.

"Is that safe?" asked Eugene.

"No reason to think it's not," said Enzo. "There are no people up here to pollute it. I never get sick from bad water anyway."

Eugene joined him and drank deeply. The freezing water trickled down his throat and into his belly. Several times he pulled himself up and spat out morsels of silt.

From this end of the valley, the landscape was magnificent and vast. Thousands of yards to either side stood the slopes of the mountain peaks, white and gray-speckled on the top, while lower down, thin, glistening waterfalls gave the mountains a vaporous, polychromatic grandeur. In the valley itself the interspersed groves of beech trees stood like cities of skyscrapers in the otherwise deserted plain. Each grove had hundreds of trees, and rarely were two clusters less than half a mile apart. The sky had the color and consistency of paraffin wax. The candle flame at the apex of the dome was the midday sun. For once Enzo had stopped weeping.

"It's so happy," he was saying to himself. "It's so happy. Happiness. Happy."

"Why? As far as I can tell, we're completely lost."

"I'm close to her again. I'm sure of it. She's returned. And I've returned. We'll be united again. I haven't seen her since the bus station. That day was so long ago it seems like another life."

Enzo explained that the town was not here but far away, on the opposite side of the valley. They skirted a dense grove and Eugene could make out a distinct, sharp odor that was neither floral nor atmospheric in nature.

"Do you smell juniper berries?" asked Enzo. "There must be a patch of them nearby."

"I smell something all right."

The air darkened slightly, and beneath their muddy feet the blades of heather cast shadows onto one another. A loud, roaring belch froze them in their tracks.

"There might be bears in these woods," said Enzo.

The trees beside them rubbed together and dislodged a filthy, barefoot, hunched-over figure. He wore a ragged military jacket, a whitish shirt the size of a mainsail, and a grimy pair of khaki pants.

"A gadda lye?" said the man.

"I thought no one came down into the valley," whispered Eugene.

"They don't," said Enzo. "He's from Idaville."

"A gadda lye?" the man asked again. He opened his lips in a grinning leer, revealing rotted incisors and a black tongue. He looked oddly familiar, but Eugene couldn't place him.

"This man's drunk," said Enzo, his brows crinkling.

"Amma gadda lig?" said the pickled man. He reached into his back pocket and withdrew a greased, withered cigarette with a broken, dangling tip. Enzo nodded and removed from his jacket a box of matches. He struck a match and, with an unsteady hand, lit the man's cigarette.

The drunk inhaled and his eyes rolled up in bliss.

"Aaaah," he said. "Nigh."

"You're welcome," said Enzo.

"Are you from Idaville?" asked Eugene.

"Ha!" said the drunk, clapping his free hand to his shoulder. "A lookin' far Eakins, arny?"

"Well, sort of—there's a girl named Sonia—"

"Oh ya DINda sai?" The drunk's eyes were shut, and saliva dripped from his gums. Before he could say anything else, he spun about and fell face forward into the grove. As he fell, one of his pantlegs caught on his knee, revealing a calf made of wood—a peg leg.

"Wait—" said Eugene, grabbing his friend's shoulder. "Who is this man?"

"It's no use. He's always like this."

"You know him?" asked Eugene.

"Yeah, he's Idaville's town drunk. I would see him around, he leaves sometimes for Trieste and who knows where else. He ends up in all kinds of unusual places. They call him Bazlen."

Eugene shook his head, trying to remember how he knew this name. Memory is an animal with tentacles, and Eugene's were already occupied, juggling other objects from his past.

They left the drunk collapsed in the grove and hiked on. The floor of the valley rose and fell in green waves. Dark islands of poplars and beech were scattered about. Several times they heard a rustling behind them and, turning, would see Bazlen swirling in the heather, warbling an Irish drinking song and sinking back down.

Eugene furiously tried to put everything together. He had been carried along this far without fully understanding what he had become a part of. Since arriving in Italy he had felt, at times, like he was brushing up against some other realm. Only now did he realize that, at some point, he had crossed an invisible border and was now trespassing on a foreign territory. He groped into his bag to make sure he still had Alvaro's manuscript. It was there, thick and frayed around the edges.

Just before sundown they reached the far edge of the valley, where two rock faces met in a jagged, vertical crevice. The top of the gap was obscured by a wispy blue-gray cloud. There, in front of a gleaming patch of wild convolvuli, they spotted an elderly man. Slumped over his cane, he strode defiantly, but not without some infirmity, in a long arc through the red flowerbeds. At first, Eugene thought that the man was looking directly at him, but when he got closer, he saw that the man's expression was blank, so that it seemed he was staring through Eugene, right on to the other side of the valley.

"Ah! I know this man too," said Enzo. "He is a beautiful artist. He made a portrait for me of my beloved. I carry it around with me."

"You have a painting of her?"

"He painted the portrait based entirely on my description of her. It was difficult at first, perhaps because I was a little hazy on her exact features. What I described was not exactly a person, just . . . a type of glow. But then he asked me to describe my feelings about her, how she affected me—you see what I mean? And so I described my feelings just as I did to you. He began sketching even as I spoke. I have to admit that he created a brilliant portrait. It is my only keepsake from Idaville."

Enzo reached into his jacket's inner pocket and took out a piece of yellow paper that had been folded into quarters. With great care he flattened it, but he could not part with it immediately, and held it pressed against his chest.

"Sometimes, it makes me sad to admit, the image of her face goes out of my mind. This usually happens first thing in the morning after a long sleep. Or I find myself turning a street corner and I become completely disoriented. I don't always remember who I am, let alone what I'm searching for. In these moments I look at the portrait. It reminds me why I go walking. It reminds me why I'm here."

"Will you let me see her? It'd mean a lot to me."

Enzo extended the fragile paper with a quivering hand.

The drawing was a blizzard of thick hash marks colored in light blues and greens. They extended from the base of the page to a horizon just an inch below the top of the frame, where the cream-colored paper was left to show through. There was nothing else on the page except several strands of yellow, dancing in the bottom corner—entwined blond tendrils drawn on top of the chaos of blue, almost as an afterthought.

"That's her," said Enzo, pointing to the yellow curls. He was frowning and one corner of his mouth twitched benevolently. "She is looking down at the sea from the cliff's edge. The edge of the Carso." He pointed to the ridge above him. "There."

At the sound of the two men rustling the meadow grass, the old artist stopped and waved his cane out before him with a looping gesture, as if to ward off an evil spirit. But he didn't say a word. There was no pride in his posture.

"Keftir," shouted Enzo. "I can't tell you how much your portrait has comforted me during my exile. It's Enzo, your old friend. I'm back."

Keftir lowered his cane and bowed his head. Eugene could see that the pockets of his velvet robe were stuffed with pastel crayons; they had smeared the fabric with bright chalk.

"You've strayed pretty far from Idaville," said Enzo, as if the thought had just occurred to him. "Maybe a mile."

"I was just observing the flowers," replied Keftir, then he mumbled something under his breath.

"What did you say?" asked Enzo, who had been staring off into the rock crevice ahead of him.

"Nothing," said Keftir. Though Eugene had heard him perfectly. The old man had said, "Will I never leave this godforsaken place?"

Keftir balled up his free hand and rubbed his eyes with the back of his fist.

"We'll lead you back," said Enzo. "But first let me introduce you to my friend, Eugene."

"What are you doing here?" asked Keftir, swiveling so that his empty eyes stared straight at Eugene. This caught Eugene by surprise, and he couldn't formulate a response right away.

"I'm looking for a friend of mine. Her name is Sonia. Do you know her?"

"You mean . . . you're not from Idaville?"

"He's a huge fan of Eakins," said Enzo. "He has helped me. We are hoping to find our beloveds in town. Do you know if mine has passed through?"

"Oh yes, you'll find them both there," said Keftir. He spoke in a subdued voice, interrupted by frequent pauses. "But if I were you, I'd turn back. There's a whole world behind you. Love alone won't carry you."

"Nonsense!" shouted Enzo. "She's there! Let's find her!"

Eugene nodded, even though he felt, somewhere deep down, a powerful impulse to turn around and run.

Enzo gave Keftir his arm, and the painter, with a shrug of resignation, took it. As they walked the final distance of the moor, it became clear to Eugene that Idaville exerted some power of magnetism on Enzo. The closer Enzo got, the more he talked about the town, its inhabitants, and finally, its Mayor. Then he grew silent for a while, and refused to look at either man. Tears filled his eyes for the last time.

"Do you think the Mayor might be happy to see me?" Enzo asked, at once terrified and hopeful.

"I think," said Keftir, "that the Mayor . . . will welcome you back . . . with great enthusiasm and . . . delight."

Before Keftir could finish this sentence, Enzo jumped out ahead of them, his burst of speed knocking Keftir back. The old man's shoulders shuddered at the jolt, and Eugene rushed to hold him up. Eugene watched, stunned, as Enzo ran, then skipped, then hopped into the rock crevice. He whooped like a phantom and pulled on his hair, so excited was he to reach Idaville.

PART III

THE CARSO

1

It is Sunday in Italy, so all the doctors' offices are closed. In the hospital, the emergency room has nearly as many patients as usual, but there are no doctors to be seen. There is only a single receptionist, who takes frequent cigarette breaks in the building's interior courtyard, where she flirts with a swarthy young Sicilian who carries, as a prop, a mop—but no bucket. The long, chartreuse halls are vacant, the overhead lights flicker defectively, and the crowded waiting room is silent except for a steady mechanical hum and a patient's occasional moan. A grim institutional pallor has settled over the room's vinyl seats, the vomit-green floor, the walls covered with a coral print that reminds Mr. Schmitz of Agnes's seahorses. He is sitting there alongside Daniel. In the seats opposite them are a rotund woman with stringy white hair and persimmon cheeks who is heaving for breath, and a mother whose ten-year-old son has had a nosebleed for the last three hours.

A nurse appears in the waiting room sporadically and capriciously. Her white smock recalls to Mr. Schmitz the shapeless

uniform worn by his Quaker teachers in Lancaster County, and
she wears the same dismayed expression. Every hour or so, with
evident reluctance, she admits a new patient. Mr. Schmitz in-
quires about the status of his friend each time, but the nurse
never answers. She's not a native Italian herself—Filipina perhaps—
and she pretends, unconvincingly, that she can't understand his
Italian. The boy, Daniel, is no help. He just stares idiotically at
the glossy pages of a women's fashion magazine. A bulky smock,
identical to the one worn by the nurse, is draped over his bare
chest—the receptionist has explained that, by hospital policy, all
visitors must wear shirts.

*"Can you ask the woman what is happening with Rutherford?
The next time she comes?"*

Daniel does not respond. He is busy examining, cross-eyed, a
photo spread of models posing with thoroughbreds at an eques-
trian club.

"Why can't you be more helpful? Aren't you a friend of Rutherford's?"

Daniel traces with his forefinger the outline of a female model's body. She is sitting barebacked on a horse in a checkered
skullcap and a creamy rider's jacket. A drop of saliva dangles from
the boy's lips and falls to the page, without ever severing its silky
trail from his mouth.

Mr. Schmitz takes the magazine out of the boy's hands and
throws it on the floor. He waits until Daniel returns his eye contact, but when he does, Daniel's stare is cold and dead.

"I'm not—so tight—with the old geezer," says Daniel at last,
overenunciating each word so that Mr. Schmitz can understand
him. He slowly rises, and retrieves the magazine.

At this moment a gaunt, weathered man stumbles through the
waiting room's double doors, clutching one of his arms. His white

T-shirt is torn at the neck and speckled by purple droplets. He falls to one knee, then gets up again, and walks to the reception desk. The arm he clutches appears to have been bent backward at the elbow joint.

"What happened to you?" asks the receptionist, in a lazy monotone.

"I fell," says the man. He looks stupidly around the room.

"Sign this sheet and the doctor will be with you shortly."

"I fell. My arm."

The nurse comes out of the emergency room and, seeing the unnatural angle of the man's arm, admits him ahead of the others.

"Rutherford must be in stable condition," says Mr. Schmitz to his silent companion. He is trying hard to keep his spirits high.

A minute later, the man with the broken arm returns to the waiting room. The arm is in the same awkward position, but now a white bandage is tied around it from elbow to shoulder, cinched in a bow. He thanks the nurse and, after pausing to brace himself against the wall for support, he slowly makes his way out of the waiting room, sighing quietly in brave, shut-eyed agony.

"Some doctor," says Daniel, thumbing open the page of another fashion glossy.

"If you don't want to be here, you can leave, I don't care at all."

Daniel pauses to consider Mr. Schmitz's offer.

"He thought I was his son," he finally says. *"But I'm not his son, of course. I was born to a poor woman in an industrial park outside of Brescia. She wept when I left for Milan, but I knew I could make a better living in a big city. This man who thought I was his son— your friend—cooked for me. He let me use the shower, too—even his*

nail clippers. He gave me money to buy food. He trusted me, man to man. So I listened to his stories."

"*Stories?*"

"*Yeah, stories. Stories about the woman, his wife. Who died with his son.*"

"*Carlita.*"

"*I listened to the stories, and he took care of me.*"

"*But what did he want from you?*"

"*He was haunted. He told me all about the woman, Carlita, and he thought he could see her still. He would notice some lady at a café and think it was her. It was worse when he got sick, when he started to speak more Italian—and forget English. He finally stopped living the apartment, but every time he looked out the window he saw her in the street. Though anyone who wasn't old and blind and crazy could see that they were all different women and none of them his dead wife.*"

"*So you . . . took care of him?*"

"*I had my reasons for staying there,*" says Daniel, grinning like he has a happy secret. He turns his attention to the magazine on his lap; the cover story is about some famous old American writer who has just died in Italy. He opens to a two-page spread of a young Italian film actress, photographed while sunbathing topless on a private beach in Ibiza.

"*What are you saying?*" asks Mr. Schmitz. A fury runs through him like an electrical charge.

"*His downstairs neighbor. She was older than me, maybe twenty-five, thirty. She once came up to see how the old man was feeling. She had heard him fall to the floor, during one of his attacks.*"

"*What attacks?*"

"*I lied to her and said he was fine—that he was my grandfather and I would inherit all his money, as soon as he croaked. She slapped me. Can you believe it? But soon I was fucking her in the old man's living room while he was passed out. She knew to come upstairs when she heard the sound of his fat ass dropping against her ceiling. She'd tell her parents that she was going to help the old man. But I'd be waiting at the door for her."*

Mr. Schmitz struggles to understand, and wonders whether his weak Italian is responsible for his confusion. Daniel, meanwhile, has become uncharacteristically still. When he speaks again, he uses a clear, measured tone that invests his features with a nobility Mr. Schmitz has not observed there before.

"If he got on my nerves with his fantasies and blabber, I'd bring on an attack. I would call him to the window and point out a woman in the street, and I'd ask him if he recognized her. 'Is it Carlita?' he'd ask, all foolish. He'd point his finger at her, and sometimes bang his flabby arms against the glass, and finally start his convulsions. I was nice, though. When he fell, I caught him and guided him to the bed. And then I myself would do a cannonball on the floor to get my girlfriend's attention and soon I'd hear her footsteps on the stairs."

"Rutherford—he would fall down often?"

"He might have stopped believing me about seeing Carlita, but by then he was too tired to leave his bed. I would cannonball myself anyway and the girl would come up and I'd take her onto the couch in the front room. I'd hush her up at first, put my hand over her mouth so her screams wouldn't wake him up. But then we stopped caring. I think the old man secretly loved it. Lying there in his stupor, he probably imagined it was him and his dead puttana.*"*

"He was my friend," says Mr. Schmitz in English, turning away from Daniel. He can think of nothing else to say, and is overcome by a fatigue so thick and woolly that he begins to slide down in his seat. His knees flex and buckle just in time to prevent his body from sliding onto the linoleum floor. For the first time he feels the weight of his mission—the puddles and marshes and the ocean he crossed and the cold sweat of long-distance travel that clings to his underclothes and makes his skin clammy.

"Finally, one time, he managed to get off his ass and dawdle down the hall, where he caught us in the act. The slob probably got the whole dirty view. In his imbecility he started shouting the name of his dead wife—Carlita, Carlita—like she was a dog that had run away from him in the street. The girl screamed and rushed out of the apartment, and the old man began to cry. He mumbled something about his life feeling unnatural and strange. Then he went back to his bed and didn't move for a couple of days. That's where you found him.

"This is the first time he's been out of bed since. I hope he gets better. I like his apartment. I like his neighbor."

"He was my friend."

With a shudder, Mr. Schmitz slaps Daniel in the face. The boy blinks in surprise, and then grins.

"Get out of here," says Mr. Schmitz, glaring darkly at the teenager. *"Go back to the apartment."*

Daniel is gone when the nurse reappears. Her arms are outstretched in a gesture of benediction. Signor Rutherford is ready to be seen, she says. Mr. Schmitz follows her to a room at the end of the hall where Rutherford lies on a hospital bed, covered by thin paper sheets. His arm is tethered to an intravenous bag. There is a black LED screen on the wall over the bed, like a headboard, casting pale electric green light down onto Rutherford's face, which his stroke has hollowed into a rare and uncanny topography. It is troubling to see that Rutherford bears a greater likeness to Agnes in the months before she died than to his previous self. Mr. Schmitz knows better than to blame Daniel. But if it is not Daniel's fault—may he suffer worse than a thousand infarctions—then whose is it?

Mr. Schmitz leans over the bed, so close that his breath moistens Rutherford's cheek. Nerves jump in Rutherford's eyelids, and Mr. Schmitz is sure he has animated some part of his friend that has fallen dormant. Then the nurse orders Mr. Schmitz to stand back from the patient, and Rutherford's eyelids freeze over once more. The brainwave monitor pops erratically, and the nurse bows her head in pity and leaves the room.

As soon as the door closes, Mr. Schmitz notices a change. The monitor seems to respond to his voice, and whenever he says Rutherford's name, the green line spikes. Mr. Schmitz repeats his friend's name over and over with increasing volume and frequency, until the LED screen looks like an emerald crown. Even when the nurse orders Mr. Schmitz to leave, he's ecstatic at the thought that he has found a new way to communicate with his friend. Because there is so much that Mr. Schmitz needs to tell him.

2 The rock faces stood as high and sturdy as two adjacent skyscrapers. Eugene and Keftir followed a corkscrew path between them.

Eugene feared that Keftir might stumble, but the blind man swatted at him every time Eugene extended a hand. Keftir seemed to know the way by heart. He stepped cleanly over obstacles without even tapping them aside with his cane.

Keftir did not answer any of Eugene's questions about Idaville or about Eakins, but walked on, his head cocked to one side.

"Some people are watchers," said Keftir, all of a sudden. "Others are watched."

"What on earth—"

"I'm leaving for good," said Keftir. He turned sharply to face Eugene. "If you're smart you'll join me."

"Please tell me—what happens in this town?"

"They worship the Mayor."

"You mean Eakins? So he *is* alive?"

"He's as virile as a seventeen-year-old. He feeds off of the adulation and love of his minions. He is a glutton of life. He eats and eats and eats. He is a wildcat. A lion. Goliath."

"Wait!" said Eugene. "Before you go—I have to ask. Are you the model for 'Keftir the Blind'? Or do you just take your name from him?"

"Ha!" said Keftir, flashing his vitreous eyeballs. "I *am* Keftir the Blind."

The painter turned and walked herky-jerky down the rock path to the long valley beyond.

Eugene clutched Alvaro's manuscript through his book bag like a talisman and decided he wouldn't be worth much if he didn't keep going. After all, does Jacinto give up, in the middle of the Dominican jungle, when he's confronted with shinefish bites or cannibal attacks or mud paths overrun by jungle vermin? Of course not. Alsa is awaiting him.

Eugene went on, and after several minutes he found himself at the end of the trail. The rock faces ended abruptly in a high scrabbly cliff. Eugene was standing at the edge of town.

Idaville stood on flat ground. Two rows of houses faced each other across a main road paved with loose gravel. This road ran the length of the town, about two hundred meters, where it ended at a large black iron gate. Every house was painted red and had been built with identical dimensions, porches, and backyards. A breeze from the Adriatic, smelling faintly of cleaning chemicals, shifted the gravel and swept debris down the street toward Eugene. This debris, he soon realized, was notebook paper—ripped, stripped, balled, and ink-stained.

There was no sign of Enzo, but the street was busy with pedestrians, out for an afternoon stroll. Many of them seemed familiar with one another, and ambled together in leisurely clusters. That is, until they noticed Eugene, standing alone at the end of the street. He felt acutely aware of the holes in his slacks and the stains covering his shirt. The townspeople stopped and cautiously turned to face him, hiding their mouths behind curled hands, whispering to each other and shaking their heads. A disproportionate number of the citizens, Eugene realized, were young, stunningly beautiful women.

"Hello," said Eugene. He lifted his hand in greeting. A ruddy-faced Chinese boy, no older than seven, charged a few steps forward and tossed a twig, which landed by Eugene's feet. The boy's mother grabbed him by the collar, slapped him twice, and pulled him close to her chest. She gave Eugene a sharp look of reproach.

A cocky young man, about Eugene's age, called out to him.

"Who are you? Where did you come from?"

"I'm Eugene," he said. The crowd instinctively lurched back. Muffled conversations broke out all around him.

"I hiked up through the Carso," he added. "I'm from America."

Eugene caught fragments of confused dialogue here and there. He was relieved, if puzzled, that they all spoke English. "But he hasn't published for years," said one woman.

"What's your story?" one woman asked Eugene.

"Who're you with?" asked another.

"What's it like in America now?"

"Do you know why you're here?"

"What's your story?"

Eugene began to notice how diversely attired the townspeople were. One woman had a gray fleece and purple sneakers with untied laces; another woman, caramel-skinned with piercing green eyes, wore what looked like an ancient Mexican headdress; a small band of rosy-cheeked men, each of them about three feet tall, dressed in green tunics and carried pickaxes.

"I'm Eugene Brentani," said Eugene, and the crowd grew quiet and attentive. "I'm looking for a girl named Alison Chisholm. She also goes by Sonia, Alicia, Alice, or Agata."

He received looks of skepticism and pity. A kindly, wide-eyed man, dressed in a doctor's white coat, stepped forward.

"If she's from your story, she should be along soon," he said. "Just be patient."

Eugene tried again.

"She's about twenty-two years old, with auburn hair and gray eyes, and she has a little white scar under her left eye. She's beautiful."

"Sounds like the Mayoress," said one teenage girl, and several women tittered.

"What's your story, anyway?" asked the doctor.

"My story is just that I met Sonia, she disappeared, and I want to find her."

"But what happens exactly? What comes next?"

"I don't know yet. That's why I'm looking for her."

"He's still doped," someone suggested. "He doesn't realize what's happened to him."

Furious debate broke out everywhere.

"She has a small overbite," Eugene continued, raising his voice in an effort to regain the crowd's attention. "She has a long neck. She laughs very loudly."

"Maybe he's a real tourist," said someone, and the conversational din redoubled.

"If you're really from America, then tell us something about your childhood there," someone else called out—a tall, dark man wearing a fedora and a trench coat.

"What does that have to do with anything?"

"See! Told you—"

"No reason to worry—"

"He's one of us, one of us—"

"OK!" said Eugene. "I was born at New York Hospital on a leap year. My mother died when I was young and I was raised by my father, who is Italian and speaks very little English. We didn't have a great relationship."

"The most predictable details!"

"He's barely his own person. A cliché. The Mayor is getting senile."

"My first-grade teacher was Ms. Martin," continued Eugene. "My second-grade teacher was Ms. Murphy. My third-grade teacher . . ."

He could tell that this was rattling some of the townspeople. He recited all the phone numbers of his high school friends that he could remember, and then their birthdays.

"A long story, perhaps."

"A novella. Maybe a realist novel. Facts and meaningless minutiae posing as reality."

Eugene gave his Social Security number; his mother's maiden name; his birthday; his zip code; his shoe size; his SAT scores; the name of every girl he had ever kissed. The crowd listened intently, straining to hear every word. Finally, to the great consternation of his audience, Eugene recited historical facts and math equations; he gave the names of the last five Super Bowl champions and the members of the New York Mets' starting rotation. He listed Supreme Court justices, gave Alvaro's recipe for rice and beans, and talked about the last movie he'd seen. His audience went silent.

"He's not one of us."

"He's an intruder."

"Villain! Outsider! Alien!"

The crowd moved in closer. A bodybuilder was pounding his fist into his open palm. A cowboy reached for his holster. A matronly woman with blood in her eye rolled up her sleeves.

"Criminal!"

"Gangster!"

"Demon!"

"Chiseler! Pornographer! Slave!"

"Thief!"

"Wait! Wait!" A hoarse, bright female voice rang out. "Leave him alone!"

She jostled through the churning crowd, rushing toward Eugene. He yelled her name.

"Sonia!"

3

For one, Mr. Schmitz has to tell Rutherford about Daniel. Daniel is a fraud, a demon. He is *not* a friend—and he's certainly not his son.

Mr. Schmitz then has to explain to Rutherford that he sent Daniel back to the apartment to squat there until the cops, whom he telephoned, come to arrest him. A nice man from the hospital will, for a small fee, collect all Rutherford's clothes, private effects, and necessary books (the American ones, that is) and he will send them to our new home as soon as we give him an address.

And Mr. Schmitz has to tell him about his trip to Italy, and the funeral that preceded it, and the long months of nighttime visits to the hospital and cereal dinners and catatonic walks through the midsummer swelter around Central Park's Harlem Meer, during which, in his mindless state, he sometimes dropped his cigarette and broke into a sprint.

But most of all, he has to tell Rutherford about Agnes. Now that she's gone, he can discuss with his friend her irrational anxieties and fears. He can explain how, though there was little tenderness between them most of the day, there was a stretch of night—from about midnight until five in the morning—in which she became a different person altogether. Rutherford never saw this side of her. During these hours she would weep or laugh loudly while writing in a small blue leather journal. Mr. Schmitz couldn't find the journal while she was alive, or after her death, despite ransacking the house for it. Her inner thoughts had been beyond his reach, like a star that only came out in the early hours before dawn, spectral and distant.

Mr. Schmitz also has a number of questions for Rutherford. How, for instance, has he managed to forget his native language completely, while acquiring perfect fluency in Italian? But Schmitz will wait until Rutherford regains his speech faculties. And his consciousness.

Mr. Schmitz feels uneasy with the responsiblity of controlling the flow of conversation. He is used to Rutherford's booming, authoritative tones, his tall tales, jokes, and antic digressions. His first few monologic sallies are delivered in a high-pitched stutter, interrupted by long, painful stretches of silence.

"Oh Rutherford? Are you listening?

"Should I just start talking? Like *this*?" His voice cracks. Then, in a baritone: "Like this?"

He is encouraged by the way Rutherford's brainwave levels respond to his voice, jumping and jagging at each syllable. Mr. Schmitz flattens his rumpled sweater against his chest with the edge of his palm, swallows a small ball of phlegm, and leans toward his friend.

"When I first met Agnes," he says, "I was a sophomore at Lancaster County High School, playing the trombone for the school band. She was just a freshman, but she came over to me across the football field, grabbed the instrument out of my hands, and started playing a fanfare right in my face. You didn't know it, but she was once spontaneous and alive. One thing I've learned in these last months, while you've been gone, is that grief can take different shapes. And if it's powerful enough, it can deform you."

On the LED display, the blips skid and burst into green fireworks. And when he tells the story of his first visit to the home of Agnes's parents—when he inexplicably addressed his future mother-in-law as "sir"—Rutherford's brainwaves ignite into playful, rolling currents. At Mr. Schmitz's account of their first night of lovemaking—a comedy of horrors more than errors—the green light wiggles sympathetically, even though the comatose Rutherford lies insensible, breathing at long, regular intervals.

We can go anywhere in the world," says Mr. Schmitz the next day, during visiting hours, after the nurse has left the room. "Ferrara, for instance, where the bicycles glide. Or Perugia, with that endless view."

The LED is unresponsive this morning. Its desultory squiggles indicate a state of minimal—fetal, really—brain activity.

"What about an eating tour of Italy? Just like after the war. Bologna first, then Florence . . . Rome and Capri?"

Nothing. It occurs to Mr. Schmitz that Rutherford may not particularly relish the idea of a culinary tour if the meals have to be fed to him intravenously. Mr. Schmitz begins to despair.

"Are you there, Rutherford?" He thumps his friend's chest with a meaty forefinger. The brainwaves undulate as indistinctly as the surface of the sea.

The nurse enters to find the American visitor sobbing silently.

Tears fall from the pouches of his cheeks, splattering on the linoleum floor and splashing on his beige slacks. She apologizes for her interruption and politely reminds him that visiting hours will end in five minutes.

"It feels like it was just the other day that we met in Udine, and danced with the country girls in Ternova," says Mr. Schmitz, more to himself than to his friend. "I was so innocent then. Brave too."

Through his pall of tears, he catches some kind of blurry activity over Rutherford's head. He wipes his eyes and looks more closely—it's an LED supernova, green flares exploding in a dark cathode sky. Mr. Schmitz knows where he has to take Rutherford. He just needs to figure out how to get him out of the hospital.

4

Sonia grabbed Eugene by the back of his neck and pulled him close, in a gesture that seemed tinged with equal parts affection and protection.

"Hold on to me," she said into his ear. "No matter what they do."

"You smell nice," he said, closing his eyes.

She touched his hand. They passed through the crowd and down the street beyond. The townspeople turned and watched them.

"Let's stop them!" someone yelled.

"Are you crazy? That's the Mayor's woman!"

"She can do whatever she wants."

"What she wants, the Mayor wants. So shut it!"

"I . . . I don't know what to say," said Eugene. He moved closer to her, put his fingers lightly on her hip.

"Don't say anything foolish," said Sonia. "C'mon."

"I've thought about you every day since you left. When you

stopped sending your letters I got worried. I thought you'd vanished. I think about you all the time. Every day."

"I'm fine," she said, looking at her feet. Her speech was wary and short. She wore her hair in a new style. It had increased in volume as well as length, curls piled on curls. It bobbed on her shoulders in ringlets, all golden except for a single one near the back of her head, which had turned bright white. The difference surprised him, made him uneasy. He wondered if it indicated any internal change.

"I had to leave," she said. "I couldn't take care of my father anymore. I love him, of course I do, but as you know, he's a demanding, difficult man. He needed more than I had. He required someone full-time who could cater to him. I'm twenty-two. I love him but I can't do that."

"But why'd you come here?"

"Why? Because the Mayor is here." She paused, taking him in, his soiled clothes and rough, unshaven face. Eugene could never grow a beard correctly, but the bristles over his lip were dark and full, giving him an unintentional resemblance to Alvaro.

"It's so good to see you," she said.

"So he's here? Eakins?"

"He's here. I was wrong before. He never died. I feel ridiculous that I made up all those letters to my dad. He was probably getting real letters from Eakins at the same time."

"I don't believe it. He's still alive? Can I meet him?"

"Actually, he wants to meet you."

"Did you tell him about me?" Eugene was suddenly envious of Sonia for being able to spend so much time with the old master. "Why do you call him the Mayor?"

"That's what he's called here. It's amazing how easily one accepts the unacceptable in Idaville."

She gave him a sad, crooked smile. Eugene took her hand, touched those slim cold fingers. He thought she might say something else, but then she glanced away and absently rubbed the scar below her eye.

"Do you think about me?" he said.

"I think about you always," she said, turning to face him again. She seemed to relax for the first time. "But why did you come here? Did my father send you?"

"I wanted to come. I wanted to find you."

"I'm not how you remember, probably."

"You're even more beautiful." Eugene felt mindlessly, pleasantly adrift. "Do you remember the morning we spent walking through Riverside Park? Stanka and the mud people?"

She turned her hand over in his, so that their fingers interlocked. He gripped her tight. They passed house after house, each painted the same dark red hue, the color of a bloodstain.

"There's someone you should meet."

"I just want to be with you."

"Follow me," she said. He recognized something in her expression that reminded him of the look she gave him on the muddy marble floor, when the silt was dripping down her calves in rivulets.

"Look ahead," she said. "That's where he lives. The Casa Contenta. Isn't it unworldly?"

Fifty yards ahead, past the black iron gate, the gravel gave way to a redbrick lane. Spruce trees, planted close together, picked up on either side of the road where the houses ended. Through the leaves the yellowing horizon shone through with sharp pinpricks of light. Farther ahead, Eugene could make out a dark, hulking stone immensity, veiled by a faint blue mist.

"This is good," said Sonia. "To see you." She slowed her pace and regarded him closely, as if she was trying to detect something in his expression. "I didn't expect it would be like this."

"Me neither," said Eugene. "But I'm happy now."

She gave him a wide smile.

"You smell nice," he said.

"Oh yeah? Like what?"

"Like clean clothes, skin, apricot shampoo . . . a sleepy type of smell."

"You should have seen me when I first got here. I was covered in moss and mud and slime."

"How did you get here, anyway? Did you come up the Carso all by yourself?"

"I had a funny trip up here. A girl I met in Trieste, who was from Idaville, led me here. She was . . . strange. Different from anyone I've ever met. It takes a long time to adjust to this place." She brushed the hair off her eyes. Eugene touched her hip again and this time she let his fingers stay there, lightly perched, a finger-shaped butterfly.

"Who is this girl?" he asked.

"You'll meet her. She was born here. Her name is Stasia. She wants to meet you too."

Sonia torqued several pulleys and pressed a panel hidden in the wall behind a thicket of ivy. The gate swung open. As they walked onto the Mayor's property, Sonia told Eugene all that had happened since she arrived in Italy; of her days spent with Frank Lang; of Kasia and Marco and Poldi; of her night flight with Stasia and their trip through the Carso—a vineyard, a lurking vintner named Goran, and their rocky descent into the valley. As they walked, the red bricks seemed to brighten in the falling light, turning orange and pink. Eugene felt as though he had lost control of himself. He could only follow Sonia wherever she led him. It was a liberating, if harrowing, sensation.

"When we got to Idaville, Stasia ran through the town but couldn't find her boyfriend. I was afraid to be left alone, but the villagers greeted me like some kind of princess—it was like they had been prepared for my arrival. I didn't really know how to respond. Then they led me to the mansion." She gestured ahead. "I entered a huge hall, with a long table lit by candles and walls covered with tapestries. Connie was sitting at the end of the table." She laughed nervously. "The first thing you notice is his size. I thought I knew everything there was to know about him, but I wasn't expecting this. He's gargantuan. I had never seen anything like it. He's even bigger than my father said he was. I think . . ." Her laughter died, and she fell silent for a moment. "I think he never stopped growing."

The mansion lurched out of the mist. Eugene's initial impression was that it looked better suited for purposes of fortification than domestication. Bright white walls rose three stories from grass to sky, broken by gold and green stained-glass windows divided by transoms, and high freestone ramparts, capped by embattled parapets and machicolations decorated with Gothic details. A single tower rose high on one side, like the Uffizi. Sonia pointed to this tower and said, with a mixture of pride and embarrassment, "That's where I'm staying."

They pushed through the heavy black door and entered an airless, claustrophobic foyer that was dark except for the flicker of candles. Sonia led him by the hand through heavy velvet curtains and into a long, high-ceilinged hall, which felt cramped despite its capacious volume, because of a gridlock of heavy, ornate furniture. Colored-glass windows admitted, through their heavy panes, dim maculae of light that settled on the cushions and tables like sludge. The wall opposite the windows was paneled with faded, ancient tapestries, from which Eugene could make out faint details here and there—a sword, a bucking horse, a scroll of ancient text. A wooden banquet table some hundred places long, covered with a yellowed dimity tablecloth, ran the length of the hall. Sofas and chairs stood along the walls. They did not look as if they had been sat upon in many years. Swirls of dust seemed to emanate from every surface and shifted slowly in the air.

And through the gloom, on the far side of the long hall, Eugene could sense a presence, if not see it—a massive, indiscernible shadow lurking over the end of the table. He grabbed Sonia's arm and dragged her back out of the room.

"Was that him?" he said in a whisper.

"He's expecting you."

"You're coming, right?"

"No. I think you should have some time alone."

"But we've barely had any time together yet. There's so much we have to talk about."

"I know, darling," she said, and held his neck in her cool hands. He flushed and leaned in to her. She pressed her hips against him. They kissed, close, and a current ran down Eugene's spine, tapping each vertebra as it passed through.

Behind them, the front door opened with an explosion of

light, and Enzo and Stasia appeared. Their arms were wrapped around each other in what appeared an uncomfortable pose, as if they had been afraid to withdraw from their initial embrace.

"Eugene!" shouted Enzo, ecstatic to see him again. "LOOK WHO I FOUND!" Eugene tried to smile, but it felt awkward on his face. "I heard you were here. I'm sorry not to have greeted you when you arrived—we've been reacquainting ourselves."

At this Stasia kissed Enzo on his neck and, as if she had tasted something of surprising richness, moved lip by lip up to his jaw and ear, the lingering spread of saliva marking her path.

"Eugene is going to meet the Mayor," said Sonia, glaring at Stasia. Stasia did not notice this, her eyes buried in the scruff of Enzo's nape.

"The Mayor is a remarkable man," said Enzo. "I was wrong before. He is a glory. He loves all of his children."

"I'm not his child," said Eugene.

"We're all the Mayor's children," said Enzo, reassuring him.

"Enzo, Stasia—let's go outside." Sonia pushed the couple back to the front door. "I'm sorry, Eugene, but you need to talk to him alone. Isn't this what you always wanted? To meet your hero, face to face?"

"I guess so," said Eugene. "Though not like this." But it was true—he had often imagined meeting Eakins before, had played the scene over in his head. He had a sick feeling about it now, however. Like he was walking into a trap. He couldn't quite tell whether Sonia's tone was sincere or mocking.

Sonia looked deep into him, as if to fix the image in her memory. "I'll see you as soon as you're done."

"And then we'll leave together?"

"Come here." She was clearly moved, and hugged him close.

And then she left with Enzo and Stasia, so that Eugene was alone in the foyer's flickering darkness. He tried to open the front door again, but it was locked from the outside and the laughing voices of Sonia and the others already seemed far away.

While he waited for his eyes to adjust, he stared deep into the shadows that flashed against the wall. He saw in them Alvaro and nurse Betty, mid-chrysalis; next to this he saw Sonia as she once was, mud dripping from her shoulders and belly, her hand groping toward him; he saw a winding trail through a cave embedded in a cliff; a jungle village in the Cordillera Central foothills, where Jacinto and Alsa hid from her evil father; and finally, most clearly now, an old man leaning against a balustrade, looking off into a dirty river, and dreaming of his son. When this image became so clear that he could not bear it anymore, Eugene let out a low growl and pushed through the door to the great hall, racing toward the enormous presence that was seated at the end of the table, awaiting him.

5

Mr. Schmitz drives up the Carso's dirt access road with a gym bag on his lap. The bag contains a laptop computer, an electroencephalogram control module with an LED screen, a receiver box, a plastic baggie stuffed with tangled electrode wires, a battery pack, a four-ounce tube of Lectron conductivity gel, a twenty-milliliter syringe, and a fourteen-gauge needle, all bought from a disgruntled nurse at the hospital for the equivalent, in lire, of $400, thanks to the strength of the American dollar. For an extra $400, she took a cigarette break while Mr. Schmitz rolled Rutherford out in a wheelchair through the back door. Using Rutherford's passport and Italian driver's license, he rented a car—a supermini turquoise Fiat Punto. Mr. Schmitz clutches the gym bag to his chest in the tightest and most gentle embrace he can manage while guiding the steering wheel with his other hand, but the mountain road doesn't make it easy for him. The car halts and jitters, and the gym bag hits so violently against Mr. Schmitz's chest that he wonders whether the subsequent rattling noises, indicative of severe dislodgment and fracture, are emanating from the medical equipment or from his rib cage. Rutherford's face falls flush against the window, then against his friend's shoulder—in a misplaced pose of affection—and finally it is sent nodding forward and back, giving him the aspect of a man who is completely satisfied with the course his life is taking.

Several hours into the ascent, all the hubcaps are gone. The Punto coughs warnings of irreparable engine damage, to add to its other injuries: scratched roof (courtesy of a low-hanging pine branch), a smashed headlight (from an errant tree stump that encroached on the edge of the road), a cracked, bloodstained windshield (crashed into by an idiot sparrow, fatally surprised by the hard reflective surface), and a deflating tire that makes the chassis tilt toward the cliff side of the road, which would afford Rutherford, were he sensate, a breathtaking view of the steep valley directly below them.

With one final lurch, the Punto arrives on a level roadway, and the brick houses of Ternova appear alongside it. To Mr. Schmitz, it's like seeing a childhood friend for the first time as an adult: slightly corrupted, wizened, but recognizable at last. The town—if such an honorific can be applied to it—is six dilapidated brick cottages, each two stories high, standing side-by-side along the road skirting the cliff's edge. The cottages are just as Mr. Schmitz remembers them, only their walls are darker and pockmarked, and their roofs' terra-cotta shingles have blanched in the sun. Two newer buildings have been adjoined, their slate-gray walls and flat roofs representative of a particular architectural vogue popular in Italy during the 1970s; but the arrangement of cottages, and the stone paths leading between them, up into the hills, are just as Mr. Schmitz recalls. What he remembers most vividly lies beyond the last of these buildings, at the end of the town, where the street rises on a slight incline to its highest point: the piazza. It is paved in red-and-yellow checkerboard squares, and at its crest there stands a small monastery. More than fifty years earlier, Mr. Schmitz and Rutherford held dances there, entertaining the daughters of the local farmers. Roused by the twinkle of the church organ playing a profane tune, the girls would sneak out in the middle of the night and head to the monastery, giddy at their own audacity. There they danced with the American soldiers, cheek to cheek, lit by the yellow glow of a hundred candles.

Mr. Schmitz recalls how the local farmers and winemakers would convene after dinner each night for involved debates in the piazza; how a group of women would cluck their tongues and promenade arm-in-arm down the stone paths, calling up to other women, who leaned out of second-story windows, their arms crossed and perched on the sills. There was so much commotion that they could pretend not to notice the regiment of American soldiers bivouacked in the town, crowding the local tavern. But this late summer afternoon, the town is silent. The grocery is closed, even though it is midweek; so is the old tavern. There is no one in the street. There aren't even any parked cars.

"Do you remember all this?" asks Mr. Schmitz. "Rutherford?" Rutherford's eyes are open, staring upward.

"To our left the old taverna," continues Mr. Schmitz. "To our right the red-and-yellow marble piazza. It's still shiny and smooth, just as it was. And the monastery—our private dance hall!"

At the foot of the piazza, Mr. Schmitz opens the trunk of the Punto and pulls out a collapsed wheelchair. He painstakingly reassembles it, forcing the metal joints into place, smoothing the blue canvas seat, and clucking to himself with satisfaction when it all clicks together. Under great physical strain, he drags Rutherford's heavy body into the chair, the patient's floppy limbs thwacking Mr. Schmitz across the mouth and chest. Mr. Schmitz wheels Rutherford through the piazza so that he can face the view.

"Ternova," he says into Rutherford's ear. "We're back, old boy."

Mr. Schmitz hustles to retrieve the gym bag from the car. He sets it on the marble tiles and pulls down on the zipper, his mouth screwed up and spittled with concentration. Out of the bag spill shattered electrodes, loose screws, and torn tubing. A round plastic widget springs up at Mr. Schmitz, leaps over his shoulder, and rolls down the remaining length of the piazza, where it slides under the barricade and over the cliff. Mr. Schmitz looks at Rutherford and, for the first time all day, begins to think about where they are, and how far away that is.

6

Constance Eakins spoke, and his voice was legend.

"Speak," he said in a gentle tone, though it seemed as loud as the shout of a hundred hale men. "Don't come any closer. Stand there—if you're a man—and SPEAK to the Mayor."

Eugene couldn't say a thing. He couldn't even walk—the man's voice had stopped him so abruptly that the soles of his sneakers made a squeaking noise against the floor. He had to remind himself to inhale. As he did, he noticed that a vast pile of plates, bowls, glasses, and cutlery was amassed before him, bearing a quantity of food and drink fit for a full banquet. Except for one plate, on which there lay a black revolver.

"The whores at the Trieste naval base," said the voice, "call me 'Constant' Eakins. But you can call me Connie." In addition to its sheer volume, the man's voice was distinguished by a patrician inflection, a modulation that resembled a British accent—though Eugene could detect in his powerful baritone, especially at the end of sentences, a Southern lilt.

"Is it really you?"

"Are you a man?" The giant chortled. It occurred to Eugene that this person, whoever he was, was drunk.

"Mr. Eakins," he began, "my name is Eugene. I work as an assistant for Abe Chisholm. I'm also good friends with his daughter, Sonia."

"Isn't she a beautiful child?" said Eakins, sighing.

"Yes. I'm also a great admirer of your work. *Dolman Hardy* is my favorite novel, and the essay 'Why Men Live' was really important to me too."

Eakins did not reply at first, but Eugene could hear him breathing through his mouth—a reverberant, quavering huff. An arm like an elephant's trunk, reticulated by blue, ropelike veins, emerged from the gloom in a pardoning gesture.

"It is always gratifying to learn that one's vision has been greeted by a glimmer of recognition in the mind of a reader," said Eakins, yawning ferociously as he did so. Then his voice deepened. "It's almost as sweet," he continued, "as the sight of one's private phantoms writhing and clawing into existence, becoming real. Walking straight out of your brain and onto the earth.

"Would you like a glass of cold white wine? I always drink one at sundown. Secret of my longevity. Cold wine and a raw onion each day. The Slovenians taught me that."

Eugene tried to guess at Eakins's proportions from the darkened shapes that heaved and settled over the table. Not knowing exactly where he should direct his gaze, he looked searchingly up and down—though mostly up. Despite being seated, Eakins seemed to be speaking from a height greater than Eugene's six feet.

"It's an honor to meet you," said Eugene. He struggled to find the right words. "No writer has had such a tremendous impact

on my views of the world, on the way I perceive human relation-
ships, and on the possibilities of the English language."

Again Eakins's hand lifted, as if to grant a supplication, and
lowered again. It landed in a giant bowl of porridge. The bowl
was lifted into the darkness where his face might have been.
There was then a loud and prolonged slurping noise. When the
bowl was placed back on the table, it was empty.

"Can I offer you something to eat?"

"No, thank you. But that's very generous of you."

"More than enough here, if you change your mind," said Eakins, and another platter—over a dozen stalks of asparagus indi-
vidually wrapped in prosciutto—rose from the table, was emptied
into the shadows, and set back down, the serving fork clattering
against the china.

"I've been expecting you," said Eakins. "Abe mentioned you'd
be here in several of his letters, but I didn't respond to any of
them. He's rather sore at me over this point, I'm afraid. But I can't
constantly be menaced by his project."

"The biography? I've been helping him conduct research for
it. That's the reason Sonia came here in the first place—to make
sure that you were still receiving his letters. And capable of responding."

"I am *beyond* capable," said Eakins, in a sullen drawl. "Agata
learned that as soon as she got here." Eakins laughed and shifted
magnificently in his chair.

"I have something for you," he said, and his meaty fist swung into
the arc of light again, this time clutching a sheaf of envelopes.

"Abe's letters to you," observed Eugene.

"Wrong. The letters are addressed to you. From your father."

The fist flung the package onto the table. It landed on top of a silver tray that had been cleared of all its contents except the garnish. The envelopes bore the Florida address Eugene had given his father and were marked with so many forwarding stamps that the different inks bled together. Each envelope had been bounced from Florida to Alvaro's apartment in New York, as Eugene had arranged; from there Alvaro had forwarded them to Chisholm's brownstone; Abe had requested forwarding service to Frank Lang's bookstore in Trieste, at which point they bounced up to Eakins. The final forwarding address read simply:

> The Mayor
> Casa Contenta
> Idaville
> Carso
> Italy
> DELIVER BY HAND—BOBBY BAZLEN

Eugene's hands trembled as he removed a crumpled, food-stained letter from the first envelope. He was acutely conscious of Eakins's heavy breaths, each one like the shudder of a dying sea mammal.

In the first letter, Eugene's father sent best wishes for his move to Florida, and reported that life in New York was quiet and peaceful. He said that he was trying to adapt to life without his son—a statement that struck Eugene as uncharacteristically warm and personal. In the second letter, mailed seven days later, his father said that he had spent a lot of the previous week walking around his neighborhood, and taking in the fine views of the river. The next letters, each a week apart—he seemed to write every Sunday—detailed the worsening state of his chronic lower-back pain, his efforts to join an Italian-American community center, and his burgeoning relationship with a female friend he had met in physical therapy. In the last paragraph of each letter he inquired after Eugene with growing desperation. Was he happy? Was he making friends? Would he deign to respond to one of his father's letters? Eugene flipped faster and faster through the packet, watching as this final paragraph grew in length and ultimately overtook the rest of the letters' contents. Where are you? Why don't you reply? I think I can understand your silence, because—and here his father would come up with various explanations, ranging from the practical to the wildly imaginative. Anger at me; sadness at not ever having a mother; natural post-adolescent rebelliousness or carelessness; self-imposed exile, taking after his father. Ultimately, Signor Brentani settled on the justification that seemed most logical, and most horrible, to him. Eugene's silence was punishment for his father's own silence, his inability to communicate with Eugene throughout his childhood. Signor Brentani hoped that this punishment—Eugene's refusal to respond to his letters—would lead the way to some sort of resolution. If not now, then in the future. If not in his lifetime, then perhaps in Eugene's. He begged Eugene not to make the same mistake, and pass on this legacy of silence to his own children. Eugene was shocked at his father's sudden outpouring of speech, of emotion, of self-analysis. He shuffled through the letters, rereading passages and leaning against the banquet table for support.

As much as Eugene was absorbed in the letters, he could not help but feel that he was being closely watched by the giant seated in the darkness several feet away from him. Eakins's breathing grew ever louder.

"Have a drink," said Eakins. Eugene tipped a nearby carafe into a large goblet and knocked it back, splashing his neck with the wine in the process. He noticed two of Eakins's fingers reaching for a plate of overstuffed sausages, and for a moment he could not distinguish between the digits and the meat tubes.

"Silence from a parent," said Eakins, "is a form of abuse. I bet you'll wish you never received those letters. To realize how invested he is in your relationship only now—and now it is too late—it must be terrifying."

"It's true," said Eugene, in a whisper. But was it really too late?

Eakins moved into the light. The cushion of his chair wheezed pneumatically, the table jolted, and plates shook and smashed to the ground, spilling wild boar terrine, fried mozzarella, and moist, pockmarked strips of tripe. Eugene realized that many of these dishes had been resting in the valley of Eakins's lap.

Eugene directed his gaze at the place where he expected Eakins's face would appear, but he could not make shape of the form—squat and cylindrical like a drum. Only after scrutiny did Eugene realize that he was staring at Eakins's chest, swaddled in a black velvet robe the size of a theater curtain. Recalibrating, Eugene looked higher, and still higher, until he finally arrived at the great man's ferocious countenance. It was shocking to behold.

Eugene could just barely recognize Eakins from the author photographs that appeared on the dust jackets of his books. Amazingly, his face didn't seem to have aged very greatly. It only seemed to have gotten larger, as if it had been injected with steroids, or intubated with balloons. Certainly he no longer had the pure, fair skin of his youth; it was drier now—saurian, but not wrinkled. Nor did he still have the famously pale blond hair; it was now an orangey white. The thin, wiry eyelashes were gone entirely and his nose had taken on the dimensions of a Friulian turnip. His chin was no longer cleft, but ditched; the dime-sized mole had appreciated tenfold into a silver dollar. His cheeks were ripe blankets of flesh, his ears like giant barnacled oysters. Even his hair had been subjected to this principle of expansion. Though neatly arrayed on his head in a classic style—parted on the left and smoothly combed over—its bulk was such that it gave his head a tangerine aura.

But most gruesome were his eyes, which bore out of his enlarged skull with a manic, fervent propulsion, as if they wanted to pounce on Eugene—or punch him, since they were each the size of a small fist.

"Did you really come all this way just to see Agata?" asked Eakins. "Or to meet me? Or were you trying to escape your father?"

"I want to be with Sonia."

Eakins smiled, revealing two shining fleets of white teeth the size of dominoes.

"I know that's not true. Don't say that again. If you weren't running away from your father, then there's one other likely justification for your leaving. Pothos."

Eugene couldn't bear to stare into Eakins's face any longer. Those bulging eyes conveyed a haunting combination of acute concentration and internal rage. Eugene focused instead on a platter of stuffed pheasant.

"Lust?" asked Eugene. "You mean lust?"

"No! But just as noble. Pothos. It describes a kind of restlessness: the burning desire to see and to know new things and places for the sake of knowing."

"I know what I want. She's here." The stuffed pheasant was missing its head. Judging from the bite marks, it seemed to have been taken in a single chomp.

"I was young once too," said Eakins. His voice grew less severe—became jaunty, even—when he fell into speeches about his past, or when he wanted to impart wisdom. "Sure, I chased women across continents, but these pursuits were all made in the service of my pothos. The women were taken, in time, but I was after the thrill of the quest, the adventures along the way, the false starts and dead ends. That is how I found myself hunting for wild moose with a one-armed man outside Bratislava. Eating brains in Kathmandu. Murdering a prostitute in Nairobi."

Eugene stared at the revolver on its china dish.

"You murdered a prostitute? I don't remember that from any of your memoirs."

"It was suppressed. The point is, I was after experience, and although I had terrific amounts of sex along the way, I found it. From those experiences were born my first books. And my first bastard children. You see, you can't have anything valuable to say until you suffer—at least a little bit—the outrages of the world."

"Who said I wanted to say anything?"

"I'm no detective, but I see you've carried some papers up all this way."

Eugene regarded Alvaro's legal pad manuscript, and the dog-eared pages of his translation in his book bag. He was almost finished with it. The cannibals had seized Alsa's father, but Jacinto had saved him, earning his respect and trust. Jacinto and Alsa would be married on top of Pico Duarte, the highest mountain on the island.

"It's not mine," he said. "It's a friend's. I'm translating it for him."

"Can I take a look?"

Eugene looked up at the man's hands, filthy with some kind of yellow sauce—Hollandaise, perhaps—and flecked with chicken gristle.

"I'll wash up first," said Eakins. "Follow me."

With a small moan and several enormous gasps of breath—the way he was breathing, he would have choked in a room any smaller than the banquet hall—Eakins rose from the table, dropping the revolver into his vast velvet pocket, where it fell as silently as a penny. Eugene followed for several steps, trying to avoid looking at all the other food piled on the edge of the table: a pig's head, stewed tomatoes, blood pudding, a whole swordfish, stuffed potatoes, olives, apples, butter. A trail of breadcrumbs followed Eakins's feet, and it was only when he turned around that Eugene realized Eakins had carried some sort of baguette sandwich with him to the next room. Eakins patiently stuffed it, with both hands, deep into his throat. Then he turned on a faucet.

"Enter!" ordered Eakins, through a mouth of bread.

The room was a small bathroom, which Eakins's flesh filled nearly to capacity. He had cinched closed his bathrobe and he washed his hands in a white sink with gold faucets—though only one hand fit at a time. When he was done, Eakins led Eugene through a door into a garden behind the house. Now, in the fading sunlight, Eugene could see Eakins at his full height. His head momentarily blocked out the sun.

"I suggest you remove your sneakers," said Eakins. "The fresh grass feels lovely between the toes."

Eakins kicked off his slippers—velvet, to match his robe—and strolled into the garden, which was really a long grass field bound by boulders. Beyond the boulders lay the horizon. Under the boulders, the side of the cliff, and a thousand-foot drop to the churning waves.

"What kind of book is it?" asked Eakins, plucking the manuscript and its translation from Eugene's book bag.

"A fictionalized memoir—not my own, a friend's. He's written a story about life in a remote region of the Dominican Republic. I'm translating it into English."

They strolled across the field. The soil was moist against the soles of Eugene's feet. Over the cliff's edge ahead of them, a cloud floated at eye level, expanding and compressing like a single-celled organism.

"So you speak a good Spanish?"

"Actually it's not written in Spanish, but in an obscure dialect from the region he's from. He's talked enough about it with me, and I get the gist. He's my closest friend. We have an understanding."

"Funny," said Eakins, "I'm at work on a similar project. A new memoir. My goal is to beat Abe to finishing it. So I haven't revealed to him what happens to me in my last chapter. That's my own. He can only speculate." He flipped through the pages of Eugene's text.

"In a funny way, Eugenio, I have some paternal feeling toward you. After reading your father's correspondence, and hearing Agata talk of you—"

"Sonia? What did she say?"

"Oh, the usual, that you are a bright, charming, shy, directionless *boy*," said Eakins, emphasizing the last word. "That you may achieve something of value one day, as soon as you make up your mind to do it. And anyone dear to Agata earns my affection, given the nature of my relationship with her."

"She's like a daughter to you," said Eugene, nodding.

"Hmm. I can tell you this. You won't go home to New York after this little meeting here."

"Why do you say that? My life is there. My job with Abe. Alvaro is there."

"You don't mention your father. No matter. You would never have left if you weren't seeking something important. And I don't think it was Agata. At least not only Agata."

"Sonia."

"Not her either. I see in you something of myself when I was your age. Of course I don't mean your age exactly. What are you, nineteen?"

"Twenty-three."

"When I was twenty-three I had sired children in over three continents, trained as a merchant marine for the Yugoslavian armed forces, and published a story collection, two volumes of poetry, and my first memoir. I had been tried for treason in Jakarta, broke out of jail in Cairo, whupped Ernie within an inch of his life in a Havana mudflat—"

"I get it."

"That said, I remember when I shared your state of mind. I was seven then, and had just left home. I wish I had had some wise person to advise me. It certainly couldn't have been my father: an ineffectual underling at a seafood cannery on Lake Pontchartrain, a small, greedy, and yes, *silent* man, whose body smelled like tunafish and acrid tin and who once saved for three years to buy a shack made of wood."

Eakins was heaving uncontrollably now, and leaned on Eugene's shoulder. Eugene strained to support his prodigious weight. The breeze from the sea flared up and lifted the ends of Eakins's orange hair off his healthy bronze scalp. Eakins recovered his breath, and gradually the pressure on Eugene's shoulder subsided.

"You mentioned the last chapter of your memoir," said Eugene. "Will that explain why you live in the same town as Keftir the Blind? That he's actually a real human being?"

"Ha! I'm flattered. I'll tell you about my last chapter, all right."

"Why?"

"You're ideally suited to hear my secret. That's why I brought you here."

7

A warm, powerful wind curls up the side of the cliff, making the shutters of Ternova's houses clatter and the pine trees whistle. Mr. Schmitz can't see anyone behind these shutters but he feels the presence of watchful eyes.

He wheels Rutherford back from the precipice of the piazza to the town's main street. At the door to the old tavern he knocks, but no one answers. He leans his forehead against the darkened storefront window, his eyes darting about in a vain effort to locate some evidence of life.

"What a funny thing has happened to our poor Ternova."

Rutherford sits still in his wheelchair. His head hangs over to one side and his eyelashes are stuck together with dried mucus. The down on the tongue-shaped mark on his face has grown coarser.

Mr. Schmitz throws his body against the door. No response, just the hollow echo of his collision. Do not panic, he tells himself, but he has a feeling of something crawling behind his ears. He leans his full weight against the door and it creaks open.

Mr. Schmitz finds himself in a living room, furnished with a kind of shabby luxury. There is a musty sofa that is missing all of its cushions but one, a chipped bronze floor lamp with a torn green shade, and two pink damask chairs facing away from each other, next to a baize-topped poker table. A long filthy mirror in a dark oak frame reflects to the room an obscure image of itself. On one side of the room, there is a small door that leads to the tavern.

"You'll be fine right here," says Mr. Schmitz, wheeling Rutherford into the room. He pulls the floor lamp's gold bead chain and, to his surprise—and momentary alarm—the bulb casts the room in a dim marigold hue.

"Hello?" he calls out. "Buongiorno? *Is there anyone here?*"

Mr. Schmitz walks through the side door into the tavern. The room smells like stale hops. Chairs are stacked upside down on all the tables, and a newspaper is spread out on the bar. It's *Il Poliglotto*, containing articles written in Italian, Slovenian, English, and German, and a Sunday supplement written in Triestino dialect. The date on the top of the page is nearly two years earlier. The headline reads, in Italian:

TONGUE TRANSPLANT SUCCESSFUL:
LIFE IS SWEET AGAIN FOR MEDEAZZA MAN

Mr. Schmitz puzzles over this for a minute, scanning the photograph—a smiling man eating gelato—for meaning. But then, at the bottom of the page, a single column of text catches his attention:

TERNOVA ABANDONED

by Carla Boccata

Ternova, a far-flung hamlet hidden in the southern-facing side of the Carso, will be abandoned at the end of this year's harvest by its three remaining citizens, Giovanni Pertucci, 72; Lucia Lancarotto, 90; and Graziella Faenza, 73.

"We're too old to spend another winter up here on our own," said Ms. Faenza. "What would happen if there's an emergency, or if Lucia has another attack?" she asked, alluding to a stroke suffered by Ms. Lancarotto last spring. "When would they find us?"

The three remaining Ternoviani say that they will move in with their children, who long ago relocated to Trieste to raise their own families.

The rugged terrain of the Carso has never yielded great amounts of produce, and life in its villages has always been isolated and meager. But since the construction of paved roads in the 1980s, the towns of this mountainous region have been put into regular contact with modern life, often with negative results. Ternova joins a growing list of Carsican villages that have been abandoned in recent years, as younger generations head to the city in search of a higher standard of living and better opportunities for prosperity.

Ternova was best known for its small cathedral, the San Giusto di Trieste, celebrated for its checkered marble piazza, which overlooks the Carso plateau and the Adriatic Sea. High points of Ternova's history included:

a mention of the village by the great Friulian poet Lan-gustino (1205–1234), in his ode, "There are so many small towns in the mountains/in which of them hides my love?" It was the birthplace of noted mountain climber Anton di Brusca (1860–1934), the third man in recorded history to climb Marmolada, the highest point of the Dolomites, in 1887. And it served as a staging post for an auxiliary regiment of the Allied military forces during World War II.

"We are sad to leave our beautiful village," said Ms. Faenza. "But it would be sadder to die here. Because no one would find us for a very, very long time."

Mr. Schmitz sets the paper down on the bar, looks up, and shudders. Rutherford is staring at him from his wheelchair in the living room. His eyes are wide open and his mouth is twisted into something resembling a grin.

But Rutherford is not awake. It is a trick, perhaps, of the nervous system, or the product of an errant synapse firing in his addled brain, that has made Rutherford's features take this shape. He has shifted in his chair, like anyone might during sleep. And that makes sense to Mr. Schmitz. Why, after all, should an unconscious body behave any more predictably than a normal slumbering one? And yet . . .

Mr. Schmitz spends the better part of the next hour trying to provoke Rutherford into moving again.

"Did you think I was going to leave you?" he asks, checking for a reaction. Rutherford gazes dumbly ahead, his wide smile raising the points of his fraying mustache.

"Are you afraid? Lonely? *Rutherford?*"

Rutherford's eyes do not move. They do not even dilate.

"Do you think we might . . . die here?"

Rutherford stares on.

". . . and that no one . . . no one . . ."

Mr. Schmitz concludes that Rutherford spent whatever was left of his strength when he moved his face into its current contortion.

Mr. Schmitz tries to assemble the EEG machine. But the electrodes are hopelessly tangled, the control module rattles, and the Lectron tube has been punctured, smearing conductivity gel all over the battery pack. Mr. Schmitz is at a loss. He leaves Rutherford and returns to the tavern. He finds a refrigerator behind the bar, opens it, and sees a six-pack of Peroni. He drinks three bottles while standing at the bar. He sits down to read the newspaper article again, and drinks a fourth. He sips the last two back in the living room, beside Rutherford, who has not stopped grinning.

Mr. Schmitz puts his hand on Rutherford's shoulder to steady himself. It occurs to Mr. Schmitz: does he really trust a machine to tell him what his friend is thinking? Mr. Schmitz is not even certain, after all, that he would know how to interpret the LED signals. There must be other ways for paralyzed men to speak. The alternative is too horrific.

From now on, Mr. Schmitz would look for other signs. He'd monitor the modulations of his friend's breathing, his pulse, the moistness of his eyes, and the temperature of his skin, in the hope of discovering new codes and signs. Even in his sleep he'd listen for Rutherford's voice.

First, however, he has to secure their new home. He raids the tavern for canned goods, tests the sink to make sure the pipes still work, and prepares the bedroom on the second floor, finding two pillows and a clean set of sheets in the closet. It is late now, but Mr. Schmitz is too excited to sleep.

He runs out into the street and knocks on the door of every house, breaking down a front gate in the process, with a shoulder-first bodythrust. He finds nothing but more canned food, which he retrieves and brings back to the tavern.

"It's better this way," says Mr. Schmitz. "We will build this town anew."

Mr. Schmitz lies in fetal position on the pool table for some time after that, passing in and out of sleep throughout the night. At one point he retrieves the blanket from upstairs and spreads it so that it covers Rutherford and, to a lesser extent, himself. Night up here in the mountains is long and silent. It's as if even the sparrows are afraid to fly so high.

8

"Every time you reveal a secret to someone," said Eakins, "part of you dies. One knows oneself by one's secrets. If you reveal everything, you're empty—just a collection of facts in other people's minds.

"For years, I've been giving away my secrets in my books. Sometimes directly, as in my memoirs, and sometimes indirectly, as in my poetry and fiction. I reveal my darkest perversions, my guilt, my fear, and my anger, no matter how irrational or poorly it reflects upon me. I have been killing myself slowly. But it's not all a loss. In return, I have gained the secret of eternal life. What I'm going to tell you is not only my most coveted secret, it is also the key to my immortality."

Eugene did not listen without skepticism to this line of talk, but he nodded along, not wishing to betray Eakins's trust—or arouse his anger.

"Please go on. I promise not to repeat anything you tell me."

"I don't really care what you repeat, God *damn* it," said Eakins. "I'm writing all this down in the last chapter of my next book, so soon the world will know it. No one, however, will believe it. Except you.

"As it was reported in the press, I disappeared from public view one summer thirty years ago. I had last been seen in Duino, on my way to hike in the Carso mountains. The trip went as planned—I found a trail leading up from the Timavo River, and followed it through the forest, past Aurisina and Ternova. The path led in a loop, but when I spotted the peak of a limestone mountain through a clear patch in the woods, I decided to chop through the brush to reach it. At the edge of the precipice, I spotted this inland valley, with its beech groves and crisscrossing streams, surrounded by four additional mountain peaks. And at the rear end of the valley, I saw a gateway to the sea. As far as I could tell, the valley was completely uninhabited.

"People assume that man has trampled every single square inch of earth, but this isn't true. There are lots of places on this world that are unexplored, and not just the peaks of the Rocky Mountains in British Columbia or the polar ice cap or the ocean floor of the Marianas Trench. Most men, when faced with the option, choose to trample land that has been already heavily trampled over. There are far more Alexanders and Corteses than there are Lewises and Clarks. Even so, few explorers would ever think of trekking into a region so travel-worn as this one, a swath of land that sits on the border of the most heavily touristed country in the world.

"I hiked down the cliff face into the valley, my traveling sack full of enough provisions to last me another month. I was stunned by the rough beauty of the land—the scattered plane trees, the rangy cordgrass, the shrubs of juniper and cashew.

"I was walking through this valley when I heard, from behind a little mound, a horrible, wet cough. It was a man—a disheveled, wounded drunk with purple sores on his mouth and his arm in a paper sling. He coughed and spat and tumbled gently down the hill, finally rolling to a rest at my feet. I realized—and had even known from the moment I had heard his cough—that I had met this man before. And yet I could not remember where.

"'Hello there,' he said. And then, 'Gawdamnit! Izityew?'

"I stared at his cast, then at his face, and then at his cast again. His cast was an impediment—it seemed out of place, but everything else looked familiar to me. And then, when I saw that one of his legs was a wooden stump, I knew who he was: Bobby Bazlen, the alcoholic bum whom I always try to fit into my novels. Despite his inanition, incoherence, and general sloppiness, his presence signifies some dramatic transformation in the main character, or some foolhardy leap of plot.

"And so my first thought, while staring at this wreck of a man, was: have I gone insane? Followed shortly by: I have hallucinated myself into my own fiction. And that is the insanity.

"Bazlen gasped at me, his breath reeking of gin. *'Eakins,'* he said. His voice was badly obscured by liquor, but I understood him. Each word was accompanied by a shudder. 'Eakins! Eakins! You've come! To! Join us! To! Save! Us!'

"The grove behind him rustled and for a moment appeared to come slowly toward me—like Birnam Wood to Dunsinane. The noise grew louder and louder, until it differentiated into a number of human voices. Some were beatific, some frightened, and others were venomous and filled with loathing. There were sighs and benedictions and I think one woman was even ululating. I heard words like Blessed Cursed Praise Be to Our Damn This Father Monster Lord Our God Lucifer Savior Zeus Loki Judas

The-One-and-Only Son of Man. Chaos had descended over this tranquil landscape."

Eakins was looking off in the distance now, over the cliff. He seemed to have forgotten about Eugene.

"A crowd of people rushed at me, bowing and swooning; another group ran screaming into the hills. Some came with malice, but they were restrained by cooler heads and pinned to the ground. I tried to ward them off as respectfully as I could, but as soon as I raised my hands, everyone fell to the ground. Out of fear, perhaps, or awe, or some unidentifiable spiritual fervor. But who were these people? They were parents and children and grandchildren. They were lovers and enemies, rivals and friends; they were explorers, college students, scientists, doctors, patients, academics, writers, firemen, and steel mill workers. Mississippian poets, New Orleans river salesmen, New York admen, French plumbers, Aztec princesses, Slavic mobsters, and South African schoolteachers. The largest group, of course, was the throng of beautiful women, who seemed to have stepped right out of my own fantasies.

"There were hundreds of them and they kept racing through the shadowy grove from the valley behind it, running toward me and falling before they came too close. And I recognized every one. Because I had created them all. They were my characters, from my books—the heroes and the extras alike, all together in that valley, praying to me and bowing and laughing and screaming and chanting as if they had witnessed the coming of the Lord."

Eugene narrowed his eyes at Eakins, trying to figure out whether he was joking. But Eakins looked solemn and determined. His breath had settled into a normal rhythm and he grew increasingly animated, punctuating his speech with forceful air punches.

"They led me in a dancing, jangling procession through the grove." His voice was booming. "We came to a muddy, godforsaken pit at the back of the valley. It looked like a refugee camp. Several fallen trees, covered by rags blowing in the sea breeze, were propped up in ramshackle lean-tos. Small children played in the dirt, their faces covered with mud and their feet cut by pebbles. Elderly people, too ill or decrepit to have joined the procession, glared balefully from under their tents. Lazy flies circled their heads. It was painful to see such disgraceful indigence in this bright and healthful setting.

"Yet despite their altered appearances and torn garments, I knew them all. These children here were the nephews of Squire Froth from *The House of Leicester*—and there were the Squire and Baronet Leicester themselves, warming their hands by a dying bonfire. The whole Botton family was there, old blind Keftir and his nurses, little Twiffle and his milk maidens were debating something fierce with Octavian Caesar and Franklin Acton, and there, in loose groups, were Esquire and Jeb Pickett and the private eye Jaymes Silk and Marie Mallon, the young thief Turk and his little girlfriend Alcida, Trace Burnhoof, and Audrey, the inbred cousin of the revolutionary hero Jean D'Artagnan, who was then yelling something at me in a crude, hysteric French. I could go on and on, but you get the point. They were all there, all of my characters, living together in this ragtag camp in various stages of disintegration, prostration, and decrepitude.

"From the congregation competing for my attention I pulled aside someone I knew I could trust: Conroy Eaker, the protagonist of my autobiographical first novel. He was too much like me to deceive me. What he told me disturbed me so greatly that I had to sit down in the mud.

"He said that everyone in the camp had been there as long as they could remember. The people here never grew old, but stayed frozen at the same age. They never slept, they ate juniper berries and wild heather, and they drank from the streams in the valley—dropping their heads into the water like pigs at a trough. Many believed that they were in some sort of afterlife, because they each had faint memories of a previous existence. Several others had gone completely mad and a few—the most depressive of the bunch—had jumped over the cliff into the sea. Only as soon as they hit the water, they would find themselves on the ground back in the middle of the town, lying down peacefully as if they were just awakening from a nap. (Several of the more adventurous citizens started to jump over the cliff as sport, confident in the knowledge that upon contact with the sea, they'd be restored intact to the town. But they got tired of that after a while, and the townspeople now only tossed one another over as a practical joke. Especially the newcomers.) Then there were a brave few—the detective Jaymes Silk led the charge—who tried to escape by hiking over the mountains. But as soon as they walked across the edge of the valley and into the mountains, they would pass seamlessly right back into the Idaville mudflat.

"Newcomers would appear in town, materializing overnight, once every six months or so. They would be oblivious and confused, having only fleeting memories of the world from which they had come. While some old-timers would toss them over the cliff for fun, others tried to console them. No one, however, could offer them an explanation, because no one knew where they had come from, and when they might be able to return, if ever.

"There had been rumors, though, of a godhead, wandering the heavens in search of them, for all of time. A creator who would appear one day and care for them. When I showed up—the only man to walk into the town from the valley, and not to materialize in the middle of town—they knew that I was the divinity they had prayed for. In my voice they recognized the source of all their speech. They spoke in a universal tongue of my own creation.

"I resisted, of course. I had a life back home, in Paris. And in New York, and Prague and New Orleans and San Francisco and London. I had lives—and families—in all those places. And women in many, many more. But it's true that I had lost interest in those lives, and those women. I'm a creature of experience and adventure. And nothing on earth could equal this experience. I could still write here—I would write better, in fact, since I would be in complete isolation, without any company except my own creations. I'd stay here because it is like a native country for me. All of my life is here. I thought, If this isn't heaven, then I don't want to go there.

"So I answered their prayers. I taught them to hunt and gather and chop trees for houses. I planned this town. The houses, all identical, match the one in which I was raised—in St. Rose, Louisiana—though these are well maintained and not dilapidated. And the women: they came to me willingly."

"Is . . . Bonnie here? From *Love in Pittsburgh*?"

"She's here. And her schoolmates Dara, Lisa, and Phlox. The sisters Dobbs and the twin Janets and even poor fat Betsy Loraine—you'd have to roll her around in flour to find her wet spot. Keftir's nurses. A gaggle of strippers, dyspeptic housewives. And most of all, the whores—I hadn't realized how dominant this motif had been in my work—the whores Daisy, Gorazda, Sasha Z., Laura Burns, Aqua-Girl . . . let's see . . . Julip the Wizardess and Kai the Pink Blossom Warrior Temptress—"

"All of them, in other words."

"Yes." Eakins smiled, inhaling deeply. "All of them. Also Allie Apples and Lemony Lil. Can you believe it?"

"Yes," lied Eugene.

"I built this town for all of them—my children—so they didn't have to live in the mud. And they called me the Mayor. I hiked to Duino and brought back for them tools and supplies and books. My books. I read them to my children and they learned the myths of their creation. Imagine their surprise when they discovered they were characters in their own bibles. But of course it couldn't have been any other way.

"To some of them, I gave an even greater gift: I allowed them—a select few, granted—to leave town. And some did. Most of them rushed back right away, terrified of the outside world. They felt as if they had been cast out of the Garden. Or they feared old age, and disease, and other misfortunes of life beyond Idaville. Or, like Enzo, they came back for love. I send others out, from time to time, to report on the world to me. One of them is the drunk, Bazlen, who is especially effective since no one except for me can understand what he's saying. In the real world he is shunned and ignored.

"Some of my children, however, never return. Frank Lang is one of them. A bit character from a murder mystery I wrote under a pseudonym, *Murder in the Mojave*. Those like Frank have their reasons and their pride. Out of my beneficence, I let them go. I take as a compliment their ability to pass for real. It means I've succeeded. Of course if they don't come back, they lose all the privileges and charms of Idaville."

Eugene felt something close and dark rise like smoke in his heart. He couldn't follow where this madman's tirade was going, but seeing the bulge of the gun in Eakins's bathrobe pocket, he knew he would have to wait it out. Eakins was likely insane, but how then could Eugene account for the mansion, or the town in the middle of nowhere? Or the slavish townspeople, living in abject awe of Eakins, their Mayor?

"Now let's take a better look at this manuscript," said Eakins. He leafed through Alvaro's manuscript and then Eugene's, slowing to read a paragraph here and there.

"Not terrible."

"That's kind of you," said Eugene, "but as I said before, the book was written by a friend, Alvaro. I'm sure he'll be happy to hear your compliments."

Eakins gave him a baffled look.

"I don't think you understand."

"Why?"

"You already admitted you can't read Cibaeño."

"Yes, but I get the gist," said Eugene, less sure of himself. He felt uncomfortable articulating these things out loud. "I'm very close to finishing. I get the gist."

He gave Eakins a brief plot summary, and the author laughed, his voice a loud, reverberant trombone.

"As it so happens," said Eakins, "I know how to speak Cibaeño. If you had read my collection of essays on the Caribbean, you would have known that I spent two winters on Hispaniola in the late fifties with a Cibaeño girlfriend and her family. I speak that pidgin tongue fluently. Your friend's story has nothing to do with shinefish, or an apartment building in Inwood, or a surgeon priest named Jacinto and his adventures with his true love, Alsa, in Cibao. It's a letter from your friend, Alvaro, to his wife. He wants a divorce."

"A divorce?"

"A divorce, no more or less. He's begging for forgiveness for his infidelities, and asking for partial custody of his children. The stories, those ridiculous stories, are yours alone."

Eakins gave Eugene a broad, venomous grin. They had come full circle around the field. The waves were quiet in the distance and the horizon had dimmed to a dull magenta.

"Why don't you come back to the house? It's time for dessert, and I'm starving."

Was Eakins right? Eugene had followed what he thought Alvaro had in mind, and written it down. He realized, of course, that he was taking some artistic license—it would be impossible to replicate in English exactly what Alvaro had written. But he felt confident that he had captured the essence of the text, that he had faithfully performed the task of the translator. It was more than confidence, in fact; deep in his blood, he knew he was writing the truth. The thought that he had subverted the manuscript entirely and had made up everything— The guilt hammered at his gut. He had been disloyal to his friend. What shameless gobbledygook had he scrawled across those pages?

Back inside the mansion, the banquet table had been cleared and reset with plates piled with banana splits, puddings, pies and cakes, and bottles of port, sherry, and cognac, even crème de cacao. Eakins began to gorge without hesitation or mercy.

"Have some," he said. A curtain of chocolate sauce fell from his mouth onto his chest, clinging to the forest of hair there. "It's good."

"Mr. Eakins—"

"Call me Connie!"

"Connie—"

"That's much better. Because we're friends, you know."

"Thank you. Connie, I have a lot of respect for you." He paused, distracted by the sight of Eakins kneading the crust of a cheesecake with one hand; with his other hand he lifted to his mouth a chocolate mousse.

"But I need to say again," continued Eugene, "that I came here for Sonia. She's coming home with me."

Eakins spat out what was then in his mouth—a jet of cognac, viscous with cake crumbs and chocolate mush.

"DAMN IT!" he yelled. Eakins gulped down a snifter of the cognac, threw the glass into the corner—where it shattered—and then lifted the bottle to his mouth and chugged vigorously. He licked his lips. "WHAT DID I TELL YOU? She came here for me."

Eugene realized he was shivering.

"Yes, Mr. Eakins," he said. "She came here for you, but she came because her father sent her. It was not . . . an offering."

Eakins smiled at Eugene.

"I don't think you understand," he said. "Agata may have come here for all kinds of reasons. But she has stayed here because she wants to be with me. She's mine. Do I need to explain to you what that means?"

"I think you should," said Eugene. He immediately regretted it. Because the next moment Eakins began to explain, in a tender, almost effeminate tone, what it meant: that Sonia had performed on Eakins a series of acts so full of depravity that Eugene could do nothing but laugh in response—a miserable, shocked laughter. Eakins took no notice and kept going, pausing only to take large swooping mouthfuls of air. The details became more horrible, and more specific, and Eugene began to recognize several of them from his own experience—a birthmark on Sonia's upper thigh, the feline way in which she arched her back, a certain kind of laughing sigh she made. Eugene wanted him to stop, but he also could not help wanting to hear more, the way a cuckolded man will become an implacable detective, continuing his investigation until he reveals every last sordid detail. Eakins was a talented storyteller. But it became too much to bear when he began describing certain freakish aspects of his own anatomy, most disturbingly, the prodigious length of his purple-black tongue, which he now let hang from his lips, in all its glory. It looked like an infant was reaching its leg out of his mouth; it was muscular and seemed to be coated with very fine down.

"Stop," cried a voice from the other end of the hall. It was Sonia.

"Sonia! You didn't tell me he was insane."

"It's not . . ." Her eyes locked with Eakins's, and her voice faded out.

"She's a beautiful child," said Eakins, his evil appendage withdrawn and his voice returned to his normal bass. "She should be in a place where she's made to feel beautiful."

"But what about all your whores? Peachy Peach and Betsy Loraine and Gorazda—"

"They're not exciting to me anymore. Agata is more real to me than any of them. She's the first person I've let in. It's as if I dreamt up this whole town for her. She makes me feel real again."

Sonia was looking at Eugene with a look of pity.

"Sonia?" said Eugene, his voice rising. "What's happened to you?"

She came over and put her hand on his arm. "I can see why you're reacting this way," she said. "But I'm happy here. He understands me." She turned to Connie. "Can you leave us and go out in the garden for a minute?"

"Yes, Agata. And Eugene, for God's sake, don't leave without this."

He held out Alvaro's manuscript, and Eugene's translation. Eugene snapped them out of his hands. Eakins bowed and went into his garden.

"If you need me," he called out behind him, "I'll be staring at the sea."

When Eugene and Sonia left the mansion, the sun was setting over the horizon and hot in their eyes.

"I came all the way here for you," said Eugene.

Sonia sighed.

"Look," she said. "I do like being here, but if you want to know the truth, I may not even stay for that much longer."

"So you'll come back with me? To New York?"

"That's not what I said. I was sorry to leave you in New York, but I realized, once I got here, that I barely knew you."

"What does that mean? I—I love you. I came here for you. *I* understand you, not him. Come on, let's leave. Together."

Sonia bit the inside of her lip, and then gave him a sideways smile.

"You're wrong about Connie," she said. "And you're wrong about yourself. You didn't come here for me. How could you have? I was like a story you wrote in your head. A dream you had."

"That's not true. Don't you remember our time together?"

"Of course, but did those moments carry you all the way here? Please, Eugene. You should go off, by yourself, and try to figure out why you came to Italy. It wasn't for me. You won't think about me too much longer. And if you see my father before I do," said Sonia, "tell him I'm happy again."

"Please, Sonia—"

"That's not even my name," she said. "It's Alison. You're the only one who calls me Sonia."

"I thought your friends called you Sonia."

"I never said that. I said that *you* could call me Sonia. My friends call me Alice."

Eugene looked one more time at Sonia. Her features seemed to be rearranging themselves before his eyes even as he watched her. Then he turned and fled from the Casa Contenta. He ran down the main street of Idaville—where Eakins's creations stared and cowered and cursed—through the narrow ravine and into the great valley, surrounded by the mountains of the Carso. It was black night now and the crisscrossing streams reflected the yellow moonlight. Eugene grasped his notebook close to his chest and wiped his eyes with his sleeves. He was exhausted and weepy and the valley was so expansive that he could not imagine crossing the whole thing. He tripped and fell in a wet patch of grass. He felt his notebook; it was damp, and he feared the ink would bleed. He'd have to pause here, in the middle of the valley, under a small thicket of beech trees.

He rested his head on his bag and lay down. Before he closed his eyes he thought he could see, among the distant groves, the silhouettes of several of Eakins's children. They seemed to be watching him with great curiosity, and fear.

9

At first light, when the sky turns dim and blue, Mr. Schmitz rouses himself. He puts his head very close to Rutherford's, so close that their noses brush each other for an instant, giving Mr. Schmitz a minor static shock. It has a galvanizing effect.

Mr. Schmitz rededicates himself to Rutherford's speech therapy. When he exhausts the familiar conversation topics, he moves to monologues, then diatribes and rants. He can sense that he has Rutherford's attention, but has no tangible proof—Rutherford's slow breaths and his heavy pulse are the only signs of life. Mr. Schmitz decides that he needs to find a subject that can last him indefinitely. He paces furiously around the room, grows tired, and sits on the floor. For many minutes he agitates his chin with determination and then flicks dandruff from the shoulders of his navy polo shirt.

Then it comes to him—he knows what he will talk about. His eyes glimmer darkly and his chin is rosy.

Rutherford's head has slumped over at some point in the

night. Mr. Schmitz now pushes it up into place with a not entirely gentle nudge.

"You're perking up already," he says. "Listen here: I'll tell you about the cities of another country we know. Maybe it'll bring you back to your past. To yourself."

Rutherford glares back, in what Mr. Schmitz interprets as an expression of deep amusement and curiosity. Mr. Schmitz begins:

"In my capacity as vice president for Alliance Equity Insurance Corporation, for instance, I often had to travel to Hartford on the Amtrak—that is, a silver-sided train."

He pauses, trying to channel Rutherford's own storytelling style.

"I took a silver-sided train to a city of glass buildings, where men of many industries—though most of them insurance—gather for their annual meetings. This city, Hartford, is the Mecca of the American Insurance industry. It was there that, just over two hundred years ago, a wealthy textile merchant named Jeremiah Wadsworth opened the first insurance company, a fire insurance concern. The city's reputation was made when, during New York City's fire of 1835, Hartford companies were the only ones to pay out.

"Yet this reliability came at a cost. Take, for instance, the case of Henry Aetna Wadsworth, a descendant of Jeremiah's. Mr. Henry Wadsworth was known to rise every morning at six-fifteen, shower and shave by six forty-five, and at seven, feed the family cat—a Cheshire named Traveler. At a quarter-past he sat for breakfast with his wife, Agatha, and his two sons, Jeremiah and Henry Jr. At Mr. Wadsworth's insurance firm, his day was planned to a meticulous degree by two assistants—a primary and an alternate, in case the primary happened to fall ill. He left the office at five sharp, in time to be home for dinner with his family at six. After dinner Mr. Wadsworth set out at exactly seven with his wife and two sons for a thirty-minute walk around the neighborhood. Mr. Wadsworth was known to tell any interested parties that this constitutional, if repeated every day, was known to prolong the human life by 1.4 years. In a city in which everyone knew or was an actuary, this practice earned the Wadsworths a great measure of social prestige. As the family strolled about the city, their fellow citizens would wave spiritedly from their porches and remark, 'There go the Wadsworths again. A model Hartford family.'"

Mr. Schmitz glances at his friend. Rutherford's Halloween-mask face registers no change. The purple-black tongue on his jaw seems to have only grown darker, as if charred by some inner flame.

"Not all Hartforders could be model citizens, however. One John Browning, a recidivist house burglar, learned of the Wadsworths' nightly routine from a Hartford inmate in Somers State Prison, where Browning was serving his third consecutive jail sentence. When Browning was released, he took a bus to Hartford. For three days, Browning trailed Mr. Wadsworth around the city, marking in a notebook the insurance man's movements and the times at which they took place.

"And so it happened that Mr. Wadsworth and his family came home one night to find that his house was empty. All valuables, paintings, and furniture were gone, including an extremely dear family heirloom: a miniature model of America's first woolen mill, constructed by Mr. Wadsworth's great-grandfather. Most horribly, their cat Traveler was dead. He had attacked the intruder, and Browning had cut his throat.

"As you may have guessed, Mr. Wadsworth's house was covered by a comprehensive insurance policy. So the settlement allowed the family to repurchase everything that was stolen—with the exception of the miniature wooden mill, which was priceless. They even bought a new cat, which they named Traveler 2.

"Mr. Wadsworth refused to let such an unfortunate and random event deter him from leading his nightly walks, and the family was greeted with renewed esteem by their Hartford neighbors, who admired Wadsworth's unswerving reliability in the face of tragedy.

"John Browning admired Mr. Wadsworth's reliability as well. After three days of careful observations, Browning struck again. Between seven and seven-thirty he stole all the Wadsworth family's new possessions. This time Browning made an even greater profit on the black market, because the goods were all recently purchased."

Even though Rutherford's expression hasn't changed, Mr. Schmitz notices with satisfaction that his friend's eyes have dilated slightly. Mr. Schmitz presses a finger to Rutherford's wrist, and rejoices to find that his pulse rate has increased.

"The Wadsworths recouped their belongings in a second windfall settlement, but Mr. Wadsworth's insurance company took note. They refused to give him the same coverage, and sold him a plan with much higher premiums. After Wadsworth's house was robbed a third time, no insurance company would take his claim. Now when the Wadsworths took their fateful evening walk through the city, they were greeted not by waves, but frowns and saddened brows.

"As you've probably guessed, Mr. Wadsworth came under immense pressure from his business associates, his wife (who was sick of repurchasing their possessions), and his sons (who had been dramatically altered by the violent deaths of Travelers 1, 2, and 3) to change his routine. With great inner turmoil and regret, Mr. Wadsworth finally gave in. He decided that he would leave early from work, at four-thirty, so that he could have dinner with his family at five-thirty. This ended, for once and for all, the Wadsworth family's seven-o'clock walk. From now on they would walk at six-thirty.

"Sometime after the death of Traveler 6—or was it Traveler 7?—Mr. Wadsworth made one final alteration to his daily schedule. After work one evening, he came home for dinner at five-thirty, led his family on their walk at six-thirty sharp, tucked his boys into bed at eight, kissed his wife good night at nine, and at ten, the hour he normally went to bed himself, Mr. Wadsworth walked out through his home's backyard and down the street. He kept walking until he reached Keney Park Pond, at the edge of town. There, at approximately ten forty-eight, he tore out his throat with his fingernails. With the payout from Mr. Wadsworth's well-apportioned life insurance policy, his family moved to California."

Rutherford's face is haggard and unfamiliar.

"You probably don't remember this, but I first took Mrs. Schmitz on one of my annual trips to Hartford in 1947. I took her to Keney Park Pond, in fact, and we kissed under a tall elm tree. That was the first time she told me that she loved me. You never asked me about that. You never asked me about her at all, really. You were off in your world of doting women, culinary extravagance, and complimentary hotel rooms. Maybe that's where you are now."

Rutherford's eyelids have closed halfway. When Mr. Schmitz carefully lifts the lids with his forefinger, Rutherford's eyes seem to focus on a space somewhere in the middle distance, between the poker table and the splotchy mirror on the far wall.

"You'd be lucky," says Mr. Schmitz, "if that's the world you're in, floating about carefree in perpetuity. You won't have to suffer the insults of age, of broken organs and damaged spirits. You can just eat and eat and never get full. Me, I have to keep eating. And I keep coughing up dust."

After sundown Mr. Schmitz lays a sheet over the couch, so that he can sleep next to Rutherford. This way he can monitor any progress Rutherford might make over the course of the night, and can change his bedpan when necessary. He finds an extra blanket upstairs, which he pats tight around Rutherford's diminishing form. The night passes like this, with Mr. Schmitz rising each half-hour to check on his friend. Every once in a while, Mr. Schmitz paces around the room, his elbows bouncing, as if he is under the spell of some unseen spirit. Despite his anxiety, he's lost all desire to smoke. Instead he opens the front door to the house and goes outside, where the air is wet with cold drizzle. He can't see anything but cracked cobblestones, the dull brass of the door handle, and the pale blue striations in the building's slate walls. The fog blurs the night sky; the stars scoot around the heavens like water mites. He loses himself in memories of long Lancaster nights spent with Agnes before the war. When her parents fell asleep, he would appear on her porch and they would go walking through the cornfields behind her house. They didn't know anything about astronomy, so they'd point up at the sky and invent their own constellations.

Over breakfast the next day—canned peas, mushed, and a glass of condensed milk that Mr. Schmitz delicately tilts down his friend's throat—Mr. Schmitz continues the therapy.

"On a thin peninsula on the Pacific Coast," he begins, "Americans built their most beautiful city on their most treacherous landmass. San Francisco, named after the Christian saint of nature, is a city of forty-two hills. Because of the terrain, each home looks out over the roof of its neighbor. The views extend over a great bay to the east; green hills to the south; the ocean to the west; and to the north, a bridge made of solid gold that leads to another peninsula, reaching out to the first like Adam to his creator in the Sistine Chapel. This land erupts from the ocean in mountain ranges and wild forests populated by the world's tallest trees.

"Since San Franciscans realize that all of this beauty can be snatched from them at any time, and that they could be pulled, along with their hills-houses-views, headfirst into the surf, they cherish their city the way a dying man does the scoop of sky visible outside his hospital window.

"The city is the missing-persons capital of the world. It collects orphans, runaways, discontents, people without pasts. Some of them return to their old existences, with contrived identities and different clothing. But many never leave. They remain there forever, in a perpetually tumultuous state of vibrant life.

"Agnes asked me to take her there to celebrate our thirtieth anniversary. I don't why. Neither of us had been there before. In fact, it had been years since we had traveled anywhere together. You'll remember the week I'm talking about—it was during your eating tour of South America. We left while you were in Buenos Aires and returned before you had left Montevideo.

"When we got to San Francisco we followed the guidebook to Lombard, a crooked street, and then to Vermont, an even more crooked street. We ate Thai food in the Mission District, burritos in Japantown, and Vietnamese food in Chinatown. We visited the locations of old wartime movies: an abandoned military fort, a glowing glass elevator, and most spectacular, the ruins of the world's largest natatorium, perched at the edge of the city where the land abruptly falls off into the ocean.

"It was once a crystal palace, with a glittering glass roof standing high over seven pools, each heated to a different temperature. The structure burned down in the 1950s, but the ruins remained, nestled in a cove between two high cliffs. The largest pool was still filled with water, though it was brackish and littered with garbage. On the steep hill above the ruins there were wild plants and shrubs in all different colors. Agnes taught me the names for wild rose madder, jonquils, and acacia root.

"Hidden in the cliffs behind the pool's ruins, we found a damp cave. Although it was the middle of the day, the cave was pitch-black, lit only by bright white halos of light on either end. The air inside was moist and clingy, and echoed with the sound of the crashing waves. It got very cool in there, about twenty degrees colder than outside. I was in my orange tartan sweater and my trusty old fedora, which I was then in the habit of wearing whenever I left the house—you know the one, Rutherford, you called it my 'weather helmet.'"

To Mr. Schmitz's delight, Rutherford's eyes show a glint of recognition.

"We had been so busy sightseeing that we hadn't spent any time together in silence. But we were quiet in the cave and I could tell that she was ruminating on something difficult. We were watching the waves frothing below us, through a head-shaped hole in the cave wall, and her face was colored with a dim bluish glow. Without ever looking at me, she said, 'That's a beautiful hat you have. You should wear it more often. It makes you look sincere.'

"I wondered if she had become deranged by the miasmic cave fumes. I pointed out to her that I wore the hat every day of my life, put it on as soon as I left the house each morning.

"'That explains it,' she said. 'That's why I've never seen it before.'

"I didn't understand her then, though I think I do now."

Mr. Schmitz looks at Rutherford, an expression of hope playing across his cheeks. This is the part in the conversation where Mr. Schmitz would normally have relied on a well-timed interruption from Rutherford, distracting him from the pain of confession, but Rutherford offers no help now. His paralytic, tongue-marked face does, however, seem to urge Mr. Schmitz on, encouraging him to reach the conclusion himself. Mr. Schmitz nods reluctantly, and worries at his chin.

"What she was trying to say, I think," continues Mr. Schmitz, "she was trying to say that I was not sincere with her. Or that I didn't spend enough time with her. Or, perhaps . . . that she could not recognize in me the man she married."

With a start, Mr. Schmitz notices that Rutherford's mouth has opened slightly. More than that—a drop of sweat is falling down from his brow. Since it is cool in the shadowy house, and Rutherford has no recourse to physical activity, he must have worked very hard—internally—to produce that single bead of perspiration. Mr. Schmitz is elated.

"You're right," he says to Rutherford. "I've felt a lot of sadness about that moment, and now I know why."

It has been months since Rutherford forgot how to speak English, over a week since he lost his ability to speak Italian, and several days since he could communicate through the spasms of his brainwaves on the EEG machine, but Mr. Schmitz is now convinced that Rutherford is beginning to recover. When his somatic nervous system failed, Rutherford had somehow learned to rely on his autonomic nervous system. Rutherford, liberated from his hospital confinement, has, after being assailed by who knows what kind of aphasias, strokes, and brain injuries, turned his nervous system into an organ of speech. Mr. Schmitz is overcome by pride for his friend and, as if buffeted by a tremendous gust, has to lean against the wall for several moments in order to right himself.

Days pass, and the two men settle into a routine. Every few mornings, Mr. Schmitz takes the Punto down to Medeazza to stock up on groceries and canned goods. He is greeted with curiosity and suspicion by the grocer in the local market, and is the object of brazen stares in the town square. One young mother hugs her tottering son close to her legs when he passes. A pair of teenage girls point at him and run away, calling him a word he doesn't recognize. Mr. Schmitz is careful not to make eye contact. He feigns ignorance of the Italian language to ensure that, when he is asked why he's traveled so far away from Trieste—not exactly a tourist destination in itself—to this mountain village, he can avoid having to prepare a response. Finally, miraculously, Mr. Schmitz has found a quiet, secluded, and gorgeous retreat where Rutherford can retire. And perhaps, after Mr. Schmitz talks through his life story with Rutherford, he can at last get down to the business of writing his memoir.

There are moments, however, while walking through town, when Mr. Schmitz is hit by a strange urge that vanishes as quickly as it appears, yet leaves a dark impression on him. One such moment comes after Mr. Schmitz has stored his grocery bags in the Punto's small backseat, and is walking around to the driver's side, his keychain dangling from his forefinger. He glances to his left, over the row of blackthorn hedge that lines the road, to the falling hills that end in the curve of the Triestine coast. The clouds passing over the sea seem to inflate and merge with the sea. It's a lonely, foreboding view, and Mr. Schmitz feels sweeping over the terrain, like the wind from the Adriatic, an emotion he can only identify as dread. It pushes him back against the car, until his shoulders press against the driver's-side window. He fears that if he doesn't watch himself, this sensation might push him all the way down the mountain and back to Trieste—back even to Milan and then Manhattan. The desire to leave Rutherford behind, no matter how perverse and slight it might be, scares him badly. Without taking his eyes off of the view, he pulls open the door and falls into the seat. He doesn't dare place the key in the ignition until his heart stops pounding.

Mr. Schmitz calms down, but his guilt flares again when he returns to Ternova. He enters backside-first into the cottage, a joyful tune in his throat and overstuffed grocery bags in his arms. Rutherford is slumped over in the wheelchair in an unnaturally lithe posture, so that his bowed forehead nearly touches the top of his knees. Only the wheelchair's seatbelt prevents him from collapsing onto the floor.

With great effort, Mr. Schmitz squats under Rutherford and, pressing against his shoulders, pushes him back into a normal sitting position. Rutherford's head is red, even purple, nearly to the point of lividity. His eyes are purple too.

Mr. Schmitz slowly steps away and heads to the tavern. He takes out the groceries and places them in the refrigerator; he scrubs the cupboards and fills them with cans of food; and he makes himself a small snack of celery and peanut butter, washing it down with cold, fresh milk he drinks straight out of a glass jug. For a long time he doesn't know what to do. He sits at the bar, pressing the jug to his hot cheek, his tears mixing with the condensation on the glass.

Chicago, Los Angeles, Miami, Detroit, Houston. Each week another set of North American cities pass by, making a kind of patchwork map of the country in Mr. Schmitz's mind. He begins to run out of major cities. But as his tales of Seattle, Pittsburgh, Tucson, Cleveland, and Minneapolis unfold, Mr. Schmitz gains confidence in his storytelling. His voice begins to sound unusual in his ears. Its pitch deepens, and it becomes inflected with a bouncy, musical quality that seems to recall some faraway place or bygone era. It is like the voice of a lost friend.

Portland, Des Moines, Tacoma, Santa Fe, Charlottesville. He has begun to write his memoir now, whenever he is not tending to Rutherford. He thinks how odd it is that Rutherford forgot how to speak English while living in Italy; for Mr. Schmitz, the muteness of his isolation has caused the language to surge out of him. The stories he tells Rutherford grow longer and longer, and reflect more of his own experience and his thoughts. He begins to take notes on what he says, and incorporates them into his writing. In the silence of their forsaken hamlet the rhythms and patterns of language swirl around the two men, reverberating off the walls of the house and in Mr. Schmitz's head. At night, when he lies down in the upstairs bedroom, the words rise into a chorus, growing in volume and radiance, drowning out the waking world and carrying him softly to sleep.

Baton Rouge, Norfolk, Augusta, Reno, and Tuscaloosa. The long summer is coming to an end, the nights are cooling, and he's just about run out of cities. He paces about the house, talking to himself and rubbing his chin, and he feels as if he is walking along the precipice of the Carso's tall cliffs, bracing against the seawind that wants to pull him over. One evening his nerves carry him to the red-and-yellow checkerboard piazza at the end of town. The high fog shifts the outlines of the rocks and trees until it's impossible to see beginnings and endings, heres and theres. He stands in the shadow of the monastery and feels the cragged mass of the mountains loom behind him with a menacing force. When he turns to look at them he thinks he can see, over the ridge in the distance, another isolated town—a smudged yellow square at the edge of a broad green valley. There must be plenty of sleepy towns like this in the Carso, each suffering its own battle against the monotonies and mirages of loneliness.

Towns, like people, can dream, and this one down in the valley, cut off from the world by mountains on all sides, looks as though it has been in a trance for many years.

He thinks of Rutherford, lost in his own reveries. What cities must he be exploring now? What dream people populate them? Carlita, the dream girl herself? It occurs to Mr. Schmitz that he knows what he'd say to Rutherford should his friend wake up again, but he hasn't considered what Rutherford might want to tell him. Focusing on the town deep in the distance of the valley, he tries to listen for his friend's voice. Finally it comes, hoarse but firm in his inner ear. And then Mr. Schmitz's eyes go blank and a pain shakes his ribs because he realizes what he has to do.

The next morning he packs his suitcase and brings it downstairs, joining Rutherford in the living room. Several minutes pass before he's able to speak.

"There's one more city I meant to talk about with you," he says at last, unable to look directly at his friend. "We lived there for, oh, so much of our lives."

Mr. Schmitz quickly glances over. Rutherford's neck is bent. He doesn't look well.

"New York is, in many ways, the opposite of San Francisco. If San Franciscans live with the knowledge that their city may fall into ruin at any moment, New Yorkers live as if their buildings are impregnable, that the city will never fall, that it will prosper forever. No one realizes that a great disaster can occur at any time, that we are the most susceptible because of our pride.

"I learned how quickly things can change, how something can destroy life out of the blue. It happened twice, in fact. Two pillars, destroyed one right after the other. First, you left for Italy. Then Agnes fell ill and died. And I've been left alone. Meanwhile, New Yorkers go about as if nothing has happened, each of them king of the city. You know how New York is. I don't need to list its qualities. It is the city of the dead. The noise of the crowds overwhelms the introspective mind. But in its incessant destruction of the old, it is a strange paradise of renewal.

"Now I'll have time to remember, to organize my memories, to write everything down. If I want to talk to you, you'll be right beside me, even though you'll be here, with Carlita, and I'll be returning home."

Mr. Schmitz turns to look one more time at his friend. And then, as if on cue, the purple tip of Rutherford's tongue slips slowly out of his mouth.

Mr. Schmitz drives quickly through the Carso's narrow switchbacks and dirt lanes, his eyes on the road but seeing nothing. It's not until the pavement comes to an abrupt end against the trunk of a giant pine tree that Mr. Schmitz realizes he's utterly, desperately lost. As he's putting the Punto into reverse, he notices a footpath through the forest. He has no idea where the nearest town might be, so he decides to get out and see whether there is a house there.

He follows the meandering path down an incline crowded with gossamer weeds until it ends in a cul-de-sac adjacent to a turquoise pond. The water is fed by a natural tunnel that gurgles out from a bed of white rocks in the mountainside. The sound of rushing water fills the air. Mr. Schmitz finds a boulder next to the pool and uses it as a bench. In the water's reflection he sees the pale skin of his cheek, a wrinkled eye socket, a carbuncled nose, a gray spray of hair. Then he looks deeper, and the shapes become abstract—a curl of light, a swirl of pond sediment, a lily pad spinning in the current—until he can make out what lies beneath.

He hears a voice so high-pitched that he mistakes it for a scream.

"Hello, friend." The voice belongs to a small man. He sits Indian-style on a boulder at the other side of the pond, facing Mr. Schmitz. His shirt is wet around the collar; he has been drinking from the pond.

"I'm lost," says Mr. Schmitz. He wants to say something else but can't think of what. "I'm lost."

"Where are you trying to go?" says the man. Something in his throat makes a clicking sound. His bare feet dangle in the pond, twirling this way and that.

"I badly want to go home."

"Where is that? Mountains or city? I'd advise the latter. Up in the mountains, the air is too thin for a man of your age. Even your dreams might asphyxiate and you could find yourself float-ing away in the atmosphere like a man-balloon. Down in the city you're near water and are immersed in the sounds of people in motion. You can lay your head down on bedrock and know the substance of the earth."

"I'd like to go home to the city where I used to live with my wife. But I have to fly through the airport in Trieste."

The man splashes his feet in the water like a child sitting on his mother's lap in a bathtub. "It's easy. The road up there is in need of repair, so turn around, take the next right, and you'll see a tunnel. After the tunnel, a series of road signs will direct you all the way down."

"Would you like a ride?" asks Mr. Schmitz. A quiet joy is creeping over him now at the thought of escaping from the Carso, and from Italy. "Is that where you're heading?"

"Thanks, but I'm taking a shortcut down. Through the woods."

Mr. Schmitz waves once and skips up the path to his bruised and dented car. The rushing water hushes into a whisper, and then disappears. He finds the tunnel easily and presses down on the accelerator. The windows are open and the air rushes over him, sending his wayward tuft of hair jogging in the breeze. He is speeding now, going toward the city, going home.

10

The next morning Eugene paced back and forth along the edge of the valley for nearly an hour, in search of the narrow path in the cliffs he and Enzo had descended. He couldn't find it, but he did see a slip in the rock face that seemed to lead out. It was a narrow, twisting dirt pass, accessible to so little sky that it was almost a tunnel. When it didn't end up anywhere after thirty minutes, Eugene panicked, and fumbled through his meager food supplies—all he had left were three of Lang's granola bars, an overripe apple, and a square of dark chocolate. He should have taken food from Idaville. Would he have to go back there to beg? Would they accept him? What further indignities would he be made to suffer? But perhaps it wasn't a bad idea. Maybe Sonia would have changed her mind. And yet he was surprised to realize that he didn't want her back anymore. She was changed. What had she been to him anyway? A fever dream of intimate laughter, an auburn swatch of hair, eyes soft and gray, a wiry voice in a long pale throat, and a curved white scar under one eye. He wanted someone else back. He wanted the girl he had dreamt up. A girl like Alsa.

The path led up an incline to the top of a hill. As he climbed the slope, other hills—some of which were topped by medieval towns and country estates—came into view. Tractors moved slowly through the plains, and solitary cars crept along dirt roads. The four mountain peaks towered behind him—he could see them clearly now, their summits obscured by a thick mass of cloud. Somewhere, within their confines, lay the valley, and at the valley's edge, between the mountains and the sea, Idaville. He removed his manuscript, to make sure it was all still there. It was, and it had dried. Looking over his work, he wondered if the monster was right. Maybe he should go on.

He reached the top of the hill. It was covered by short grass and cashew shrubs. A loose ring of cypress trees formed its perimeter, thin patches of fog dragging in their branches like cotton caught on brambles. Eugene lay down, laughing with relief, his back pressing into the warm softness of the field. He took out his manuscript and opened it to the final page. A sheaf of envelopes fell out: his father's letters, stained here and there by giant grimy, food-stained fingerprints—Eakins's mark. He reread them, more slowly this time. He felt a desperate pull to go back to Trieste and catch the next flight to New York, and find his father. But after Idaville, he couldn't imagine returning home. Besides, what good would it do? His father would be no more articulate. It would be better, he decided, to reciprocate the correspondence. On a new page in the notebook, he began to compose a letter:

Dear Father, it began.

You won't ever believe what has happened to me.

He must have fallen asleep, because the next thing he knew, his head lying on the ground and the sun was right over him, so bright that it pierced through his eyelids. When he sat up, he could not make out anything in the glare. Finally forms began to materialize before him, and with a start, he saw that he was surrounded by strangers. There were nearly a dozen of them—muddied, bedraggled, half-naked forms, squatting on their haunches like apes, observing him closely, and grunting to themselves, half-formed words spoken by half-formed people. They stared at him intently, their filthy faces stricken by fear and something almost religious—something like wonder. Two of them, a woman and a man, seemed to be the chosen emissaries, and they approached him.

"Good morning," said Eugene. He didn't know what else to say.

His visitors flinched, as if they had been struck a blow. Several of the group stood and scurried several yards away, before looking back and, with great apprehension, returning.

"I'm Eugene." These people didn't scare him. It wasn't just that they appeared harmless and timid, but also that he recognized in them something deeply familiar—friendly even. He gestured to the man and the woman, and they obeyed cautiously, coming close again.

"Who are you?" He wondered how savages—if that was what they were—could still exist in Italy, almost within view of towns and roads.

The girl whispered something, hoarsely, that he could not quite make out. "And he is Jacinto."

Then the man spoke, though he seemed startled at the sound of his own halting, croaking voice. "We've been waiting for you," he said. "Please. What is happening to us? We have vague memories of the jungle, and of an enormous steel city, and of our wedding, on a high mountaintop. But how did we get here?"

The man, he realized, bore a startling resemblance to Alvaro. And the girl, he saw, was beautiful, and had a white, crescent-shaped scar below one eye. Eugene looked down at his notebook, and then he looked up at them, and he realized who they were, and he understood what they were saying.